Joanne Simms was born in Lichfield. She attended the city's famous Friary School and Marple Hall School, but she was educated at the Reporter Group of Newspapers, Ashton-under-Lyne, where she was apprenticed at the age of 16 during the last heady days of hot metal. She is news editor of the *Oban Times* because she believes that if you have to earn a living you should do so in the most beautiful place on earth.

Big Fibs
Little Fibs

Joanne Simms

PIATKUS

First published in Great Britain in 2000 by
Judy Piatkus (Publishers) Ltd of
5 Windmill Street, London W1P 1HF
email: info@piatkus.co.uk

The moral right of the author has been asserted

A catalogue record for this book is available from the British Library

ISBN 0 7499 3190 6

Set in 11/13 Times by
Action Publishing Technology, Northgate Street, Gloucester
Printed and bound in Great Britain by
Mackays of Chatham plc, Chatham, Kent

This book is dedicated to my family and to anyone who has ever told a fib.

Author's Note

This story is a work of fiction. It is set in a given place and at a given time; Lichfield in 1961. As such the characters and the story are set against a background of real places and people.

I would contend that if you lived in Lichfield in 1961 you would have bought pork pies from Garrett's, a radio from Bradshaw's, had coffee in the Tudor Café or Melia's and gone for a drink at the Malt Shovel.

Likewise you would have seen Pauline Sneyd crowned as Bower queen, heard about Little Johnny's death and watched Miss McGuinness and the Westgate girls marching down the street towards The Friary School; you would have got a dog from Miss Macmillan.

You can still find some of the shops and most of the pubs mentioned in Lichfield today. The city and its people are fact; this story and its characters are not. I hope you can't see the stitches where I have sewn my story into the fabric of real life, but don't forget they are there.

My thanks to the staff of the local history archives, record office and library in Lichfield for helping me and the *Lichfield Mercury's* files were invaluable.

My Godmother got used to telephone calls at all hours of the day or night asking her for street plans and a good place to go for lunch ... 38 years later, her reward has been fictional. God bless you and save you, darling. I'd never have finished this if you hadn't told me I could and should.

Chapter 1

Edie-The-Fence

Mummy choked on Auntie Edie's offer. 'Three bleeding quid!' Then, remembering she was an actress, clutching her pearls for effect, 'I mean darling, they're pure silk.'

Daisy kept looking out of the window, back turned. On the lawn Aunt Edie's cat killed a thrush. Death is a part of life, Daddy told her as he coughed out his lungs in hospital, you mustn't get upset. So she didn't.

She heard Aunt Ruth stirring her tea, the spoon's delicate note against fine china.

'Three pounds.' Aunt Edie sounded final. Daisy decided this was her cue. She hitched her gymslip, fished the package from her knickers, and crossed the room to the three women.

'Five, and we'll throw in the Chanel,' she said, putting the perfume on the stolen scarves.

Mummy recovered first as the eight-year-old held Edie's gaze.

'Whendidja lift that, I mean darling, you mustn't take things.'

'You do.'

Aunt Ruth's elegantly plucked eyebrows rose heaven-

1

ward. 'Explain *that*, my dear.' Daisy looked at her mother in expectation.

'Well, darling, it's like this, when Mummy takes things—'

'Steals,' Aunt Ruth cut in, and would have gone further, but Mummy felled her with a look Daisy frequently saw her use on the landlord if he dared suggest she should pay some rent.

'If Mummy has to take things, it is sort of borrowing because we need the money so we don't upset Mr Pickup with the rent. Now, if you take something . . .

'Steal,' said Aunt Ruth, sitting back, looking over her teacup and thoroughly enjoying the proceedings. Mummy shot her The Look again, but Daisy had to admit to herself, if there was ever anyone impervious to Mummy's best witherer, it had to be Aunt Ruth.

Mummy started again. 'But if you take something, darling, it would be a fib, a really big fib, and you know you mustn't do that, don't you?'

Daisy nodded silently, and all three women seemed, to her, to breathe a faint sigh of relief. She didn't understand, really, but decided to save it up to ask Daddy when they went to visit him that afternoon.

'All right then, a fiver.' Auntie Edie produced the notes and in one smooth, well-practised action Mummy nearly had her hand off, put down her teacup, pocketed the cash and had herself and Daisy on the front doorstep so fast that the child's teeth rattled in her head. Daisy knew Mummy always moved fast once the deal was over, but today, for some reason, she seemed in more of a rush than usual.

As Mummy dragged her towards the gate, Daisy noticed Aunt Edie's cat, sitting chewing its bloody prey on the gravel. It stared right into her eyes, and Daisy stared back. The cat looked away first.

2

Mummy was so quick that Aunt Ruth had to move to catch them up, her long dancer's legs gliding in ridiculously high heels, her fox fur falling over one shoulder. 'Slow down Alice for God's sake.'

'Three quid, three quid!' Mummy kept striding out, heading towards Bore Street.

'She's a good fence, the best in Lichfield.' Ruth and Mummy were in stride now. Daisy was being dragged along behind, her arm nearly out of its socket.

'The bitch knows how I'm fixed, with Fred and the child and everything.'

Daisy noted the bit about 'the child' and didn't like it.

'But you got five!' Mummy came to an abrupt halt, wrapped her arms around Ruth and the pair of them collapsed into laughter. Daisy, breathless, was just glad they had come to a halt, Mummy's outrage at Auntie Edie having worked itself out.

'You mean Dorothy did! Christ, Ruth, I never saw the little bugger lift it! Hadn't the slightest idea. Oh God, what am I doing? What am I raising? How the hell will I ever get through this?'

As the two women wiped the tears from their eyes, neither was sure if they were laughing or crying, and decided they were laughing, because crying would have been too hard for either of them to bear.

Daisy watched. She wasn't sure what Mummy was talking about, but it probably had something to do with her taking the perfume. She felt uncomfortable that it had been a fib, and a big one at that, but it had got them a fiver, instead of three quid. She stored it all up to tell Daddy, but then thought the better of it; Daddy got upset if he found out she had been fibbing, and if he got upset he started coughing and that was something they fought against all the time. No, this was one Daddy didn't have to know about. She'd tell Gran. Perhaps not. Gran got pretty upset about fibs as well; more so about the ones Mummy told, though she could get pretty fierce if she found out about any of Daisy's.

Nan. Nana Rosen, Aunt Ruth's mummy. Daisy decided she'd tell her. Nana Rosen always knew what things meant. Daisy felt much better now she had decided what to do.

Mummy and Aunt Ruth straightened up and Mummy held out a hand to Daisy. They set off down the road at a steadier pace; men who passed them by as they walked into the Market Square and headed for the Malt Shovel all took a second look. They saw a tall, slim Jewess with bobbed hair, in an impeccable grey suit topped with a fox fur, and a stunning Katharine Hepburn lookalike who was perhaps a little too gaunt for their taste, wrapped in a man's gabardine mac, its belt knotted tightly. Holding her hand was a plain little sparrow of a girl, wearing a beautiful camel coat. Patent button shoes and dazzling white socks, just like a princess, her father always told her; even if she did have another bottle of Chanel stuffed up her knickers to give to her mummy when they got home.

The warmth, noise and smell of the public bar washed around Daisy as the door opened. She felt engulfed as she was towed, at knee height, to the bar.

Mummy went to order.

'Now Alice, you know the rules, you can't bring that nipper in here.' The barman leaned over and a big, beer-stinking ham of a hand tousled Daisy's hair.

Aunt Ruth just flashed one of her perfect smiles as she hoisted Daisy up onto a barstool. 'Why not, it's her round, she's paying for it.'

Mummy got two gin and tonics, a Vimto with a straw in it and a packet of crisps. Daisy took a big drink, looked round delightedly as she opened the crisps, with a big beaming smile for everyone in the bar. She loved pubs, and they loved her. The Malt was almost as good as her own pub, the Horse and Jockey, but they didn't live there any more. Not since Daddy had been ill. Mummy got upset if you talked about it, so Daisy didn't mention it any more.

Besides, she had been back once, when Uncle Charlie went to get some beer at the off sales. It hadn't been the same; it hadn't smelt the same. It was sad, but she could understand why Mummy got upset. Daisy decided not to think about the Horse and Jockey. Why spoil a perfectly good visit to a pub? She turned to the barman and gave him the smile that Mummy called her 'melter'.

'All right, she can stay but keep her tucked out of sight in the snug.'

Once they were settled, Aunt Ruth opened her handbag and pulled out her tin. Daisy always felt that all that grace and charm should have had a long cigarette holder, a gold case and lighter, like Mummy had when she was in a play once. Aunt Ruth settled for an Old Holborn tin and rolled her own, or rather started to when in public. Before the tobacco ever left her gloriously red-painted fingernails a man always leaned over, offering his packet.

On this occasion the two women both gave their practised hesitation for what they hoped was long enough to be seemly, and then accepted, smiling delightedly at him, as though he had just suggested lunch, and a trip to the races at Uttoxeter tomorrow. He did that by the time he had bought the third round of drinks, and he even thought it had been his own idea.

By the time they left the Malt Shovel for Lichfield City station and the journey to visit Daddy, Daisy was three Vimtos, two packets of crisps, a cheese sandwich from

5

the barman and a bag of chocolate buttons better off. Mummy and Aunt Ruth had the benefit of some generously poured gin. They sat contentedly in the compartment, until Aunt Ruth cocked her ear.

'Tickets please!'

They bolted for the lavatory at the end of the carriage and the two women dived inside. The engaged sign clicked in place. Daisy stood patiently outside.

'Hello me duck,' said the ticket collector as Daisy handed him tickets for one adult and one child.

'Mummy's in the toilet.' Daisy turned on her melting smile, which appeared from such a plain little face like sun from behind rain clouds.

'What's the matter darling, I'll be with you in a moment,' Mummy called from inside.

'It's the gentleman for the tickets, Mummy.'

It was the word 'gentleman' which clinched it for them every time. Daisy continued to beam, and watched as the ticket collector went on his way with a smile and a spring in his step, at the thought of such a nicely brought-up little girl calling him a gentleman. Only when she could see the sucker was halfway down the next carriage did she give a knock on the door. Mummy and Aunt Ruth reappeared, faces repaired, leaving behind a heady scent of face powder, Coty L'Aimant and roll-ups in the lavatory.

As Mummy herded them back to their seats she told Daisy, 'Don't say toilet dear, it's common.'

Chapter 2

Visiting Day

All her life Daisy would feel uneasy when in and around hospitals, and she could only put it down to visiting day at the chest hospital.

They would arrive, exhausted from two long train journeys, each time on edge in case the ticket collector caught them, or browbeaten after a lift from Aunty Betty. If forced to choose, Daisy would have gone for the train and the risk of incarceration every time.

Aunt Betty was Mummy's older tight-lipped sister. She was the only woman in the family who could drive, and had a car during the day because her husband was a long-distance lorry driver. Even though Mummy gave her money for petrol and picked up the bill when they stopped at a tea room near Sutton Coldfield on the way back, Aunt Betty let it be known how kind she was being to them. With each crunch of the gear lever, each peering cautiously out of a junction with a 'clear your side, Alice?' she managed to imply that they could never repay such charity.

The bus dropped them off at the gates of the hospital, and then began the long walk up the drive of what once had been a private mansion. In amongst overgrown grass and strangled young trees Daisy could pick out remnants of garden borders and statuary.

Daisy braced herself. Soon they would go into a building so big that the very walls and ceilings appeared to loom over her, ready to pounce; the smell of polish and disinfectant clung to her nose. The sound of coughing struck her with terror. Coughing must not happen, coughing was Daddy bent double, face puce, eyes watering, with Mummy, full of fear, holding him, trying to soothe him, trying to make the dreadful noise stop.

Hospitals and coughing. Across the years they would polaxe the adult Daisy with fear.

Soon they were in the corridor. It went on for ever; long, hollow, creating echoes from their footsteps and the whispered voices of other visitors. At the end of the corridor and through the swing doors was Daddy's bed.

As they drew nearer, Mummy began to prepare for their performance.

'Now remember, darling, Daddy wouldn't want to see unhappy, would he? He's far too poorly to be bothered with that. Let me see you.'

She bent down to the child, tucked a strand of hair here, wiped her face just there, adjusted her coat and gave a quick flick of the handkerchief across the patent button shoes. Then she accepted the compact and lipstick that Aunt Ruth held out.

'Perfect, come on, darling.'

As Daisy was shooed towards the ward door, she saw Aunt Ruth grip her mother's arm.

'God knows, Ruth, he hasn't got much left. Let him see pretty, let him see happy,' Mummy whispered.

'Pretty and happy,' confirmed Ruth, who snapped the compact shut after checking her own face, linked arms with her friend, switched on a smile to match hers as they walked in, wife and mistress to see their man.

Daisy got to the bed first. From the minute she had completed her dreaded journey and opened the ward door, the sight of her father made all fear vanish.

In a perfect mimicry of her mother she cried 'Darling!' and ran to his bedside, arms outstretched. It was a performance which all but brought her a round of applause each visiting day.

Though cancer-ravaged and in his mid sixties, Fred was still a handsome man, and it would take more than a devouring illness and radium to kill his charm. Daisy clung tightly to his arm, intoxicated with love for him, and just looked and looked at her wonderful father.

Alice thought he had grown so frail and grey that it was hard to tell where he ended and the starched hospital sheets began, as though he was simply fading away from life. Ruth looked at him and remembered she had seen too many people die, fought to control the shudder of horror, and stamped the lid shut on her own personal box of nightmares. She lifted the child up onto the bed and into his arms.

'Up you go Daisy.'

'Dorothy,' Fred corrected, 'are we still with this Daisy business?'

Daisy nodded solemnly, 'I like Daisy, I want to be Daisy.'

Fred just smiled and tutted, stroking the little girl's hair.

'You're Dorothy, and don't forget it. You can't have people just changing their names left, right and centre because they feel like it. How would we keep up with who was who?'

Daisy knew to nod in agreement. No point in upsetting visiting day. She would be a Dorothy in here and start being a Daisy again when they were outside. Then, when Daddy got better and came home, and they lived in the Horse and Jockey again, she'd be a Dorothy once more. That was a Dorothy sort of life.

You needed to be a Daisy when you lived in rooms at Mr Pickup's, with horrible silverfish things on the lino when you turned the light on at night; got driven crazy with large portions of Aunt Betty and left with Gran for bread-and-marg teas with sugar sprinkled on the top. Not to mention visits to Edie-the-Fence, who Mummy insisted you were nice to and called Auntie. Daisy could teach Dorothy a thing or two, that was for sure.

Daisy resurfaced from the glory of Daddy's arms and began to listen to the conversation.

'George says he has got some work for me again. Vi's mother's had another do with her legs and so she's gone home to Northampton to look after her. He's got two weeks at the Hippodrome.'

Daisy could feel the disapproval in her father's body.

'Getting sawn in half again? Nothing else?'

'She was offered a tour. *Hay Fever* with Derek's lot,' Aunt Ruth cut in.

'You should have taken it, my dear.'

'I'd have had to tour, and I'm not leaving you, or her.'

'She could have stayed with my mother, you know that, and she loves Nana Rosen, don't you?' Ruth turned to Daisy who felt obliged to nod, but every fibre of her body screamed at the thought of being left.

'Then my mother would give me hell for not leaving her there, our Betty would have to put in her threepenny-worth and I'd have a war on my hands. Variety's all right, and I might be able to pick up some more work at the Hippodrome. I'm staying local.'

Fred admitted defeat and turned to his daughter. 'Your

10

mother is going to be sawn in half instead of Vi. Oh, don't put your mother on the stage, Daisy Worthington, don't put your mother on the stage.'

Both women laughed.

'Our name isn't Worthington,' Daisy pointed out.

Daddy shot her a serious look, 'And your name isn't Daisy, try to remember that.'

Daisy nodded. The day had turned out better than expected. She had been in a pub, got one over on the ticket collector, seen Daddy and now Mummy had announced she was going back working with Uncle George.

The last time Mummy had worked with Uncle George there had been another man on the bill who was the most wonderful man in the whole world, except for Daddy. Would he be there again? Daisy snuggled into her daddy's arms with delight. He held her close, and even through the dreaded hospital smells, Daisy could breathe in the scent of her father and the Pears soap he always used.

All too soon it came time for Aunt Ruth to say, 'Come on, let's see if we can get a bar of chocolate out of that funny machine downstairs.'

Daisy wanted to scream and cling to her daddy, but she knew she mustn't. She had done it once and it had set him coughing, and both he and Mummy started to cry. Mummy had made her promise never to do that again and upset Daddy. So she gave him a big hug and a kiss.

Daddy hugged and kissed her back so hard he was breathless and the little girl was afraid he would start to cough.

'Bye-bye Dorothy,' he said, stroking her hair, blue veins standing out on the paper-thin skin of his hands.

'Bye-bye Daddy,' said Daisy. Taking hold of Aunt Ruth's hand she headed for the door, after Ruth gave Daddy a goodbye kiss.

Ruth squeezed her hand so hard Daisy looked up at her in surprise. For some reason her aunt had gone pale.

'Never look,' the woman whispered, more to herself than to the girl, as she fought to stop visions of guard dogs and barbed wire flooding over her. 'Never let them see you need to look back.'

Daisy nodded solemnly, and squeezed Aunt Ruth's hand hard in reply. The child was pleased to note it seemed to break the spell her aunt was under. Once through the door, Ruth returned the compliment and chased away Daisy's own corridor demons by playing at *The Wizard of Oz*.

This involved linking arms and doing the funny little dance that Dorothy did in the film while singing the song.

Aunt Ruth draped her fox fur round Daisy's shoulders and they took a half-step back, paused and began: 'We're off to see the wizard . . .'

Chapter 3

Mr Pickup's

Waking up at Mr Pickup's was horrible, Daisy had come to that conclusion on the first morning, and nothing in the following seven months had happened to make her change her mind.

What made it worse was the realisation she was there and not in her pretty bedroom with roses on the walls, looking out over the back yard of the pub with its stacks of crates and barrels, over to the dog kennels, and the fields beyond.

Each morning tricked her. She would slowly come awake, cuddled up to the delicious warmth and smell of her mother, still expecting to open her eyes and see her bedroom. Then the awfulness of the situation would creep in. She would realise that she was alongside Mummy who should be in another room in bed with Daddy, not in her lovely bed with her. Then the shock of it all would hit her anew, as fresh and as terrible as it was every morning: this wasn't home, this wasn't the Horse and Jockey on the Tamworth Road. This was Mr Pickup's place. She was in a lumpy bed, in a damp room, with crumbling lino on the floor, a po under the bed, and a sink and a gas ring behind Mummy's old dressing-room screen. Dorothy felt indignant that she had to wash in the same sink as the dinner pots.

As she shivered and cuddled up tightly to her still-sleeping mother, it was Dorothy who felt indignant; Daisy could deal with it.

She peered over the top of her mother to where the other bottle of Chanel stood on the table. When they got back Daisy had given it to Mummy. She had been so happy she cried. Dorothy could never have done that; she had to admit that Daisy did have her uses.

Mummy began to stir, and, unbeknown to the child, awoke to the same hellish flood of reality. Her comfort was to turn over and hug her daughter closely to her, her part of Fred that would never leave her.

'Good morning, darling.'

It was useful having a Mummy who called everyone darling; it made it so much easier to keep the armour plating of Daisy in place throughout each uncertain, if entertaining, day.

'Ruth and I are going to the races with . . .' Mummy gave a laugh to herself and hugged Daisy even more tightly to her. 'Do you know, darling, I can't remember his name. Let's hope Ruth does. Who would you like to stay with?'

Dorothy acted as though she was trying to make a very hard decision. Sometimes she thought she was a better actress than Mummy herself.

'Let me see,' she paused for dramatic effect, 'I think I would like to stay, best of all, with Nana Rosen.'

Alice hugged her daughter to her. 'Well I didn't think you were going to say Aunt Betty.' They both laughed in horror at the thought of anyone ever going to stay voluntarily with Aunt Betty.

Mummy soon had breakfast on the table. In her bright

14

yellow kimono, she sat, teacup in one hand, as she lit a cigarette and watched her daughter eat. Daisy had to admit that she always had a very Dorothy breakfast, her own silver eggcup and its matching spoon along with the napkin in its silver ring with *Dorothy* engraved on it. They were all her christening presents from her godparents and unbeknown to her they had, as such, escaped the route to the pawnshop taken by Alice's cherished table silver.

Hostilities with life had to be suspended at breakfast-time; it was hard to be anything but Dorothy when eating your egg from a silver spoon. Daisy would be back soon enough, conning a cheese sandwich at the Malt Shovel, tucking into a bag of chips in newspaper or bread and dripping with pepper on it for tea.

Mother and daughter were quickly washed and dressed, for it was too chilly to linger in the mornings at Mr Pickup's. Then followed the breakfast pots, bed-making, and emptying of the dreaded po from under the bed.

Daisy liked this part of the day best, when she did not have to be rushed out of the door to school, but could sit, knees tucked under her chin, and watch as Mummy held a fashion show while deciding what to wear. She didn't have many of her clothes with her and Daisy often wondered where they had gone.

'Uncle's, darling,' Mummy said, and Daisy recognised a tone of voice which meant there would be no elaboration. Sometimes some of the clothes came back to visit for a few days but quickly disappeared again.

'Races, races, let me see, what should one wear to the races . . .' Mummy thumbed along the coat hangers in the plywood wardrobe.

'A little tweed suit's best for Uttoxeter, darling,' Daisy piped up, remembering a conversation she had once heard

15

between Mummy and Aunt Ruth, and trying her best to imitate Ruth's unlikely-sounding but exotic mixture of Viennese accent and Dudley twang.

Mummy laughed and reached for the suit. 'Tweed it is. You'll be an actress yet, my girl, though over your father's dead body.' Before the words came out she had frozen in horror, given a little shudder and then burst into a song to cover her tracks. It was the one Daisy had heard the day before.

'Don't put your daughter on the stage, Mrs Worthington, Don't . . .'

'But our name's not Worthington!' Daisy knew this was a grown-up's joke and it annoyed her because she did not understand it.

'And your name isn't Daisy,' her mother bent over and kissed the top of her head, 'do try to remember that.'

By the time Mummy had put on her make-up, found the right shoes and made sure that Daisy's own pair was polished to her satisfaction, they were late for the bus. This meant they had to face a terrible dilemma.

Did they charge down the stairs, make a noise, and disturb Mr Pickup, who might come out from his room by the door and challenge them about the rent? Or did they creep slowly and silently trying to remember each of the floorboards and stairs which creaked, and run the risk of missing the bus?

In the end they tried to do both, and made themselves look like a comic turn Daisy had seen when Mummy, Daddy, Aunt Ruth and Nan Rosen took her to see a pantomime one Boxing Day. It nearly worked. They had made it outside onto the top step and Mummy had just given a dramatic mime of mopping her brow in relief when they heard Mr Pickup open his front door.

'Mrs Smedley about the—'

'Can't stop Mr P. must dash, see you later, byee.'
Mummy whisked Daisy down the steps and at full speed
towards Bird Street.

The library, Minster Pool, the cathedral, the Swan and
George hotels went by in a blur for Daisy as they headed
for the bus station.

Daisy looked up and caught a brief glance of rooks
wheeling in the cloud-ragged sky of early spring, over the
trees which fringed Minster Pool.

Mummy called out a greeting to the lady sweeping the
step of Lucille's hairdressing salon, but tore past before
she, too, had a chance to raise the matter of money
owing.

They arrived at the bus station opposite the Friary
School just in time to hop onto the Tamworth bus. On the
other side of the crossroads workmen were starting to
demolish the old buildings at Jones's Corner. Daisy
thought it was sad to see the inside walls with their wall-
paper, as though someone had sliced off the end of the
building like a loaf's crust.

Mummy managed to act as if the bus was her own
limousine. The other passengers, mainly women, took
note of the fact that the conductor personally escorted the
elegant woman to her seat, handed over her tickets with a
flourish and walked away taller than before; Alice had
that kind of effect on men.

As the bus turned the corner onto St John's Street
Daisy looked from her seat by the window at the sand-
stone building of the school.

'I went there, your sister went there and you'll go
there,' Mummy told her, 'though I hope to God it's
changed since Miss Hodge's day.'

Mummy's Friary School stories were some of Daisy's
favourites.

17

'Tell me about your eyebrows,' she pleaded. Mummy didn't need a second prompting.

'Well, darling, I had been to the cinema with Uncle Jack and Uncle Charlie, and I had seen an old silent film starring Theda Bara. She had the most wonderful, elegant eyebrows, so romantic you know.' Mummy struck a pose from the silent film, clutching her hands to her bosom, fluttering her eyebrows, then swooning by placing the back of her hand dramatically against her forehead.

'So I decided when I got home that I wanted to look like her. Well you would, wouldn't you?' Daisy nodded, and by now most of the other passengers on the bus were nodding along with her, entranced.

'I tried plucking my eyebrows, with your Auntie Nellie's tweezers, but it hurt so and was taking ages. So, I took Grandad's razor and shaved them right off!' Even though Daisy knew the story off by heart, Mummy's fierce shaving gesture made her jump.

'Gran went crackers, as you can imagine, and gave me such a wallop, but the worst was yet to come.' Mummy gave one of her dramatic pauses.

'On Monday, when I went to school, Miss Hodge saw me and at morning prayers she made me stand on the stage and told the whole school what a disgrace I was. She made me stand there all through prayers, imagine!'

Daisy did, with a shudder. Mother and daughter fell silent now, for the story had taken up enough time for the bus to be nearing Freeford and the Horse and Jockey. Both watched as they came closer to their old home.

They strained to see if there was anyone waiting outside to board the bus. Daisy longed for there to be someone they knew, someone from what she regarded as her real life; Alice looked in dread in case there was.

Alice could not bear the thought of having to face

18

people. They were kind enough, and most were genuinely concerned about her husband's health, but she knew that they knew how bad things were for her. Lichfield was still a small enough place, even in 1961, for everyone to know your business; what you had pawned, how much rent you owed, which pubs you went into and how many drinks the men bought for you and your husband's fancy woman. Ordinarily, Alice thrived on attention, that was why she had gone on the stage; she needed it like oxygen, but there were times, especially now, when she just wanted to slink away.

Her answer was the same as to any adversity, she had learned it from her previous marriage: to sit up straight, hold up her head, radiate the beauty of her smile and let the world believe that darlings, she didn't give a damn.

She did that now, as the bone-jolting old Midland Red bus laboured past the golf course on its way up to Whittington Barracks.

By some form of telepathy or osmosis, Daisy picked up her mother's mood. She sat up and mother and daughter looked at each other and smiled.

As the bus went past Miss MacMillan's Lochranza Boarding Kennels, Daisy strained to look over the wall and see if any of the beautiful cocker spaniels were out in the runs, but it was impossible. Best not to think about dogs; the kennels at the Horse and Jockey had become silent as her father's illness worsened. When the house dog, a cantankerous, half-blind spaniel had died of old age it had not been replaced. Daisy, or rather Dorothy, had dreamed of a puppy, but it was not to be.

The lack of a dog by her side was probably the biggest hardship Dorothy had to bear. A quiet child, who did not mix easily with other children, her precocity was due to the attention of older parents, who had never expected to have a child together and delighted in her when they did. Dorothy's best friend had always been a spaniel who shared her secrets, her joys and fears. Now she did not have one she hoarded her secrets to herself, and her new invention, Daisy.

The bus was pulling away from the barracks and heading for their stop. All too soon the ride was over and they were deposited by the Whittington road end, looking at Botany Bay: a motley collection of council houses and farm cottages stuck in the middle of a sea of fields, with a shop on the opposite side of the Lichfield to Tamworth road.

Mummy glanced at her watch: just enough time to leave Daisy with Nana Rosen and catch the bus back into Lichfield with Ruth. She gave Daisy a smile, which was supposed to boost her confidence, but it didn't.

Chapter 4

Nana Rosen

Nana Rosen had been keeping an eye out for the bus's arrival, and was on the back doorstep waiting for them both with a big smile.

'Darlinks!' Nana's accent had never succumbed to the Black Country as Ruth's had. It was an accent as thick, syrupy and delicious as the mug of hot chocolate Daisy could expect when Nana sat down for afternoon tea.

She was halfway across the back yard coming towards them with her arms outstretched in welcome, beginning a slowly arthritic swoop down to Daisy, who knew from experience she had just enough time to take a big gulp of air before being engulfed by a solid eiderdown of woman.

'*Leibling*! My little darlink, how are you?'

Daisy managed a mumbled response from the depth of the embrace which pulled her down into the warm cinnamon-and-floury apron encasing Aunt Ruth's mother. At the heart of the hug Daisy was crunched up tight against the glittering stone brooch at Nana's neck, she could feel the hard edge of the case Nana kept her spectacles in digging into her ribs and yet the hug went on until Daisy could feel and hear the crack of bones in Nana's corset, like the creak of an ancient tree in the wind.

21

It was a luxuriously encompassing embrace of love but with the occasional hard edges; a bit like the woman herself. Nana Rosen had lived through two world wars, the splitting of the atom, the attempted annihilation of her race and the founding of its homeland, and amidst such wonder and horror she had never lost faith in the power of a loving embrace and good baking.

Gasping for air and fearful of broken bones, Daisy emerged, as Nana turned her attentions to Alice. No great hug here, just the same welcome as Aunt Ruth received: a kiss on one cheek and the painful pinching of the other between a vice-like thumb and forefinger.

'So pale!' cried Nana. 'How is your poor husband?'

Before Mummy could get a word in, Nana bellowed 'Ruth!' and a reply came floating downstairs.

Aunt Ruth appeared from behind the heavy chenille curtain which closed off the cottage stairwell in an attempt to deaden the howling draughts which all farm cottages breed, no matter how low the ceilings.

'Ciao,' she said, having seen a Sophia Loren film the weekend before. Daisy watched in her usual fascination as Aunt Ruth managed to relight an old roll-up from her infamous tin, while putting on a pair of stockings and fishing down to retrieve her stilettos from the gap between an ancient chintz-covered chair and the polished brass fender.

Meanwhile Mummy had turned to the old bevelled mirror, hung on a chain above the sink, and was repainting her face after Nana's assault. Daisy loved watching her put on her lipstick: Mummy applied it carefully, pressed her lips together, turned her face this way then that, and finally used her ring finger to wipe each corner of her mouth.

The two women managed to turn the kitchen into their

dressing room backstage; any second Daisy expected a knock on the door and a cry of 'Second act beginners, please!' The little girl sat and watched them, enjoying every minute and trying to forget that soon they would leave her behind, and every time that happened it felt as though someone, somewhere, had switched a light off.

Mummy and Aunt Ruth filled the room with their laughter, and as Mummy sprayed herself with perfume she leaned over and squirted Daisy, who disappeared delightedly into a cloud of contraband Chanel.

'Do you remember that time we went to the races at Nottingham?' Mummy asked Aunt Ruth, as she reached for her handbag. 'We ended up in Yates's Wine Lodge and you got so tight you finished off by dropping your fox fur down the lavvy?'

The two women looked at each other and laughed at a shared escapade.

'Oh my God! Nottingham! Don't mention it. My last attempt in rep, before I decided to stick to dancing, terrible, terrible!'

Daisy cut in, remembering something she had overhead.

'Was that when you played Belsen, Auntie?'

The kitchen stopped dead. Daisy was sure the temperature dropped; Nana Rosen gave a big shiver, like a convulsion.

'Belsen, darling?' Mummy managed to ask.

Daisy realised an explanation was called for. 'Yes, Belsen. Aunty Betty said to Gran that Aunt Ruth was in Belsen, and it was dreadful.'

'Yes, darling,' Aunt Ruth said, looking away from her while she spoke. Then she turned to Daisy and said too brightly, 'Absolutely dreadful. The houses were awful and the reviews were lousy.' Ruth leaned over, hugged the child to her and kissed her. 'No wonder it closed! Best not to talk about it.'

It must have been pretty bad, Daisy thought, because Aunt Ruth looked on the point of tears. Daisy made a mental note to herself not to mention it again: Aunt Ruth was like Mummy, she hated to be reminded of bad reviews and a show closing.

Mummy kissed Ruth on the cheek. Nana opened the kitchen door and went and stood outside.

'The bus!' Nana cried, from her lookout point on the back doorstep, which gave her a good view of the main road as far as the horizon in each direction.

The two women gathered themselves up with handbags, headscarves, gloves and an old shooting stick that Aunt Ruth always insisted on taking along when they went racing. They kissed Daisy, kissed Nana and sprinted down the path.

Their departure did not just empty and silence the kitchen, but created a void. Daisy told herself she didn't mind being left, really.

Nana came to the same conclusion, only she added to herself the words 'with a sad-faced little child', and thought that she had seen too many of them in her time.

For a few seconds they looked across the emptiness at each other, readjusting; both broke into smiles of acceptance of their lot.

'A biscuit, darlink?' Nana always filled any gaps in conversation with food. Daisy nodded, climbing onto an old kitchen chair at the table as Nana beckoned.

'Did you have breakfast?'

Daisy nodded. Nana, who made a pretty good guess at how irregular meals could be in the child's life, put a plateful of homemade biscuits and a glass of milk in front of her. Satisfied, the old lady began to bustle round her

24

kitchen, sure that whatever crisis of confidence or loneliness she had seen flash over Daisy's features at the departure of her mother had now vanished.

Daisy gave a small sigh to herself, and tucked in. Mummy would be back soon enough and have lots of stories to tell about her day out. With a bit of luck she wouldn't have lost any money, and would be what she called 'ahead of the game'.

Daisy hoped so, and in the back of her mind she knew that their landlord, Mr Pickup, probably felt the same.

'So,' said Nana, 'what are you going to do with yourself today?' She hoped Daisy would have an answer.

'Please may I help you bake?'

'How do you know I am going to bake?'

'You always bake.'

'You are one shrewd little girl, though I guess you have to be, don't you *liebling*?'

Daisy withdrew from the big glass, milky whiskers around her face, and nodded seriously in agreement. Nana smiled, and went over to the table, hugging Daisy to her and kissing the top of her head.

'What a life! What a life for us all! My little Ruth was not older than you when . . .' The scene a few minutes before had stirred up old memories both Ruth and her mother worked hard at forgetting.

'When?' Daisy was relieved the hug hadn't been of the corset-crunching variety, but now she was interested.

'Oh, just when,' said Nana. 'Now eat up! I'll bake later. When you've finished, go down the garden and tell Mr Bloum that his elevenses are ready.'

Daisy smiled. She hadn't forgotten Mr Bloum. Her lodger was another of the nice things about staying with Nana for the day. His accent was nearly as thick as Nana's. But thankfully he didn't feel obliged to hug and kiss and fuss all the time. In fact, you could have quite a good conversation with Mr Bloum. He knew about things, and knew about gardening too; he had to because he never stopped. The rain might drive him from the garden, but it sent him into the old shed by the field gate, where he continued to garden nonetheless, busying himself in pots and trays and cleaning the tools.

Face wiped, crumbs brushed, suggestion she should put on her coat declined, Daisy went into the garden to find Mr Bloum.

Nana's cottage was a corner one and as such had an extra large garden, which also went further back than its neighbours. Daisy set off down the lawn, then into the undergrowth of the fruit garden. The pungent smell of blackcurrant bushes was exciting, a little further on came the odour of chives, and the scent of thyme, escaped from its bed onto the path, floated up as she crushed it underfoot.

'Mr Bloum!'

'Hello.' He rose up from behind the tangled undergrowth of raspberry canes where he had been turning over a small bed for vegetables. It took him a little while to straighten, but he gave her a warm smile of welcome.

'So you have arrived, my dear.'

Daisy felt obliged to nod. It seemed fairy obvious to her that she was there, but then some grown-ups did have a talent for stating the obvious, even if the obvious was sometimes, more often than not in Mummy's case, a bit of a fib.

'Nana says elevenses.'

Mr Bloum's turn to nod. He rolled down his sleeves and followed her back up the garden. Another silence, which this time Daisy felt she should fill.

'I'm going to help Nana bake.'

26

Mr Bloum nodded: 'She always bakes.'

'That's what I said. I can help you if you like.' Daisy did not want him to feel left out, after all, she liked Mr Bloum.

'Thank you,' said Mr Bloum graciously. When Daisy was a woman all she could remember about Mr Bloum was his smile, and that everything he did, even if she never saw him outside the small kingdom of his garden, was done with a tremendous sense of old-fashioned graciousness. She never knew how old he was, and when she asked her mother she too could not hazard a guess. There was about him an air of timelessness. All she could recall was his smile and his kindness, and the jungle smell of the vegetable garden, she never associated him with flowers even though they grew in profusion; but she would feel good whenever she thought of him, to which there can be no better epitaph.

Elevenses over, with the benefit of another glass of milk and a round of meat-paste sandwiches inside her, as part of Nana's feeding campaign, Daisy found herself on an upturned bucket, its top padded with an unravelling jumper which belonged to Mr Bloum, watching as he set to work.

'Lettuces,' he told Daisy without looking up, as he raked the soil to a fine tilth. 'These are for later on in the summer, it is what is called a catch crop.'

'Cash crop?' she misunderstood, 'are we going to sell them?'

Now he looked up smiling: 'No, a catch crop. You could say that I'm catching the other vegetables unawares. Lettuce grows more quickly, so we can sneak a few in here without the other plants catching on to what I'm doing. They will have grown and gone, before the others are ready to harvest.'

27

Daisy wasn't really sure what he was talking about, but watched quietly as he worked methodically. The fertiliser went into the ground, then he made a line in the soil with the end of his hoe.

'This is the drill where we put the seeds, half an inch down.' Mr Bloum produced a packet from his waistcoat pocket. He then beckoned to Daisy and solemnly placed a large pinch of seed onto her hand.

'You can plant them for me, very gently down the line.' Daisy felt very important.

'There,' he said when the job had been completed to his satisfaction, 'those are your lettuces. When you come again you can thin them, and when they are grown you can cut them and give them to Nana and to your mother.'

'And Gran. We had better give one to Gran,' said Daisy, who always felt very guilty about the fact that she liked Nana Rosen far better than her own grandmother, and she was not even related to Nana at all.

'I don't think I should forget her even if . . .' her words failed. Mr Bloum read her face and finished the sentence for her.

'Even if you don't like your grandmother very much.'

Daisy blushed and nodded in agreement.

'Never mind, my dear, we can't help who we love and who we don't; it's good that you think about her and don't want to hurt her feelings, even if you don't like her very much. In a way it shows you do like her. If you didn't, you wouldn't be worried about upsetting her, now would you?'

Daisy nodded and smiled. Mr Bloum had sorted it all out for her.

'I'll let you in on a little secret of mine: I don't like lettuce.'

'But why do you grow it then?'

'Because people I like, like lettuce.'

'That's the same as me and Gran, isn't it, only a sort of other way round.'

'A sort of other way round,' he agreed. 'Now pick up your bucket and follow me, let us attend to our lettuce!'

Mr Bloum moved them along to a sunnier part of the vegetable garden. Here Daisy propped her bucket up against a low wall and felt the warmth from the bricks seep through her cardigan and into her shoulders. She remembered that it was knitted by Gran and she felt better about liking her, even though she hadn't realised she didn't know she did.

'These are ones I planted earlier, when the weather wasn't as nice, so they are in a warmer spot, to help them grow better. We all like a bit of warmth now, don't we?'

Daisy agreed. She found putting her feet out of a warm bed onto icy lino on cold mornings one of the many horrendous things about Mr Pickup's. This jogged her thoughts back, she had been going to ask Nana about the big fib of taking things, but decided Mr Bloum would do instead: hadn't he just sorted out Gran for her?

'Why is it a little fib if Mummy takes something from a shop, but a big one if I do?'

Daisy's dilemma stopped Mr Bloum in his tracks. He knew Daisy well enough, 'blunt as a mallet, quite terrifying', he told Ruth on one occasion. He also knew the problems her mother was currently facing and the unique way she had of tackling them. Not many women would join up with their dying husband's mistress to go on shoplifting expeditions, but then he had been around Alice long enough, too, to know that given the choice between the logical or the unique as a solution, Alice would steer towards the bizarre as surely as a magnet had to point north.

Mr Bloum accepted the fact that hoeing lettuce had suddenly vaporised from the morning's agenda. Slowly he seated himself on the wall and looked down at her.

Daisy looked up at him literally and physically from the bucket. She had an expectant look on her face; he knew that she knew he had the answer, she had the disturbing faith of a small child that what he was going to tell her was the truth. Not just the truth, but whatever he told her now was going to become her unswerving answer when faced with this dilemma for the rest of her life. It was going to be one of the bedrocks of her character: worse then that, it was going to be part of her morality.

That's what makes it so damned disturbing, he thought: whatever I tell her now she will treasure as the truth. Such faith to place in one, such an honour to be the recipient of such a faith, such expectations. Such responsibility.

The former rabbinical scholar, devoted student of the Torah, took a deep breath and paused.

'I think you'd better ask your Nana, don't you?'

Daisy stood on a little stool to give her height, and carefully tipped some of the dried fruit from the pear-shaped brass pan of Nana's scales into the bowl of cake mixture. Nana stirred it slowly, deliberately, and then tipped the bowl towards Daisy for some more. She continued to stir, echoing her own careful, deliberate thoughts.

Then she broke the silence: 'So what you want to know is, why is it a little fib if Mummy takes something, but a big fib if you do?'

Daisy nodded, adding some more fruit. The silence continued, the only sound the noise of the wooden spoon in the bowl.

Nana kept folding and stirring, making sure the fruit was evenly distributed. Daisy waited. She could see that

30

Nana was giving the problem as much thought and care as she gave to one of her fruit cakes. Nana nodded and Daisy let the last of the fruit fall in, save for one plump sultana, which got left behind. She popped that into her mouth.

Satisfied with the mixture, Nana signalled for the child to pass the large cake tin over. Daisy had cut out the greaseproof circle for the bottom and the long strip to go round the inside edge, rubbing them with the butter paper and dusting the tin with flour, like Nana had showed her; it was one of her favourite parts of the job.

Getting the tins ready properly was part of the magic of good baking: part of the egg, sugar, flour, spice and fruit peel which ended in a fruit cake. This was the unseen part, the part people didn't get to eat, but just as important, like knowing when to stir or fold and when the mixture was just right. Nobody ever saw the tins or the paper but they all went towards the final taste, Nana said.

Only when the tin was full, smoothed just right and in the oven, with the time noted on the mantel clock, did Nana speak.

Daisy sat on a stool, using her finger to wipe out the mixing bowl, catching up every scrap of mixture and popping it into her mouth.

'It seems to me,' Nana said, 'that a little fib for a grown-up is a big fib for a little girl; like your mummy's shoes are if you try them on. You can walk in them, can't you, your mummy's shoes? But they don't look right and you couldn't get very far.'

Daisy nodded, mouth full of raw-caked finger. She often put Mummy's shoes on and clumped across the floor. She longed for them to fit, so she could wear wonderful high heels in red or blue, with a fancy bow on the front.

31

'Will the fib fit me, when I'm grown-up?'

'It might do, or you might never grow enough to fit it. Or,' Nana paused, 'you might grow too big for the fib and it might blister and pinch you like walking in shoes which are too tight.'

Daisy nodded. She knew Nana would have the answer. She held up the bowl for Nana's inspection, wiped clean inside, before she took it over to the sink. Nana nodded in approval.

'We must keep an eye on that clock,' the old woman said.

She didn't condemn Alice's shoplifting activities. She didn't need to, because she knew that Alice, in her own mind, did that for herself. She had also done far worse to put food in Ruth's mouth.

She resisted memories she preferred to keep hidden, from herself and from the world: three soldiers, each took his turn on her kitchen table while Ruth slept upstairs. They hadn't felt particular about diluting the Aryan race.

She scrubbed the table afterwards, before preparing the food they paid for her. She scrubbed it with her tears and her hatred, but her child ate.

Nana crossed to the biscuit tin, took out a piece of her shortbread, bent over the sitting child and popped it into her mouth. 'Eat, eat,' she said.

Mr Bloum, his attention now turned to the flower beds, was putting pea-sticks round the new growth of a bushy blue geranium. He looked up in time to see Nana bend to kiss the top of Daisy's head.

The afternoon was coming to an end and heading gently towards evening, as Daisy helped Nana wash up the dishes from teatime. Daisy felt wonderfully bloated after a boiled egg, sandwiches, toast and cakes and the hot chocolate which was always a highlight of a visit to Nana's, served in her own pretty china cup which Nana kept especially for her.

Tea was a ritual for Nana Rosen. As she put away the odd pieces of jumble-sale china which Daisy had dried so carefully, the old lady could not help but remember her afternoon teas back home: her fine china and silver, the distinguished and learned university friends of her husband who came to call.

They had all vanished, from the eager, penniless young students who sat, hiding their fraying cuffs under their threadbare jacket sleeves while trying not to appear to eat too much, to the fellow professors who strove to dazzle each other with their wisdom while cramming Sachertorte into their mouths at the same time. All vanished, like her beautiful home with its paintings and furniture and the piano where a young Ruth had tried to master her lessons.

Now she was an old woman, with no husband, no status, and a mishmash of cups and saucers and plates. Each one a little piece of beauty in its own way, but each one a cast-off, an abandoned remnant of a once perfectly matched set, now unwanted because it no longer fitted in.

Just like me, she thought.

She could feel herself sliding towards melancholy, into what might have been, but for the war. Would she have grown into a contented old age with her beloved husband, or would some other of life's hellish interventions have occurred to separate them? She gave the little girl a smile, and was just about to close the china cupboard when the back door opened and Ruth and Alice burst in.

Behind them was a tall, well-built man with well-groomed ginger hair and a neatly trimmed moustache. Nana mistrusted him on sight, before he had stepped over the threshold or uttered a word.

'Have we missed tea?' Ruth hugged her mother, 'would you mind putting the kettle on again, we're all famished.'

Alice picked her daughter up in a hug.

'Hello, darling!'

'Did you have a nice time at the races?' Daisy eyed the man, who seemed to her to be as tall as a giant; she shared some of Nana's uneasiness.

'We never got to the races, darling, we bumped into your Uncle Malcie here.' Daisy looked at her new uncle. He got the benefit of her best stare, and Daisy noted with some concern that unlike many grown-ups she met for the first time he was not unnerved to be the object of such scrutiny, and gave as good as he got, staring right back. Daisy was determined not to give in and she noted that as he kept looking the beginnings of a small smile appeared, hiding under the corner of his moustache.

As much as she fought it, Daisy could feel a smile starting on her own face. He came forward and shook her hand solemnly, bending as he did. His face came up close and his hard-man expression melted slightly as he gave her a wink which no one else saw.

He smelled almost as nice as Daddy, he had a crisp white shirt, a silk tie, and a well-tailored, fine woollen suit, just like her father, all things which she wasn't aware of, but instinctively told the child to accept him, even though she did not trust him at all. By the time she had caught a glimpse of his gold cufflinks and watch, Daisy was smitten.

'How do you do,' she said in her best Dorothy voice.

'Very well thank you, how's yourself?' she was asked in warm, gravel-edged Glaswegian tones.

He straightened up and turned to Nana who was busy

preparing a second act on the tea stage.

'Mother, this is Mr Malcolm MacFadyen, he is an old friend of Fred's.' Ruth introduced and explained at the same time.

Nana turned, and he shook hands with her just as formally. Nana had seen how friendly he had been towards Daisy and the way he politely and gratefully accepted her invitation to tea, and allowed herself to thaw slightly. Yet there was something, something she could not put her finger on, something which triggered a warning deep in her that made Nana keep a very watchful and worried eye on him during his brief stay in her home.

Mr Bloum suddenly made one of his rare forays into the house; he usually only came indoors to eat and sleep.

The big man greeted him with the same grave, good manners.

Mr Bloum had seen the expensive red Jaguar car pull up outside the house and Alice and Ruth's arrival with the stranger. He had taken one look and he too felt he should inspect this newcomer to their lives.

He even thought he should make an attempt at conversation: 'That is a very fine car. I used to have a Mercedes myself, or rather my father kept one, back in Berlin.' Daisy and Alice were astonished: it was more than Mr Bloum had ever told them about himself in all the time they had known him.

MacFadyen nodded. 'I have always been a Jaguar man myself, perhaps you'd like to look her over.' His formal good manners did nothing to put anyone at ease; they were like sunshine making a rainbow glint on a piece of broken glass: attractive, but underneath you were still aware of the dangerous jagged edge.

Daisy wondered why all the grown-ups were suddenly

so stiff, the gentle, relaxed friendliness of Nana's home seemed to have vanished. She started to feel uneasy and confused around her new Uncle Malcie as well, but he couldn't be too bad, he was a lot like Daddy.

A quick inspection of the car was agreed while tea was being prepared. Nana nodded her approval, she knew that Mr Bloum had felt his own unease and this was his way of checking the big Scotsman out for himself. They had learned the hard way to take no one on trust.

Daisy was despatched to the parlour to lay the table. As she stood on tiptoe to reach past the chairs and lay the cutlery in the precise way her mother had shown her, she could hear the three women talking in the kitchen, something the request that she should lay the table was supposed to prevent.

'So who is this man then?' Nana interrogated.

'Haven't got the slightest, darling, Ruth met him one night,' Alice paused slightly, 'when she was out with Fred.' Ruth felt her friend's unease about mentioning her husband and lover together.

'We met him one night at the dogs. I think he was with one of the bookies.' Ruth rushed the information out a little too fast.

'So what does he do?'

'I'm not sure, I think he has his own business up in the north, in Scotland.'

'Glagow?' Alice's question did not get a reply. She continued, 'Well, he did seem to be genuinely concerned, and surprised to hear Fred was so ill.'

'Yes, he's said he thinks there's a way he can help, he's going to take us to see Fred one day next week, put a proposition to him, he said.'

'What kind of proposition?' Nana seemed mildly alarmed, rather than curious.

'Don't know, just said he had an idea, a proposition.'
Ruth was vague.

Daisy, table set to her satisfaction, went over to the window to look out at Mr Bloum and Uncle Malcie. New uncles and aunts came into and out of her life regularly these days. She quite liked the idea of this one, even if she was a bit scared of him.

He stood talking to Mr Bloum. One of the little boys from a cottage nearby had stolen up to look at the car. She saw Uncle Malcie reach in his pocket and give him a coin, and noted this with interest. He might be good for half a crown if she played her cards right.

Uncle Malcie joined them for tea; Mr Bloum declined and headed back to the depths of the garden and his shed, clutching a mug of tea. His head was spinning with remembered trips to the countryside as a little boy, safely cocooned in the leather seats of his father's car.

Malcie sat on the sofa, his knees almost up to his chin. He was too big, too well-built to fit into the proportions of the small parlour. The china cup and saucer were dwarfed in his hands; he could not fit his finger through the handle of the cup, but held it in a pinch between his huge finger and thumb.

He complimented Nana's baking, and tucked in, talking about his own grandmother's home baking when he was a little boy. Daisy could not help but stare and when he caught her he stared back, but not with malice, it was evolving into a little game they would play; Daisy was never sure who won.

'I was very sorry to hear about Fred's illness,' he said. Everything he said had a slow, formal deliberation. Not Mr Bloum's careful choosing of words to give them the right weight and meaning, but rather the conversation of a man who was used to only saying words once, and having them understood or obeyed. He was not ungenerous with his words, but once he had spent them in conversation he expected them to give him value for money.

'You should have come to me,' he said.

There was an awkward silence.

Alice would not have contacted him, because she did not know he existed until she and Ruth met him in the George that morning when they went for an eye-opener to try and remember the name of the man with whom they planned to go racing.

Ruth would not have thought about contacting him, because she remembered Fred's words to her as they drove home after meeting him: 'Not one you'd cross in a hurry.'

The big man finished his tea, mopped his lips with his napkin, and with polite excuses that he had other calls to make, said goodbye. The three women and Daisy went out to wave him off, Nana and Daisy both wanting to see the polished paintwork and chrome of the fabulous car for themselves.

Uncle Malcie shook hands and to Daisy's surprise bent over to giver her a gentle peck on the cheek. He popped coins into her hand and gave it a squeeze before driving off with a toot on the horn, and a wave through the open window.

Daisy opened her fingers and inspected her haul. An incredible two half-crowns sat in her palm. She looked up at the car as it sped out of sight, and it was then that she noticed. She gave her mother's sleeve an anxious tug and motioned down to the road with her head.

Neither Alice nor Ruth had seen her, they had been too preoccupied with saying goodbye.

There, coming up the road, like a crow flying against

the wind, was Gran. They could sense her disapproval in every approaching step. She must have seen or heard about the fancy car outside Nana Rosen's house, put two and two together and set off from her cottage on Jerry's Lane.

Five foot three of solid Irish Catholic contempt looked them up and down.

'I've just had the truant man round our house about Dorothy.' She spat the words at Alice, turned and marched off.

Chapter 5

School

Daisy walked up to the playground like a man to the gallows. Beside her Mummy could have been the priest reading words of comfort, but they had little effect.

'Come on now darling, it isn't so bad now, is it?'

Oh yes it is, thought Daisy, but Dorothy just smiled and said, 'No Mummy.'

School was definitely a Dorothy affair. Dorothy went to school with a wooden pencil box with Swiss flowers painted on the top; Daisy just wagged it.

At the gates Mummy bent and kissed her cheek. A finger slowly and lovingly wiped away the lipstick mark.

'Soon be over, got your dinner money?' Daisy nodded and fought the lump in her throat, as Mummy walked away and she watched her go. Mummy paused at the road end and waved, and Dorothy waved back, a small wave, which tried not to be frightened. Then she turned to face her own personal hell of the playground.

It was more than five weeks since she had last made an appearance. Her best friend Zoe, tired of being deserted and always on the edge of the other girls' games, had made new friends. Now it was Dorothy's turn to be on the outside looking in; a stranger in a strange land where she knew the vocabulary, but never seemed to have mastered the art of conversation.

Two boys came up to her, one pushed the other forward in a dare. 'Go on, tell her then.'

'You mam's a whore,' he said, repeating overheard, grown-up words he didn't understand. Dorothy didn't either, but she knew his intention was to hurt.

'Sticks and stones may break my bones, but names can never hurt me,' she told him primly and walked off.

A handful of gravel showered her legs and back.

'That break anything, heh?' one of them jeered after her.

Out of the corner of her eye Dorothy could see others watching, going over to join in. She kept walking, afraid she would become like a rabbit trapped in the headlights of Daddy's car on the way home after collecting Mummy from a play, with Dorothy in her nightie and dressing gown, tucked up under a rug on the back seat. Daddy had stopped the car and turned the lights off until the rabbit had come to its senses and hopped away. No such mercy here.

She remembered Mummy's words over her silver-eggcup breakfast: 'If Daddy can be brave in hospital, you can be brave at school.' Then Mummy added with a flourish, 'And I can be brave when Uncle George saws me in half! Cheer up, darling, soon be Friday and you can come on Saturday and watch both houses. Aunt Zita will be there.'

Not even the thought of her beloved godmother, wardrobe mistress and owner of a wonderful pincushion she would let Daisy wear on her own wrist, could bring any comfort.

Dorothy walked up to Zoe, who was turning one end of a long rope for girls to run in and skip.

'Hello.'

Zoe turned away and concentrated on the rhyme: 'B'min'h'm-Mail-Post-and-News. I-sell-edition-one.' There the rope turned faster and faster, 'Two-three-four-five-six-seven-eight.' Susan Chalmers got tangled on nine, but that was the best score: Susan was the best at skipping. Everyone wanted to be her friend and now she had claimed Zoe. As the hand-bell was rung the girls wound up their rope. Zoe, Susan and friends linked arms and marched to the line-up. Dorothy followed glumly, like a wounded animal on the edge of the pack. Tagging along behind the other girls was her safest bet, so was standing on the boundary of their games. If the boys decided they would get her, the other girls would consider it their right to defend her; but in the meantime she would stay on the outside. Different and unwanted.

In the classroom when it came to Dorothy's name being called at registration time, the teacher looked up in surprise, even though she had seen the little girl walk in.

This caused a ripple of laughter around the class, further separating Dorothy from the others. Some of the boys' laughter was tinged with admiration: no one else had such a poor attendance record. Not even the boys from the tinker's family which had been given one of the council houses near Nana at Botany Bay were as accomplished at wagging it as Dorothy Smedley.

Dorothy sat at her desk and wished the world would go away and it was Saturday. She felt like she was being sawn in half.

Watching Ruth warm up in a rehearsal room, Alice thought of her daughter and her dying husband and felt the teethmarks of the saw inside her heart.

Ruth, as she stretched and limbered up before her audition for a variety show on ATV with Russ Conway topping the bill, felt her hamstrings being sawn in half. She looked round her at the fresh young faces of the other dancers and felt too old for this damn lark.

The four dancers who were hired were all straight from school, much to Ruth and Alice's disgust.

'Ballet de bleeding Monaco, my arse! That blonde who said she spent last summer there, I doubt if she'd been south of Solihull,' Alice consoled her friend as they settled themselves in the pub across the road afterwards. There was a noise behind them as the four girls, and the show's producer, came in on a wave of euphoria and headed for the bar. Alice and Ruth noted the young faces, the glowing effect they had on the man with them, and sighed inwardly to themselves.

'Vat's left for us?' asked Ruth. In such philosophical moments her Brummy accent deserted her and she sounded more thickly Austrian than her mother, the unhappiness smothering every syllable.

'Us?' said Alice, as she threw the remains of her gin and It down her throat with an air of bravado, 'us? We get sawn in bleeding half.'

She got up and headed for the door, Ruth finished her drink and followed. She knew the mood Alice was in now, and she knew they were off to borrow a few things for Edie-the-Fence.

'Just time to pop into Rackham's, I think. We couldn't possibly go home empty-handed, imagine how let down Mr Pickup would be if we did.' Alice tightened the belt of Fred's old mac around her waist. It had such useful deep pockets.

Daisy managed to make it through the day. Through the loneliness of morning and afternoon playtime, and the lunchtime which only had treacle sponge and an

43

enormous ladleful of custard to console her.

She had made it through the lessons, and the surprised resentment of her teacher that despite weeks of absence she had got only one of her sums wrong, achieved full marks in the general knowledge test, had finished Janet and John and was now favouring Kipling's *Puck of Pook's Hill*, given to her by an actor friend of Alice's when her mother had been trying her damnedest to get a bit of legit work with a production of *A Midsummer Night's Dream*.

Daisy had confessed to Miss that her petticoat had been part of a fairy costume from the same production, until her Aunt Zita had got hold of it. The woman seemed unable to cope with persistent truants with Shakespearean underwear and left Daisy to her own devices, which suited them both fine.

The other children, however, knew a freak when they saw one, and had either ignored her or bullied her. Being ignored she could cope with; the taunts, hair-pulls and sundry playground persecutions were causing her to erode slowly. Neither Dorothy nor Daisy could cope with this. She could feel herself dissolving into a huge lake of unhappiness.

The whole class began to fidget as home time came nearer. Daisy would have liked to chance standing up and peering out to see if Mummy was there to meet her, like she said she would, but she felt too cowed by the day and the risk of catching the teacher's eye to make a move.

Suddenly it was time to stand up, hands together, eyes closed: *Thank you Jesus for this day, For our work and for our play. Thank you for the birds that sing. Thank you God for everything. Amen.*

The ones nearest the door were halfway out to the cloakroom before the end of the Amen and they had opened their eyes.

44

Daisy held back, put her coat on slowly and headed down the stairs. She hated school and it seemed hostile, or at best indifferent to her.

She trudged across the playground, satchel over her shoulder, shoe bag in her hand. She hated the way her shoes got dirty and trodden on at school.

To her delight both Mummy and Aunt Ruth were waiting for her outside the school gate.

They stood apart from the main knot of mothers as much as they stood out. Mummy was far more beautiful than any other in the whole world, Daisy knew that for a fact. All the other mothers didn't wear make-up, didn't have best friends who were just as glamorous and stood by them smoking cigarettes they had made themselves between their long red fingernails. The other mothers didn't go on stage or recite lines from plays when washing up, or dance like Mummy and Aunt Ruth did.

Daisy felt her heart swell with pride. She could see all the other children, and their mothers, looking at them.

As she walked over to Mummy she heard one of the mothers say 'Fancy woman,' and Daisy had to admit to herself that, yes, Mummy was very fancy and smart indeed.

On the bus back to Lichfield Alice asked her daughter how the day had been.

'Horrid, I hate it.'

'Well, what don't you like about it, darling?'

'Just everything. It's horrid.'

'That's not good enough, you'll have to do better than that.'

So Daisy did. All of a sudden her dam of personal sadness decided to burst. It had no warning signs or

45

leaks, but as the bus lumbered past King Edward's School, heading for the depot, every piece of misery in her life decided it was going to be aired.

'I hate the way they won't let me play, or talk to me, and laugh at me and call me names and call you names and I hate having to do sums.' Alice tried to get a word in, but Daisy was now in full flow. What had started in dryness, with a throat so tight the words could hardly come out, exploded into tears.

'And I hate it when Daddy's ill and I hate it at Mr Pickup's and I hate not having my own bedroom and I hate not being at the Horse and Jockey and I hate not having a dog and I hate it being cold in the mornings and I hate having to wash in the sink after the pots and I hate having to go on the po under the bed and I want it to be like it was and I want my daddy.'

The Daisy Dorothy had built for herself to take all the knocks and uncertainties into which her life had descended had suddenly vanished, and Alice was left clutching her child, now a raw piece of unhappiness. The little girl did not sob noisily, but silent tears poured down her cheeks.

Alice fought back her own, because she knew that if they started she was afraid they might not stop. Ruth leaned over from the seat behind and embraced them both, and without such inhibitions sobbed her mascara into black streaks.

Alice was afraid that this was where she lost her battle, her nerve and her wits. The bus would soon come to a halt at the top of Levetts Fields and she didn't know if her legs would work to carry her off the bus, let alone through the rest of her life.

'And I never, ever want to have to go to school again,' said a little voice beside her.

Alice managed to find some words.
'OK, you don't have to.'
So she didn't.

Chapter 6

Mummy Gets Sawn in Half

Daisy was intoxicated by the Birmingham Hippodrome. To her it was a cavernous palace of delights, from the stage door with its sentry in his cubbyhole, who smiled and offered sweeties, to the labyrinth of corridors and dressing rooms. Then there was the front of house. The foyer, the stairs leading to the stalls, the circle, the plush seats with their sixpence-in-the-slot opera glasses and chandeliers floating above. It was a wonderland where anything could, and did, happen.

Backstage had its own hypnotic smell: the Wills Old Flake smoked by the stagehands, the age and dust combined into a headiness tinged with faint perfume from the passing women dancers or actresses. Different corridors and turns had a smell either dry, old and venerable, or musty, damp and sad. The little girl stood and sniffed like a spaniel in the wind and absorbed it all.

The theatre seeped into her through her senses, through the uneven floorboards and ragged linoleum in the dressing rooms. She was born with Alice's lifelong romance with the stage in her blood, and nothing the theatre had shown her in her eight years had ever disappointed. She was as smitten as her mother. Here was her own philosopher's stone, which transmuted into gold the base metal of everyday life.

Mummy's stints in rep, the hard slog of variety, Aunt Ruth's chorus lines, the costumes her godmother sewed all ganged together and conspired to take Daisy out of Dorothy and transport her to a magical place where only good things happened.

'Shift yer bloody self, sixpence,' a stagehand sang out, and Daisy shot out of the way as he and a mate staggered past with an enormous papier-mâché urn with palm fronds spilling out.

All around her people were hard at work preparing the magic spells that would entrance two houses nightly with matinées Wednesday and Saturday.

Alice swept up and tucked Daisy under her wing. 'Come on, darling, let's find the dressing room and track down your Uncle George, if he's not across the road getting a few under his belt.'

Settled in the little box that passed as a dressing room, Mummy began her own part of the ritual. Out of her battered alligator grip came the slap box made of black tin, brushes, combs and pins along with her lucky yellow kimono.

'Some say yellow is unlucky, but not for me, darling,' Mummy had confided to her once, setting her daughter off into adult life with a determination for yellow dresses. Daisy would be well into her twenties before she realised they were totally unsuited for her pale complexion and made her look as sick as hell.

Aunt Zita materialised around the paint-chipped door, two mugs in hand.

'Tea up.'

'God bless you and save you, darling.'

Mummy took a few gulps and offered the tannin-stained mug for Daisy to drink.

'Seen George?'

'Over the road, love.' Aunt Zita put down her mug and added another ring to the patina of decades.

'Probably getting a few under his belt,' Daisy gave her opinion and wondered why both women roared with laughter.

'I'm quite sure, love,' said Aunt Zita and ceremonially draped her tape measure around the little girl's shoulders. Daisy noticed her godmother did not have her special pincushion with her, perhaps she'd be allowed to wear it later.

'I've got Vi's stuff ready for you, George dropped it off,' said Aunt Zita. 'Done it up for you with a bit I had left over.'

Aunt Zita's leftovers were legendary. They filled the wardrobes, professional or daily, of her many friends, unbeknown to the producers and theatre managers who footed the bill. Daisy had just grown out of a velvet coat which should have been part of a famous leading lady's dress in *The Cherry Orchard*; she was glad her fairy-costume underwear was still going strong.

Her godmother leaned over towards her conspiratorially. 'I've got a lovely party frock for you to try on later.'

A wave of mixed emotions hit Daisy: delight at the thought of a new dress and the dread of a room full of children at her cousin Graham's tenth birthday, an invitation to which Mummy had suddenly announced she had accepted without Daisy's knowledge or agreement.

'How's Vi's mother's legs, then?' Aunt Zita asked.

Mummy gave a look of measured judgement, head on one side, and waggled her hand in a so-so motion.

50

'Not that good, but not that bad.' Then came the magical words, 'If you ask me ...' She let the words hang in the air and drift slowly to the ground, as she returned her attention to her tea.

Daisy knew the code by now, Mummy was just about to indulge in one of her more harmless pastimes: that of character assassination.

'Yes?' Aunt Zita stretched the word into a cross between an honest enquiry and come-on-Alice-out-with-it.

'If you ask me.' Mummy leaned over the other side of her battered chair, rummaged in her handbag and came up with her cigarettes and, wonder of wonders for Daisy, a Kit-Kat that she pounced on.

'What do you say?'

'Thank you Mummy.'

'I should think so. That was quite rude, you know darling, and not like you at all. Never forget your manners, darling.'

'Yes?' Aunt Zita wanted to know about Vi's mother's legs, which might not now be as bad as Vi had led everyone to believe.

'I mean, darling,' Mummy continued to Daisy, 'you may have not had breakfast, you might have shoes with holes in them, but you can always have manners. Charm people, darling, charm. Even when you're hungry and your feet are wet. That's when charm matters most.'

'Well? About Vi's mother's legs?'

Mummy turned from Daisy now that she knew her audience was riveted.

Daisy turned the Kit-Kat over onto its front and undid the seam in the red paper wrapper carefully, so that it did not tear. She peeled back the silver paper, smoothing out the edges and wallowing in the first wave of chocolate aroma. Then she turned the bar over again, so that it was the right way up and she could see the writing, stopped to admire it and then carefully broke it into four fingers.

It was a big one! Usually Mummy bought the two-finger ones; but then she remembered. On the way to the station they had gone into Melia's café on Bird Street for Mummy to buy a packet of cigarettes, and she must have slipped the Kit-Kat into her bag then. That didn't take the shine off the foil wrapper Daisy had turned into a silver salver for such a treat. She shrugged mentally; she hadn't had any breakfast, just like Mummy said. The eggs had run out, and her silver eggcup and spoon had stood silently empty on the shelf. She turned instead to her silver-paper feast.

My shoes don't leak through, Daisy thought, we only got them last week at Playfers on Market Street. And we even paid for them.

They were still so new you could see the little boy and girl in their funny clothes setting off down the Start-Rite road together, printed into the heel in gold. Mummy polished them every night with the Cherry Blossom they hadn't paid for, which somehow found its way into Mummy's pocket as the nice man thanked them and opened the door as they said goodbye.

Daisy shrugged to herself again, gave up on reason and bit into the first finger. Daisy loved chocolate as much as Mummy loved a good gossip.

'If you ask me,' Mummy exhaled from the cigarette she had just lit, 'it's not Vi's mother's legs. It's George.'

'George?'

'Yes, George.'

'No?' Aunt Zita managed to stretch her 'no', just as well as her 'yes', into one long I-don't-believe-it-Alice-you'd-better-have-a-good-go-at-convincing-me syllable.

'No, it's George. I think the strain is getting to her, poor soul.'

'Really?' (What's-the-fat-drunken-lecherous-old-sod-done-to-her-now?) Aunt Zita might not have been a woman of many words, but she made each one of them work for her.

'Really. It's the stress and strain of not only being married to a magic act, but being in it as well.'

'Not to mention the drink, and the other,' said Aunt Zita darkly.

'My argument exactly, darling. I think they're symptoms, myself.'

'Symptoms?'

'Symptoms, darling. What does the audience see? A fat, jolly man on stage conjuring. They don't see the nerves, the worry, the obsession with his props, the pacing up and down before he goes on.'

'True.'

'Gospel, darling. He's, he's . . .'

'Fibbing,' said Daisy without looking up from her Kit-Kat, which she had decided was too good to rush, and she was eating very slowly, sucking the chocolate off each piece in her mouth first, before starting to chew.

'Fibbing?' Aunt Zita asked.

'Fibbing,' said Mummy. 'He's living a lie. He's two men in the one body. Fat and calm on stage and off it he worries so much, he should be a whippet. They say that inside every fat person there's a thin one trying to get out and in George's case it's a constant battle to keep the thin, frantic one locked away. He's a big fib.'

The idea stunned both Daisy and her godmother. There were big fibs and little fibs and, in Uncle George, a fib couldn't come much bigger.

Mummy paused to stub out her cigarette into a battle-scarred old tin Players Please ashtray in front of the mirror.

53

'The strain of living with George's nerves is turning Vi into a wreck herself. So no wonder she keeps bolting back to her mother's for some peace, using the old girl's legs as an alibi. Can't complain though, from my point of view it's regular money coming in. God knows, darling, we need it.'

'How's things?'

Daisy saw her mother give a glance in her direction, and she pretended to be engrossed in folding the silver paper of her Kit-Kat into something interesting.

The child kept her head down, but her ears were strained, as the two women switched to half-whisper and half-lip-reading.

'Couldn't you have done *Hay Fever* with Derek?'

'Yes, I did get an offer, but all things considered . . .'

'You mean with Fred and,' here Zita mouthed the word 'Dorothy' and gestured towards the girl.

'Yes,' Mummy continued smoothly, 'Dorothy would have to stay with my mother or Caroline, and I don't think it's best that . . .'

Daisy didn't hear any more. The mention of her older half-sister's name had the same effect as an electric shock, jolting through her body in a mixture of horror, fear and total dismay.

Daisy thought back to the three occasions they had met, and she had been on the receiving end of Caroline's cold, unpleasant stare. The look did not contain anger, it wasn't even nasty. Daisy could have coped with emotions, even hostile ones; you couldn't be with Mummy or Aunt Ruth every day and not develop some kind of immunity to emotional highs and lows. Rather, Caroline had a way of looking at her that just blanked Daisy out, as though she did not exist or even matter in the slightest, and that was far more frightening. This was

54

compounded by the fact that Caroline looked so much like Mummy in the physical sense, though in reality they were complete opposites.

No one could be more different from Mummy and her way of life than Caroline. Not even Gran with her legion of plaster saints all ready to condemn you to eternal damnation was as bad. It was as if the dour, sour young woman took everything their mother was, carried out her own inquisition and found Mummy guilty on all counts. She was determined to be an exact opposite, so thorough was her condemnation.

Not Caroline. Silent, scrub-faced Caroline, who never let the word 'darling' pass her lips, who never had adventures; to her the stage was anathema. She stood behind the walls of the fortress of respectability she had built of her semi-detached, with its striped front-lawn moat and her bank-clerk husband as its defending army, and she poured the boiling oil of her disapproval over the mother, stepfather and Dorothy, her half-sister.

'You wouldn't want me to go and stay with Caroline, would you?'

Mummy and Aunt Zita stopped talking immediately.

'Of course not darling, I mean,' Mummy rolled her eyes in mock horror, 'really!'

'Promise?'

'Cross my heart and hope to die,' her mother mimed the actions.

Daisy could feel tears beginning to rise. It was bad enough having to stop being Dorothy, without having to deal with the Grans, Aunt Bettys and Carolines of this world. Panic engulfed her at the thought of being separrated from her mother as well as her father, a panic so intense it stalled her ability to think, to the extent she just sat and felt she was dissolving, slowly melting into the chair, becoming part of the walls and floor of the shabby dressing room. Ceasing to exist would be the only way to cope, by becoming so blank that no one would be able to see her.

Alice saw the look of abject misery on her daughter's face and flung a kimono-ed arm around her, engulfing the little girl into folds of cheap, printed yellow satin, hugging her close.

'Of course not, darling, of course not, promise.'

Daisy's misery was cut short by Uncle George booming through the door.

'Alice, my dear!'

'George, darling, how the devil are you?'

He didn't bother to answer, but kissed Mummy's hand, told Zita her saxophonist husband didn't realise what a pearl among women she truly was, as he bent down to conjure a threepenny bit from behind Daisy's ear.

'Voilà!' he exclaimed.

Daisy knew very well that her aunt's name was Violet, but where money was concerned she wasn't going to argue.

'How's Vi?' Mummy enquired. 'How's Vi's mother's legs?'

George's face darkened. 'Terrible dear, terrible, Vi says she is going to go back in again, to have them drained.'

'Drained,' said Aunt Zita, weighing the word, and exchanging a meaningful look with Alice.

'Drained,' confirmed George. All three adults fell quiet, picturing the scene.

'What have the houses been like?' Mummy felt obliged to break the silence. She had never met Vi's mother, but she felt she knew her intimately; the poor woman's failing legs were currently Alice's only legal means of support.

56

'Damnable houses, damnable. Half empty, half dead like as not. Not like the old days. Television is killing the halls, Alice.'

'Ruth went for a dancer's part up at ATV,' Mummy added, turning her attention back to unpacking her slap tin and hairpiece, 'it's for the young.'

George sighed to himself, the three adults fell silent again and Daisy caught their mood. Uncle George's sandy hair was thinning slightly, and now instead of being fat and jolly like a sort of Father Christmas in a tail coat when he went on stage, she saw him diminished like a beloved teddy bear slowly losing its stuffing, with its fur wearing away to the canvas backing.

'I've done Vi's stuff up for Alice,' Zita cut in. In matters of costume and wardrobe she could be quite verbose. 'I haven't got round to doing your silks.'

'Don't worry, I'll take care of his scarves,' Mummy said. 'Would you mind if Daisy went along with you, darling?' Alice knew how grumpy George could get before he went on and wanted her daughter out of the way; the little girl could probably read as well as a child twice her age, but there were parts of her vocabulary Alice wanted to stay underdeveloped.

'Delighted. Come on, you can use my magnet. I'm running out of pins.' Daisy's godmother held out her hand and invited the child to join her in her own magic kingdom.

'I've got a little something for you to try on as well, remember?' She ushered Daisy out of the door.

Somewhere, some actress would be wondering if perhaps she was putting on a little weight, because the seams of her costume would be just slightly too tight, despite being measured, all thanks to Zita's larcenous ability to make a little fabric go a long way: usually onto

57

the back of her favourite, if impecunious, godchild.

Daisy was still wearing Aunt Zita's tape measure, like a badge of office. Now she was going to be allowed to use her magnet! Once inside the wardrobe department Aunt Zita produced an old-fashioned grey horseshoe-shaped magnet and Daisy set to work.

'You're better at bending over than I am,' Aunt Zita said. 'Never mind about Vi's mother's legs, it's my knees you should be worrying about. Off you go!'

Daisy bent over and methodically walked along, with the magnet a few inches above the worn linoleum floor. As if by magic the pins jumped onto the magnet's steel ends while Daisy clutched its grey-painted curve. It never failed to fascinate her. Halfway round the worktable Daisy had to stop and scrape the pins off the magnet into their waiting tin. They wriggled and clung to each other like maggots in an angler's can. Daisy set off again and soon the big flat tin was full.

'Splendid. Will you fill up my pincushions for me?'

The little girl hitched herself up onto a stool and set to work. The big fat strawberry full of sawdust to keep the pins from rusting was soon seeded with handfuls of pins; then the velvet square one and finally Daisy set to work on her favourite: the little pincushion Aunt Zita fastened to her wrist while she worked on a fitting. No sooner had Daisy filled it than it was called for.

'Zeet, love, come to my rescue!' A tall thin woman with a blonde beehive rushed in.

'Put me bloody stiletto through the lace,' she held up the hem of her flowing evening dress. 'Can you be an angel and sort it?'

Zita nodded to a step stool and the woman hopped up.

'Want to help?' Zita asked as she threaded a needle, which she pinned to her lapel.

Daisy nodded, excited, happy to help in an emergency. Her heart swelled with pride as Zita fastened the little pincushion to her wrist. Daisy held out her hand in an ever-so-important way, offering the pins as a lightning repair to the lace hem got under way.

The woman turned when directed, and while she waited admired herself in the huge mirror on the wall opposite, smoothing her lacquered hair, wiping an imaginary smudge from her mascara.

'I see that crazy bloody Alice is standing in for Vi with George,' she said by way of conversation. Both Zita and Daisy stiffened.

'Yes,' said Zita coolly,' and her daughter, my god-daughter, is helping me, aren't you dear?'

The woman froze, poleaxed with embarrassment.

'Say hello to the nice lady, Dorothy dear.' It was at times like these that Zita's habit of imbuing words with so much meaning came to the fore. Even Daisy was aware of how much venom and contempt the wardrobe mistress could get into the four little letters of the word 'nice'.

'How do you do,' said Daisy in her best Dorothy voice, trying to impersonate her aunt's technique, though she had to admit to herself she spoiled it by not being able to decide which word to poison: the how or the you. She resolved to work on it.

As Zita finished stitching she stood slowly and fixed the woman with a look that finished off the job. Daisy would be a grown woman with a couple of lovers, one with a hysterical wife, and a libidinous boss under her belt before she had perfected such a stare.

The woman managed a strangled, 'Ta, ever so,' as she bolted for the door, while Zita and Daisy managed a wordless that-showed-her look. From her mother Daisy inherited the ability to talk her head off; from her godmother she learned the true power of the right word, well aimed.

'Now!' said Aunt Zita and the word worked like a magic spell, banishing all trace of the beehive woman from the room. 'Time for a fitting, off with your pinny and jumper and up you hop.'

Zita helped Daisy with the buttons. 'Skin a rabbit,' she cried as the pinafore and jumper flew off and were folded in one experienced move.

'Mind the pins!' she warned as she lowered the dress over Daisy's head.

'There!'

Daisy turned to look at herself in the mirror and her heart sank. Aunt Zita might have been a model of restraint with words, but in material she talked the hind legs off a herd of donkeys.

As young as she was, Daisy knew how she should look, how a little girl with plain features and straight hair should dress: like her Aunt Ruth. Daisy did not understand what the words sophisticated or chic meant, but she knew instinctively that plain, simple, tailored black, grey or beige turned an angular, rather ordinary aunt into someone who made people stop and stare in admiration.

What Daisy dreamed of was pale grey silk taffeta, plain fitted with a slightly gathered waist falling into a full skirt. She had seen a picture in Aunt Betty's *Good Housekeeping* last Christmas of a little girl wearing the dress, holding a present behind her back, leaning forward, lips puckered, to kiss a boy beneath the mistletoe. Behind them was a Christmas tree, a spaniel in front of the fireplace and a happy Mummy and Daddy looking on. Daisy wanted to be the girl in the picture; she wanted her parents to be in it, too. She would wear the strand of pearls Daddy bought her last Christmas, which came in a plush-lined box.

That was what she wanted, but what she got was the royal blue velvet equivalent of a Blackpool tram lit up for the illuminations. It had frills, it had buttons down the front, it had a bow at the back, puffed sleeves, lace collar and net petticoat.

'Oh that does look nice, doesn't it?'

Daisy nodded to hide the fib she was telling, and could feel tears of disappointment start to well up.

Her godmother, busy tutting and fussing the dress to perfection, mistook them for tears of joy, the silence for a little girl overcome with delight.

It was the party dress that Zita had always wanted as a child. She remembered the plain little grey dress her mother made for her and how she had stared in envy at the splendid party frocks of the rich girls in her class, when she was a scholarship girl in a cast-off gymslip.

Daisy risked another look in the mirror. Yes, the dress was everything she feared, and then some more. The dress needed a flamboyant character with curly blonde hair, not a shy plain thing who hugged the wall, said nothing and watched everyone else all the time, who wasn't really sure who she was, but knew she wasn't cut out to be the owner of a dress like this. The dress cried out for Shirley Temple.

Daisy thought her heart couldn't sink any lower and then Aunt Zita said, removing the dress with care, 'It will be ready for you for Graham's party.' Her heart slipped down another couple of hitherto undiscovered notches.

Graham. Aunt Betty's adored son, who could build the Forth Rail Bridge out of Meccano, had his lifesaving badges sewn onto his trunks, and badges on his sleeve at Cubs.

61

He was a boy, a strange kind of creature Daisy never met socially. She knew them only from playground warfare; she mainly mixed with adults, so she found the company of other children slightly odd, almost threatening. She could just about cope with girls, but boys were alien to her. The only one she ever met was Graham, and she didn't like him, or rather the Graham that she came into contact with: Aunt Betty's version of her son.

Daisy didn't realise, and neither did anyone else, that Graham was a quiet, gentle, shy boy who was very unsure of himself, but what he did have, in Aunty Betty, was a mother who was sure of one thing: the world revolved around her son.

Aunt Betty was short and dumpy like the mother hen she had evolved into, cackling round Lichfield and Whittington with her shopping basket, pecking at pieces of gossip. Graham was the chick she fussed and protected and clucked about to the world. He was her pride, her reason.

Alice might have had the looks, the flash clothes and glamour that pulled the men; but Betty consoled herself she had something her sister had never had: a son. So each achievement of Graham's was amplified, each maths test, each Cubs outing was used by Aunt Betty to trumpet to the world that she had a son. Such a magnificent son that she kept her house polished to perfection, and pulled the clothes off her husband's back as he walked in after work, not out of passion but to wash and iron, so that her home and the people in it were the perfect setting for her perfect son. With Graham's arrival Betty's life had become complete, justified.

Her husband, who could never measure up to the importance of his son, made sure he got the long-distance jobs at work, driving from the paper mill at Alrewas to the one at Fort William, two days away in the Highlands. He bought an old railway goods van to put on his allotment, so he could keep out of the way of his wife and son; at least there he didn't feel an outsider. So her husband's neglect made Betty turn to Graham even more, to justify herself, and the circle spiralled.

Daisy knew nothing of that, all she knew was she never walked into her aunt's house without being met with a look of disapproval, or being told what a wonderful person her cousin Graham was, and she, by implication, was not.

Now she had to face his party, where Aunt Betty would spend the afternoon preaching the gospel of Graham.

In the midst of a room full of Grahams and their female equivalents, including some of the girls from the school she presently avoided, Daisy would be as out of place as her new party frock would be at a funeral.

They would stare, she knew they would, and their parents coming to collect them afterwards would stare at Mummy, whisper amongst themselves, then say hello with smiles just a little bit too bright.

Daisy's orbit was slowly spinning further and further away from what was accepted or expected of childhood, as her father's illness worsened, money lessened and their home vanished.

'Graham's party.' It was a flat statement from Daisy, bordering on terror.

Aunt Zita was busy tacking a seam she had altered on the dress and hardly looked up. 'Yes, next Tuesday. Your Uncle Archie and I were having tea in the Tudor Café last week, and your Aunt Betty was there and told us Caroline might be going. Do you remember the dress I made for her wedding? Wonderful!'

Daisy remembered a photograph of her half-sister,

bouquet in hand, standing outside a church, dressed like a lampshade.

Caroline. Daisy froze. Was this a plot? Would they make her dress up in this party frock to end all frocks and then make her go home with Caroline? Mummy wouldn't? She couldn't, could she? Daisy shivered in her little lace cotton vest and knickers, more from fear than cold.

The altered dress had not altered that much. It still hung on Daisy and quietly condemned her for not being able to sing 'On the Good Ship Lollipop'. Daisy tried not to look in the mirror at the dress but, like all good horrors, her eyes were drawn to it.

As she looked she saw the door open behind them.

'Tra-laaaaaa!' Mummy opened her yellow kimono and struck a pose, arms wide, the one she usually did when Uncle George produced something amazing on stage. He used to do doves, but Aunt Vi said they ponged something terrible.

'Looks great, Zita.' Mummy turned and admired herself in the mirror.

Daisy's godmother smiled with pleasure. 'Yes, it turned out nicely. Hope Vi likes the changes when she gets back.'

'If,' said Mummy conspiratorially, 'if. Remember what I said earlier? George has more or less confirmed it to me just now.'

Mummy did a couple of smart steps round the table, ending up alongside Daisy, after a kick-turn. 'And do you know what that means, darling?'

Daisy shook her head.

'I will be sawn in half full-time and we'll be in the money.'

She planted a kiss on top of Daisy's head.

'Wonderful dress that, Zita. Have you said thank you, darling?'

Daisy shook her head again, this time more solemnly. 'Thank you Auntie.'

'It's not finished yet, my love, thank me next week when I bring it over. You know, I've some lovely red zigzag braid I'm going to pop round the hem and cuffs. Finish it off a treat.'

The faint flutter of hope Daisy had of going unnoticed and unremarked upon at Graham's party finally fell off its perch with a thud and died.

Zita carefully removed the dress and Mummy helped Daisy with her jumper and pinny.

'Ready to come and watch?'

Daisy gave a nod of excitement.

'Come on then, show time!' Daisy grasped her outstretched hand in anticipation.

'Only remember, darling, keep out of Uncle George's way, you know what a rotten sod he is before he goes on.'

The earlier chaos backstage had been replaced with something that ran more smoothly, only with a frantic edge.

People knew where to go, what to do, when to be ready in the wings for their cue, but now an electric current of excitement shot through them all. The curtain was up and the show was under way.

Mummy threaded her way through the bodies backstage and tucked Daisy away with the sparky, who was busy setting lights. He barely looked up as Mummy kissed her and left, his only acknowledgement a softly grunted: 'Keep yer elbows in and don't touch bleedin' nothin'.'

After some dancers came off it was Uncle George's turn.

Mummy gave a big wink to Daisy as the compère announced, 'George Benedict, the grand illusionist extraordinaire!'

Like a butterfly emerging from a chrysalis, or perhaps a big fat moth, Uncle George shrugged off his backstage nerves, grew in stature and lost his unstuffed teddy-bear look as he walked onto the stage and transformed, right before Daisy's eyes, into the tall, magnificent conjuror she remembered. What a fibber, Daisy thought.

He led Mummy as if she was a grand empress at a ball, the sequins on her costume sparkled, the stones in her tiara dazzled as she gave a sweeping curtsy to the audience.

Mummy then held up her arms in exaltation. Her dazzling smile playing importance onto Uncle George like an extra spotlight.

No one would ever guess her long white gloves were clamped to her with safety pins to take in the slack from Vi's biceps, made muscular from humping all George's cases and props. No one, least of all Daisy, would ever guess that she was broke, terrified for the future, facing her husband's death head-on and had just lifted a fiver from the wallet of the ventriloquist going on after the interval. Alice was a conjuror in her own right.

Uncle George took a third bow, aimed at an imaginary royal box, took Alice by the hand, kissed her fingers and presented her to the applauding audience. She was halfway through her second curtsy when George gave a smooth and practised yank on her arm, which the punters didn't see, but she felt like a whiplash. As he led her offstage he hissed, 'I'm the bugger they're paying to see, not you.'

The fly came down, hiding his props from view; the smooth-talking compère came on, with a line of patter

66

which couldn't decide whether to be as smooth as Bruce Forsyth or as comical as Norman Vaughan, and chose to flounder instead. Daisy followed them down the corridor to the dressing rooms. Uncle George would not allow her to carry anything, though she offered. The backwash of adrenalin made him almost as impossible after a show as the time before he went on. Daisy knew to leave well alone for a while, so she watched and waited in Mummy's dressing room.

'Well darling, was I marvellous?' Mummy flopped down on the chair in front of the mirror, the glamorous glow of the stage slowly dimming into tiredness and spent nerves. Daisy could see a film of sweat between the greasepaint and the start of her mother's hairline as she lifted her onto her lap. Daisy gave her a kiss and stared, almost overawed, at her mother. Sometimes it was hard to see where the stage ended and real life, real Mummy, began again.

Alice then lifted her daughter up onto the dressing table, and lit a cigarette. As she exhaled she bent her head for Daisy to take off the tiara. Daisy removed the hairgrips and eased the bejwelled headband off with reverence. To her delight, Mummy took up her tail comb and combed through her hair, giving Daisy a quick back-comb here and there before popping the tiara onto her head. Another couple of flicks with the comb satisfied Alice; she helped Daisy to jump down and turn to the mirror. Alice switched the mirror lights on and handed Daisy a lipstick. Silently, not to break the spell, the child put on the lipstick, pressing her lips together and wiping the corner of her mouth, copying Alice's actions.

Daisy gazed into the illuminated mirror, entranced. Gone was the plain little girl, here shimmering in the light was a girl who could wear one of Aunt Zita's fanciful dresses;

67

here was someone who would never, ever, be afraid of going to school and would laugh in the face of the awful Graham's birthday party. Here was the power of magic, which would saw you in half and put you back together again, in time to take a bow twice nightly with a matinée on Saturday. It was the biggest and best fib in the whole world.

She could barely whisper to her mother, 'Can I go and show Uncle George and Aunt Zita?'

Alice was just as entranced as her daughter. It was the first time in what seemed liked months she had seen her truly happy. The dull, sad eyes that had followed her everywhere since Fred's illness and their flight from the Horse and Jockey were replaced with eyes that once again sparkled with joy and hope for the future.

Alice put her head alongside her daughter's and looked at the child through the mirror. She too whispered so as not to break the enchantment. 'Of course you can, darling.'

Uncle George was nearer. Daisy pushed open the door of his dressing room. He was sitting with his back to her. His dinner jacket and trousers were folded neatly over the back of a chair. The evening's success had left him, and he looked deflated, in nothing but his shirt, vest, boxer shorts and socks; a towel at his side was clogged with his stage make-up. After the splendour of the show Daisy felt sad for him.

'Look at me, Uncle George,' Daisy struck a pose like Mummy did on stage when he completed a trick.

A smile struggled to appear on his face. 'My, you look grand.'

'You could saw me in half when I'm grown-up, couldn't you?'

'I could.' He reached over for a bottle of Worthington E and began to pour it into a glass. 'I could indeed. You look proper grown-up, a big girl, don't you?'

'Yes,' Daisy nodded and gave a twirl round for him.

'My word, yes, proper grown-up. Would you like to know some magic?'

Daisy nodded again, amazed. The day was just getting better and better. As well as the party frock, she had helped Aunt Zita, seen the show, got to wear Aunt Vi's tiara and now she was going to learn how to do magic.

'Yes please, Uncle George.'

'Good girl. Now,' he paused and looked round for effect, bent close to Daisy and whispered, 'the thing about magic is that no one else must know how you do it. It's a secret, understand?'

Daisy nodded.

'No one, not Mummy, Aunt Vi, Aunt Zita, understand?'

'Or Aunt Ruth?'

Uncle George gave a wink. 'That's the idea. No one or the magic won't work.'

He brought her up, close to him, between his legs. She could smell the beer on his breath, the cold cream he had used to remove his slap.

'First of all you have to learn how to get hold of this.'

It was warm, and damp, and podgy and hairy, and Daisy had never seen anything like it before; she didn't have to have one, she hoped, because she didn't like the look of it at all.

It was starting to grow and wriggle and have life of its own.

'That's a good girl. It's nice, isn't it?'

Daisy wasn't too sure.

'It's magic,' said Uncle George, 'and like all magic you have to learn to—'

'I think she's a bit too young to learn about that kind of

69

magic, don't you, George?' Mummy was standing in the doorway, her arms folded.

The thing shot out of Daisy's hand and disappeared back into Uncle George's shorts. Part of her was disappointed Uncle George wasn't going to teach her how to produce bunches of flowers; the other half of her was relieved Mummy was there, though she wasn't quite sure why.

Aunt Zita came up behind Mummy with the inevitable mugs of tea; she took one look at the scene.

'Bastard.' As usual she gave her word its full weight and meaning.

Mummy held out her hand to Daisy. 'Off you go with Auntie. I've got to have a word with Uncle George.'

'About the magic?'

'That's right, darling, off you go.'

Zita looked down at the little girl; she carefully put one mug of tea down on the dressing table, so that she had a hand free to slip around Daisy's fingers. The other mug hit the wall above Uncle George, showering him with tea and pieces of broken crockery.

'Magic,' said Aunt Zita, with a certain amount of contempt, as she steered the child away from what was becoming a noisy dressing room. 'You'll find out about it soon enough.'

A quiet and confused Daisy followed Aunt Zita to the wardrobe department.

Most of the lights had been switched off now the show was over and people were packing up; there would be a new act topping the bill from Monday. Some of the show's acts were booked to stay another week. Most were moving on: either 'resting' or to a hard-won booking at another of the dwindling number of variety theatres scattered across the land. Television was killing variety and work was becoming as thin as a lodging-house landlady's welcome.

Only a couple of women remained in the workroom, one from the wardrobe department, and the other a dancer taking the chance to repair some fishnet tights, painstakingly picking over them with a crochet hook. They each looked up as Zita and the child walked in.

They took one look at the wardrobe mistress's face and didn't need telling twice when she semaphored by a jerk of the head that they should scarper.

Aunt Zita sank down into the battered old chintz-covered armchair that had belonged to so many wardrobe mistresses before her. Its arms were threadbare with horsehair starting to poke through the patches; the chair was a kind of badge of office, the recognised sanctuary of the one woman who was expected to stay an oasis of calm amidst the desert of theatrical tensions.

Zita lifted the unresisting child onto her lap and gently cradled her. Neither spoke for a while. Daisy slowly began to play with the buttons on her godmother's blouse. She knew something was wrong, but she wasn't sure what it was.

'Dorothy, darling,' the woman began softly.

'Daisy.'

'Daisy, darling,' she corrected herself, wondering what sort of child decided to rename herself. Or rather, what sort of life made that kind of decision for you.

'Uncle George was showing me how to do magic.' Daisy felt some kind of explanation was needed.

'Really?' Zita worked hard at keeping her voice level, as she gently took the tiara out of the child's hair and wiped away the lipstick with her handkerchief.

'Yes,' Daisy hoisted herself up on Zita's lap so that she could look at her. 'He said you had to hold that

71

thingy to do magic.'

'Really?'

'Yes.'

'Did Uncle George say you had to do anything else?'
Daisy shook her head.

'Did Uncle George do anything else to you, I mean,
did he show you any more magic?'

'No, he'd only just started to show me.' Daisy felt her
godmother sag with relief. The woman smiled, ruffled
Daisy's hair and hugged her tightly.

'Auntie Zita?'

'Yes?' Daisy felt her go tense again.

'You know that funny thing Uncle George said I had to
hold?'

'Yes?'

'Do all magicians have one?'

'Only the men ones, darling.'

'Oh. I suppose it hands him his flags and bunches of
flowers and silver balls inside his jacket.'

'Something like that.'

'Magic is just a fib, isn't it?'

Zita nodded.

'Is it a big fib or a little fib?'

'Well I think it's a big one, but people don't mind,
because it is the one time they like being fibbed to, you
know. They like to see all the coloured silks and flowers
and silver balls appear and disappear, even though they
know that you can't just conjure doves out of fresh air
inside a hat. They enjoy the fib when it's told.'

'It is a big fib to say you can make doves, isn't it.'

'Yes.'

'When Auntie Vi said Uncle George had to stop doing
doves because they ponged, where did they go?'

Ruth's ma is right, Zita thought, the child thinks too

much.

'The Great Supremo took them off his hands for his own act,' she invented, hoping that Daisy wouldn't quiz her any further. A distraction was needed.

'I wonder if there are any pins left on the floor?' Zita handed Daisy the magnet. 'Would you mind having a look, pins are expensive and I'm not made of money.'

Daisy set to work in the dim light, hunting on the dusty floor, pleased with herself every time a hidden pin jumped onto the magnet and saved her aunt a fortune. Daisy had all her questions answered and she had closed the lid and tidied away the whole incident, her curiosity satisfied. The world had far more important things than Uncle George and magic.

Zita watched as the child put each pin into the pincush-ion diligently. No harm done, thank God, though she doubted if George would be able to say the same after Alice had finished with him. Pity the bastard ducked. Poor Vi. Alice was right: no wonder she scuttled off home to her old mum's legs every chance she got.

Alice came through the door first, her hair perhaps a little more out of place than usual. She was followed by Ruth, who made a beeline for Daisy. A few steps behind came Uncle Malcie, slowly massaging the knuckles of his right hand.

Daisy saw the new arrivals and smiled. If Aunt Ruth had brought Uncle Malcie then he would no doubt be driving them back to Mr Pickup's. With a bit of luck they would stop off for a drink, and she would get a bottle of Vimto and a packet of Smith's crisps with the salt in a twist of blue paper, or even fish and chips as she sat outside in the car and waited.

'Come and see this, darlink, come with me.' Aunt Ruth led her out into the corridor, while Alice, Zita and

Malcie huddled into a conversation.

In the dimly lit corridor Ruth went into a dance step. 'I bet you can't bossa nova!' She danced a few steps under the dingy overhead light bulb, singing the music, turned round and danced back to Daisy, holding out her hands to the child to teach her the step.

'Excuse me, young man, is this a private party or can anyone join in?'

A tall thin man wearing dark-rimmed spectacles and a silly smile pantomimed pushing Daisy out of the way, and grabbed Ruth in a clinch, foxtrotted her down the corridor and back. He spun her round, turned to Daisy and looked at her through his glasses, now half on and half off his nose. He mimed staggering backwards as though Daisy had pushed him.

'Get off,' he pretended to be scared. Daisy and Ruth clung together with laughter.

'Eric! Come on, the car's here.' Another man, shorter with fair hair, put his head round the bottom of the stairs and yelled to him. 'Stop fooling about, we'll be— Oh, hello Ruth love, how's things?'

Ruth held the stair rail and leaned down to him. 'Fine Ernie, fine, considering, television is killing this business. Do you need a dancer?'

'Tell you what, I'll ditch him. We'll be Wiseman and Rosenberg. How does that sound? Like fifty-bob tailors!' He called to his partner, who had found Daisy a captive audience and had broken into a soft-shoe shuffle. 'Will you get a move on!' The two men disappeared shouting their goodbyes, and Daisy and Ruth yelled back.

'Now there's a pair who don't have to look too far for work, they're going to be on the television again,' said Ruth, with a sigh of admiration.

The next person who came up the stairs was Uncle

Archie, overcoat over his white tie and tails, long silk evening scarf and trilby hat in hand, carrying his saxophone case. Daisy always thought he looked like a film star.

'Dinner dance at the Masonic, got over soon as I could,' he said, giving Ruth a peck on the cheek, which she returned, and bestowing a big kiss on Daisy his goddaughter. 'Zita not finished yet?' Daisy's godparents were perfectly matched in the conversation department.

The wardrobe-department door opened and Alice, Zita and the big Scotsman appeared. Archie paused slightly, weighing up Malcie, and then recognising him as one of Fred's dodgy mates. They shook hands cordially. Malcie was his usual stiff, polite and formal self; Archie made sure he kept on the right side of a known hard man.

They all walked to where Uncle Malcie had parked his Jaguar. He offered Archie and Zita a lift, but they declined, politely, for Uncle Archie was going on to a club to meet up with a jazz quintet, and Daisy saw them flag down a passing taxi as Uncle Malcie drove off towards Lichfield. Daisy and Ruth sat in the back, and giggled as they played with the armrest that folded out of the seat back and the ashtrays, which popped out. They played at waving like the Queen to passers-by when the car slowed down at junctions and traffic lights. Slowly Daisy began to feel very tired, and the rhythm of the car and its warmth made her drowsy. She curled up next to Ruth, who became a willing cushion, and gently stroked the child's hair as she began to float off to sleep, slightly disappointed that they didn't seem to be stopping for a chip supper.

Ruth started to sing a soft little song under her breath to Daisy, a song her own mother used to sing to her, to send her to sleep and keep the nightmares at bay; all the while Uncle Malcie talked to Alice in the front. Ruth tried to listen.

'What? Do you mean the stuff Scotch Wally printed?'

'Aye,' the big man replied.

'Go to hell, Malcie. That stuff's rubbish. He tried passing some of it off on Fred. You can spot it a mile off: the Queen's got a bloody squint.'

Malcie laughed softly. 'The early stuff maybe. This is better. Got some help from a couple of boys down in Brighton. It's good, Alice, believe me.' His tone switched from reasonable to reassuring, 'I know how you are fixed, and this run-in with that nonce George leaves you high and dry without work. I told Fred I'd look out for you, and this is putting good money your way.'

'Putting the law my way, more like it.' Alice saw Malcie's face set hard and, remembering Ruth's warning about him not being a man to cross, she changed her approach.

'Malcie, it's kind of you. Don't think I'm not grateful, because believe you me, I am, but there's Dorothy to consider. I need to try and keep some kind or normality in her life. God knows, she's lost her home, her father's stuck miles away in hospital. What will she think if I disappear as well? I can't leave her with my mother because the child's terrified of her. I can't leave her with Ruth or her mother, because my mother would come down on me like the wrath of God.'

'What about your other girl, the one up in Manchester?'

'I don't know what I've done to make her hate me so much. She won't have me at any price, or Fred and certainly not our daughter. No, I can't help you out darling, as much as it's a generous offer, you can see how I'm fixed. Why don't you take Ruth with you, she's just as strapped for cash as I am.' Alice turned to look at him, hoping he'd bought it from her; she felt guilty about putting Ruth forward instead.

They drove in silence for a while, Malcie handling the big car and the traffic in a smooth deliberate manner.

Eventually he spoke. 'Ruth's no good for a scam like this; she's too noticeable with her accent. People would remember her. You'll do it, because you're right for it. You need the money and I can keep my word to Fred that I'm looking out for you.'

Alice tried to cut in again, but failed.

'You'll do it, or I'll tell Fred about George's little game tonight. Not exactly what you would want a dying man to hear has happened to his little girl, now is it?'

Silence filled the car. By now Daisy was asleep, and Ruth gave her a gentle hug of reassurance and love; one she wanted to give to her best friend sitting in the front seat next to 'Mad' Malcie MacFadyen. Ruth knew about being trapped without any chance of a way out.

'But what shall I do with my child?' Alice said it despairingly, not so much to Malcie, but as an unanswered question to herself.

Silence, then his face brightened as he had his good idea. 'She can come with us. People don't expect a woman, or a couple. They'd never think twice about a family, now would they?'

Chapter 7

Looking for Work

Breakfast at Nana Rosen's was something wonderful. Mummy's boiled egg and soldiers just did not match up.

Nana had not been impressed by British cuisine on her arrival in the country. True enough, she could turn out roast beef with horseradish sauce so hot it made you smart and Yorkshire puddings so light they floated off the plate and into your mouth like a dream, but there was nothing which really topped her Austrian recipes.

Then Nana discovered porridge.

Daisy knew all about porridge. Mummy's was of the no-nonsense variety, Gran's was terrifying, salt-tasting God-fearing stuff that grew back every time you took a spoonful, each plate a penance.

Nana's porridge was velvet. She conspired with the oats to make a wonderful comforting concoction, aided by Tate and Lyle's golden syrup, and topped with a liberal squeezing of Nestlé condensed milk out of a tube. Daisy finished scraping the last of her second bowl and sat back, under Nana's beaming approval, feeling contentedly full, and ready to take an interest in proceedings.

At the other end of the kitchen table Aunt Ruth had

spread the *Lichfield Mercury*. Her cigarette tin was open and she was industriously engaged in producing roll-ups: one for Mummy, one for the tin, and now one for herself.

She lit up, dragged the smoke deep into her lungs and exhaled as something in the paper caught her eye.

'The little Aves girl, Yvonne, won the fancy dress at the Regal. You know, they live up the Weston Road.'

Mummy looked over her shoulder as she flicked ash into an ashtray also on top of the paper. 'Says here she had a gypsy princess costume, we should have entered you, darling.'

Daisy shook her head. She would have won, she knew that without boasting: Aunt Zita would have summoned up a costume like a genie in a bottle, which would have left all the other kids standing. It would have also meant the other kids staring at her, and Mummy and Aunt Ruth in the background, working their charms on Mr Woodhall the manager. Before you knew it there would be an offer of drinks and free cinema passes wangled.

Daisy quite liked the idea of going somewhere quietly, unobtrusively, and paying with money for once. She remembered the time last Christmas when the children's Saturday matinée club at the cinema, the ABC Minors, had ordained that every child should bring a lump of coal so fuel could be given to pensioners.

'ABC miners more like,' Mummy had said, and to her embarrassment Daisy was the only child who took along a lump of coal that had been carefully wrapped in Christmas paper. It was Mummy's idea of a little joke, which had left the other children staring at her like she was a Martian from the *Eagle* comic, as she gave it to the commissionaire when she went in.

'Hold your foot up Alice, your worries are over.' Ruth

leaned over the *Mercury* and started to read intently. 'Women wanted for light, clean work. French Plastics Ltd, Trent Valley Works. You work either 8am to 5pm or 4.45pm to 8pm. It's on the bus route, the 112.'

Mummy looked at the advertisement. 'What would I do with Dorothy?'

'Daisy,' Daisy reminded her.

Mummy gave her an exasperated look, because she had cut in. 'Your name is Dorothy, try to remember that.'

Miraculously, over Daisy's shoulder, a huge wooden spoon appeared and refilled her porridge bowl. A teaspoon of syrup followed, swirled into a pretty pattern, and Nana handed her the tube of Nestlé. 'Finish off the pan, darlink.' Daisy felt it was her duty.

'You'd have to go back to school, darling,' Mummy told her, and Daisy tried to give her mother one of her own withering looks, but failed.

'I'm not going. You said.'

'If you went in the evening, she could stay with me,' Nana Rosen offered.

'How would I manage that? We couldn't afford the bus here and back every day. By the time I'd finished there wouldn't be time to collect her.'

'She could stay.'

It was persuasive, it was an obvious solution. Daisy's stomach said yes, but her heart said no, she wanted to be with her mummy. She felt guilty because her stomach was winning.

'No, the evening shift wouldn't do. Mornings would be just as bad; even if Dorothy went back to school, she'd be hanging about for an hour and a half at either end of the day.'

'What if you did half of one shift and half of the other?' Nana suggested.

Mummy and Ruth looked at each other. 'It's worth a try.'

'You are supposed to write,' said Aunt Ruth, consulting the paper again.

'To hell with that, let's go and see them.' Mummy was taken with the idea and, as everyone who knew her knew, once Alice had decided on something the only way between her and what she wanted was a straight line.

The line in this case involved the bus back from Botany Bay into Lichfield for Mummy, Ruth and Daisy. They crept into the rooms at Mr Pickup's on Beacon Street, for fear he should be roused and demand rent, but fortunately he was out.

'Gone to the bank,' said the quiet little man who lived in the rooms below who went in fear of Alice.

'Gone to visit his money,' said Aunt Ruth.

Ruth and Daisy sat on the bed while Mummy modelled what she should wear to get her job.

'Too cocktail,' said Aunt Ruth, 'too afternoon tea dance, try that dress.'

Mummy held it up to herself, and swished across the floor and turned. 'You don't think it makes me look too needy?'

'Darlink, you are needy. Try it, it works.'

They decided the pearls were a bit too much, and had settled on a little brooch when they heard a car door slam outside, and footsteps up the stairs.

Ruth, conditioned not to like sudden, unannounced arrivals, shot off the bed to the window, and peered out of the side of the net curtains. There was a red Jaguar.

'Malcie,' she gasped, as there came a loud knock at the door. Daisy noticed that both Mummy and Aunt Ruth had gone a little pale.

The two women hesitated and clung to each other.

81

Daisy decided to take matters into her own hands, and opened the door, looking up at her Uncle Malcie with the sort of smile she hoped deserved a couple of half-crowns. Tied up in a hankie in amongst her pile of knickers were his last gift, plus her savings; she was aiming to get thirty bob. She'd never had that much money of her own before and the sound of the sum appealed to her.

'Hello Uncle Malcie.' Her melter seemed to have the desired effect, the big man bent down to her. 'Hello wean, is your Mammy in?'

Daisy kept the smile firmly in place, nodded and opened the door. There was a half-crown there at least, no doubt about it.

'Ladies,' he nodded to them, taking off his hat as he walked into the bedsit. He made a point of looking round the room, letting them see he was inspecting it. His expression left them in no doubt he was not impressed.

'I thought I'd take you down to see Fred, stop for a spot of lunch on the way and tell him what we are going to do.'

'We can't,' Alice started, 'it's not convenient.' She saw Malcie's brows shoot up and his expression harden, and she hurriedly changed her approach.

'What I mean is, Malcie, I've got an interview for a job, a good job, at a factory, plastics factory down Trent Valley. I was, we were, just going.' Daisy watched as her mummy's mixture of explanation and apology petered out.

Even Daisy felt the temperature drop in the room.

'I'll drive you there.' Malcie's voice was cold, the cold voice of a man not used to being disobeyed; Alice and Ruth were scared. Ruth tried not to remember the stories she had heard about the razor gang he used to run with in the Gorbals.

'No, I mean, we don't want to take you out of your way.'

'It isn't. I'll take you.' Malcie's assurance was polite, even gently spoken, but underneath there was a steel edge. Both women were aware of it, and he knew they were.

They drove in silence through the city centre, up Greenhill and onto the Trent Valley Road. The livestock lorries turning into the Smithfield yard for Winterton's cattle market slowed them down. Daisy watched the big eyes of the black and white cows, mournful, resigned, peering out of the back of the smaller trailers.

They pulled up at a modern factory building. It had flower beds and a flagpole. Uncle Malcie drove right up to the front door, got out and helped Alice from the back seat with the impeccable manners of a duchess's chauffeur.

Alice, who had the good sense to know when her bluff was being called, took a deep breath and walked in with as much dignity as she could muster. Daisy watched her go. She didn't like the idea of her mother getting a job; the idea of school kept creeping up on her.

From the back of the car Daisy could see a man looking out of his office window. He thought Alice's arrival marked a visit from one of the ladies from the Red Cross or Inner Wheel, looking for a donation, so he put on his jacket, dusting it off as he called reception to send her through.

Alice was surprised to be welcomed with smiles and doors opened all the way through to such a senior manager.

He, on the other hand, was more than a little surprised to find she did not so much want a donation as a job, and one which would involve him rearranging his entire shift system to suit her. Charmed as he was, he felt he had to decline Alice's gracious offer of working for him, but he did ask her out for dinner. Alice left, but not before getting his telephone number and instructions to hang up if his wife or children answered.

Malcie all but saluted as she got back to the car and he opened the rear door. One of Alice's saving graces was her sense of the ridiculous and she broke into a grin as she took her seat, whispering in Malcie's ear so that only he could hear: 'You bastard.' Malcie discovered he had the same gift and chuckled back at her, under his breath. He knew he'd won, but not by having to give someone a beating. He'd won by laughing at, and now with them. He'd never done that before, and he liked the feeling.

'Let's go and see Fred then,' said Alice, shooting an I'll-tell-you-all-about-it-later look to Ruth.

Daisy was on the back seat, engrossed in the cat's cradle Aunt Ruth had taught her with a length of knotted wool while they had been waiting, and completely missed all this grown-up nonsense.

It was, Daisy decided, the best journey to visit Daddy she had ever had. No Aunt Betty, no dodging the ticket collector, but a magic carpet ride in the back of Uncle Malcie's Jaguar, singing songs with Aunt Ruth and Mummy.

As they made their way with 'Here a moo, there a moo' through 'Old Macdonald's Farm' Daisy noticed Uncle Malcie was watching them, but not saying anything; he wasn't even singing.

He was wondering what some of his contemporaries would have thought. 'Mad' Malcie, hard man, handy with a razor, had been known to carry a sawn-off when working, though he'd only ever used it as a frightener. A man Glasgow City polis usually sent six big lads and a van round to if they felt the need to question him.

He stole a glance in the rear-view mirror at Ruth and child on the back seat; alongside him Alice was starting on 'One Man Went to Mow' with a vengeance.

He'd always wondered what the hell a smart man like Fred Smedley had seen in a crazy woman like Alice, and now he was beginning to realise. Alice was in love with life, and at the centre was her love for Fred and their daughter. And if that love didn't have too much of a grasp on the practicalities of life, if it made up the words and sometimes the tune as well as it went along, or sang nursery rhymes to delight her child, then what the hell of it?

Yet at the same time she knew she was out of step with the rest of the parade, but that was her own private joke which she shared with Fred and the child, and Ruth, her old man's bit on the side, for Christ's sake! Now, if his Celia had known about any of the lasses he'd put it about with, she'd have got a straight razor out of her handbag and taken their faces off.

Once again Malcie felt a stab of envy for Fred and had the good sense to realise, much to his own amazement, that for the first time in his life he had met a woman he actually admired.

Daisy was going to ask him why he wasn't singing, but took a look at the scowl on his face and thought better of it.

Chapter 8

The Filth

So good was the ride to the hospital that Daisy was astonished to find that the long terrifying corridor to Daddy's ward had lost some of its horrors.

She burst through the door and went straight to his bed. She was so excited to see him that she did not notice, as Alice and Ruth did, that her father was so weak he could not lean over to her, but rather she fell into his arms.

The decline in his health in just a matter of days was frighteningly obvious to the two women. The realisation gripped Alice bitterly; Malcie saw her fade like a flower in frost as the fear sank in. Then he saw her rally to show her husband something good and happy amidst his own pain, illness and fear.

'I'll be going then, Fred, take care of yourself, and remember what I said.' A grey man in a grey raincoat held his grey trilby in one hand and picked up his bedside chair to offer it to Alice.

They had all been so caught up in Daisy's joy at seeing her father, and the shock of his decline, they had failed to notice him. He was the kind of man you might not necessarily notice; that was what he intended. That was how he worked.

'Ladies,' he said, nodding his head slightly, 'Malcie, nice to see you here, taking care of things are you?'

'Mr MacCallum.' Big Malcie's words were not so much a greeting, more stating the obvious.

The grey man turned to Fred again. 'Remember what I said.' He left without looking at any of the others again.

Malcie stood rooted to the spot and watched him leave, not taking his eyes off the door till he was long gone.

'Who was he?' Ruth sensed the men's unease.

'The filth,' said Malcie. He turned to Fred. 'What the hell did he want?'

Alice shot him a look which said you may be a hard man, and people may be frightened of you, but upset my husband right now and I'll have you.

'Nothing like trying to get you when you're down,' even Fred's voice sounded ill and tired. 'Thought he'd have a chat, so I just kept pretending to nod off.'

'Who?' Alice hauled the adoring Daisy off Fred's bed and onto her lap, while Ruth helped him to sit up a little more, and smoothed his pillows. After an initial fussing over Fred, his locker and its contents, the two women settled down.

'Birmingham City CID,' Daddy said in passing, trying not to make too big a thing of it. 'Thank you for bringing them, Malcie.'

'My pleasure,' said the big man, and he realised that strangely enough, it truly was.

Daddy opened his arms out for Daisy to get back on the bed beside him, and Mummy lifted her gently into place. 'Now don't wriggle, Daddy's tired,' Mummy whispered to her.

'How's Vi's mother's legs then?' asked Fred, anxious to have someone's health other than his own as a topic of conversation.

There was a pause, which Alice and Ruth hoped wasn't noticed, before they launched into the rehearsed steps of their formation lying routine.

'She's much better, they've got her on new tablets,' Mummy began.

'For her water retention,' Ruth cut in.

'So Vi's back with George full-time now, more's the pity.'

Daisy opened her mouth to speak, but like a chick in the nest, food was popped into it, in the form of a toffee Alice had been carrying round for just this occasion. In her mac pocket she had her fingers around the wrapper of a second, if needed.

Malcie looked at the pair of them and reckoned he knew the steps of this dance well enough to join in. 'So I've got a wee bit of work to put Alice's way, soon. It'll pay well, pal.'

Ruth was in a dilemma. She had a good idea what was coming next and knew that Alice wouldn't want Daisy to hear, so she should do the usual routine of taking the child to visit the chocolate-vending machine. She didn't want to leave her friend alone with Malcie; neither did she wish to curtail the amount of time Daisy had with her father. Each time they visited it became more obvious that Daisy's chances to see her daddy were numbered. Ruth thought of her own father, or rather the vague memories she could still summon, and she wanted to make sure that Daisy saw as much of her father as possible.

'We'll talk about it later,' Alice said coolly, 'now, what did the consultant say today?'

Malcie didn't press the point, but sat back and watched the three women adoring Fred: wife, mistress and daughter. He knew he would never inspire such devotion in a woman.

Fred recounted his morning conversation with the doctor, trying, for Alice's sake to inject some hope into the proceedings; he was well aware that Ruth would not be fooled. Ruth knew all about death because she had seen it often enough in her life.

The four adults fell silent, and then Malcie, using more tact than anyone who knew him would have ever thought possible, and more than he knew he had himself, brought up the subject of 'the wee job' he had in mind for Alice.

'Is it good gear?' asked Fred, mindful of the samples of Scotch Wally's handiwork he had seen before.

'Excellent,' Malcie assured him, 'I had a couple of boys from Brighton help out.'

Fred nodded, he remembered he had recommended them to the big Glaswegian months before.

Daisy sat on the bed, snuggled up to her father, and played with a picture book Mummy had surprisingly found in her handbag, her mouth working its way round another big wedge of toffee. The little girl was content just to be there by her father, not at all interested in the conversation going on above her head.

'You're not going to try shifting it at the races, or the dogs?' That had always been Fred's favourite way of cleaning up dirty money.

'Nah, the filth know there's the stuff around, and they're watching. I suppose that's why you had your visitor.'

'Must be, I've been out of touch, you're the only person who's been to see me, Malcie.' Here Fred paused. 'And I appreciate it and what you're doing for Alice.'

'My pleasure,' said Malcie. 'I know how you're fixed, you'd do the same for me.'

Yes he would, thought Ruth, always looking out for so-called friends and always favouring the quickest way to make money had got Fred to where he was right now: dying in hospital, with his wife and child all but on the street. She couldn't really grasp it.

After all, the Horse and Jockey should have been a gold mine. It certainly was now for the new family running it. More and more people had cars these days and driving out to have a drink at a little country pub was all the rage. The Jockey didn't just rely on locals and the occasional officers from the barracks wanting a change from the mess; the car park was always full.

Ruth felt an unusual surge of exasperation towards her friend. Alice hadn't known how lucky she was. If only she had knuckled down and got involved in running the pub, she could have created a thriving little business.

While Fred and Malcie talked, and Alice kept a watchful eye on her daughter, Ruth allowed herself to slip into her favourite daydream: her and Fred running the Jockey with her mother cooking the food and Mr Bloum growing the vegetables and turning the outside into a beautiful garden with overflowing hanging baskets and arches, which everyone would admire. She, in crisp white blouse, and nice pearl earrings would supervise the entire operation, keeping the barmaids on their toes and the potman always busy clearing tables.

She sighed inwardly. The daydream was the nearest she ever got to the security of a home, money and a man, and she felt all the more guilty about it because it would only have come true at the expense of her friend Alice, and the little girl she had grown to love like her own. The most guilt-laden version of her dream saw Alice dying in a tragic accident, and Ruth assuming the roles of landlady, mother and wife.

'That MacCallum's sharp and he knows something's on the boil; he's the one who got Paddy and Jack banged to rights over that Cradley Heath job,' Malcie said to Fred. 'It makes more sense if we go for spending it: getting some good stuff to fence and clean change. Preferably at smaller places, tedious I know but that's the only way I can see of shifting it right now. I thought of heading north, Kendal, Penrith, Carlisle, Moffat and then the bulk in Paisley and Glasgow.'

Fred nodded. 'What about the seaside?'

'Can't touch the south coast, the London boys wouldn't like it. If this goes well we might try going down the water this summer: Largs, Saltcoats, Rothesay when they're really busy, and they'll not be bothered about a lot of English notes. Blackpool's out, of course.'

Fred nodded, remembering a narrow escape when Malcie had turned over a bookie's in the big seaside town, shortly after he'd had to leave Glasgow in a hurry.

'Do you think things have quietened down enough for you to go back north?'

'Aye,' said Malcie. He said it slowly, more to convince himself.

'Are we going to the seaside?' The words had filtered through to Daisy. Both men stopped talking and looked at Alice, who put a protective arm round the child and looked at Ruth.

'Come on darlink, let's see if that machine's got any chocolate for us today.'

Relief flooded Malcie's face as he stood, fishing into his pocket for change.

'Aye, there y'go.' He promptly passed over a handful of silver to Daisy. Her eyes went out on stalks: there were sixpences, a couple of shillings and she thought she spotted a couple of half-crowns. She was rich!

'Say bye now sweetheart,' said her daddy, and it took all his effort to hold out his arms to her. The little girl

91

fell into his embrace, trying to absorb as much of him as possible, the sight and the smell and the touch of him, to last her until she saw him again.

'Bye-bye Daddy.'

'Bye-bye my little princess, take care of your Mummy and Auntie Ruth for me, and your Uncle Malcie.'

Daisy shot a doubtful look at Uncle Malcie, he always struck her as someone who could take care of himself, but if that was what her daddy wanted, who was she to argue. She nodded to him.

''Course I will, bye-bye.' Fred pulled her close and kissed and kissed his daughter: the best thing he had ever achieved in his life. She was never going to be pretty, but she was sharp even at this age, and she would always land on her feet and stay one step ahead of the game. She was going to make something of herself, he knew that in his soul, but in his heart he bitterly regretted he would never see it happen.

Ruth held out her manicured hand, and Daisy grasped it tightly, and walked towards the ward door.

Ruth always told her never to look back and Daisy never did, but on this occasion she stopped, turned round and stood staring at the wraith-like man who had sunk back into his pillows, his energy spent, now looking at her longingly.

'Bye-bye Daddy.'

He managed to raise his arm and wave.

Ruth and Daisy went and stuffed themselves with consoling chocolate.

Chapter 9

Mummy and Daisy Go Shopping

'I think we need an adventure,' Mummy said once they had got the breakfast pots washed, dried and put away, and they had decided what to wear. Mummy chose a navy dress and coat with a matching silk square; Daisy a green and black houndstooth pinafore that had come from Sadler's on the Market Square. It had belonged to a cousin before her but Mummy said she shouldn't be proud. 'And besides, darling, it looks so much better on you than her, green is much more your colour.' While Mummy brushed her hair with her Mason Pearson brush for the obligatory fifty times, Daisy looked in the mirror over the sink and had to agree that Mummy was right, as usual.

They had gone downstairs, and actually knocked on Mr Pickup's door. The little barrel of a man soon changed from being grumpy to what passed, for him, as gracious when Mummy handed over all the back rent, and then, with a flourish, produced two weeks' money in advance. He was so stunned he almost tugged his forelock in reply to Mummy's grand manner, which, had she but known it, Daisy could have compared to the Queen giving out Maundy money at Lichfield Cathedral.

They walked down Bird Street, flushed with the success of a purse full of Uncle Malcie's money, and the genuine stuff at that. Mummy repaid the lady at Lucille's and Daisy sat in the chair in front of the mirror, boosted up with a special cushion to the right height while she had her hair trimmed. Mummy sat behind her, elegantly reading an old copy of *Nova* and occasionally looking up to smile into the mirror, and Daisy smiled back at her.

They were wondering what sort of adventure they were going to have, when they caught sight of Aunt Betty getting into her Mini estate on Bore Street.

'Alice,' she said, declining to add a hello, how are you or to enquire about Fred's health; Daisy did not even merit acknowledgement. Betty viewed sisterly love as a duty, and as a good Catholic she was never one to shirk from her duty, even if her sister was bound for the depths of hell for divorce, marrying a Protestant get and consorting with his Jew mistress.

As a child Alice loved her sister so much she had been known to kick at her knees, but only when they had scabs on which would then bleed most satisfactorily. She knew that as Betty's eyes darted around as they just had, it meant she was in fear of anyone from church seeing her in such company, and decided she was never too old to go scab-kicking.

'Darling!' she cried as she flung herself round her sister's shoulders, 'you look wonderful!' It was a cry that would have carried across a noisy, drunken, backstage party and made people stop and look. On a mid-morning Bore Street, it all but stopped the traffic.

It had the desired effect: Aunt Betty was stricken with embarrassment.

'I can't stop, I'm on my way to Sutton,' she stammered, 'I've got to pick up Graham's present.'

'Too marvellous,' Mummy was really projecting now, her voice would have carried all the way to the cheap seats. 'We'll come along to keep you company.'

Aunt Betty could only be pushed so far.

'I don't need company,' she said through gritted teeth.

Daisy was impressed: she had seen some pretty good ventriloquists in her time, and seen them backstage, up close. Aunt Betty had nearly got the hang of it, even if she was chewing her pale pink lipstick off her lips and onto her teeth while she was doing it.

'All right, we'll just cadge a lift off you then.' Mummy opened the passenger door, pushed her seat back and propelled Daisy into the back seat before Betty could get another word out.

They drove past the Friary clock tower and onto the Walsall Road. Mummy said, 'Pity we didn't know you were coming, you could have picked Ruth up and we could have made a day of it.' It was the only attempt at conversation they had until Aunt Betty pulled into the car park by the railway station. It was understood they would make their own way home.

Sutton Coldfield was as good as foreign country to Daisy: it had beautiful flower beds and shops far larger than Lichfield, but it did not frighten her as much as Birmingham with its big, packed streets and buildings so tall they seemed to meet overhead.

Uncle Malcie's money bought them a fish and chip lunch at Pattison's café and afterwards Daisy wallowed through the most incredible sticky Kunzle cake, so full of chocolate it oozed all over her fingers, prompting a trip to the ladies' cloakroom and a serious wash and tidying operation.

'You need some new vests,' said Mummy, 'I think we should go and see what British Home has in store for us.'

They walked down The Parade and looked in all the windows before going into the shop where Mummy soon found a counter full of children's underclothes. Daisy stood silently and watched while Mummy asked for some judicious advice from the saleslady about cotton or wool, and plenty of 'she'll soon grow into them, they do at this age, don't they?'

Daisy was bored and she also realised she could have done with a wee as well as a wash in the café cloakroom.

'No, I don't think we're in need of any knickers today, I usually stock up just before the start of term,' said Mummy, playing the practical housewife and mother, while casually slipping a couple of extra vests into the shopping bag at her side.

Daisy just hoped no one noticed, as they thanked the nice lady and went over to look at the nylon stockings.

Mummy always favoured American tan, but she popped a couple of pairs of Bamboo into her bag for Aunt Ruth as well and headed for the door.

'Excuse me, madam.' The man in the suit was polite, but he stood between them and the door leading onto The Parade, and freedom.

'Yes?' Mummy did polite and concerned back to him.

'It would seem that you might have some items in your bag which you haven't paid for.'

'Really? I don't think so, I just came in to get some vests for my daughter, I do think your cotton ones are such good value for money.'

Daisy felt scared, her heart started to pound.

'If you would just care to come with me to the office, I am sure we can sort this out, check the goods against your receipt.'

'I really haven't got the time today, you see we must get . . .'

Daisy's heart felt like it was going to burst, and all of a sudden her bladder decided to accompany it.

'The office, madam.' The man came forward and took Mummy by the elbow. Daisy couldn't hold it all in for much longer. Her heart was going to explode with fear, tears were coming to her eyes.

'Mummy I need a wee!'

In all her life, Alice never missed a cue.

'Do forgive me, it's all such a rush, you see my daughter is in need of a lavatory and I—'

'Now Mummy!'

The man tightened his grip on Alice's elbow, his tone suddenly hardened. 'The office, or it's the police.'

Daisy panicked: she thought her heart would burst with fright, but her bladder decided to instead.

Warm pee began to seep into her knickers, no matter how hard she tried to stop it, and as the material became saturated it slowly began to trickle down her legs, before all her self-control gave way and a large puddle spread around her feet.

'I've done a wee!' All Daisy's fear of Mummy being dragged off by the police vanished, and instead humiliation and anger flooded into its place. She started to sob, half in shame and half in fury.

'Look what you made me do,' she lashed out at the man and clung to Alice's jacket, conscious of the fact that her knickers were hot and wet and so was her face, with a mixture of tears and a depth of mortification only a child can feel.

'I said I wanted a wee, but no one listened, no one helped me. Look at what I've done, look what I've done,' she sobbed piteously.

Alice realised the best form of defence was attack. 'Are you satisfied? How dare you. I tried to explain, but you . . . Look! You officious little man. Look at how you've upset my daughter. You bully boy.' She paused and all but spat the words at him: 'You Nazi!'

Daisy stopped gulping and wiped her eyes, that was the nastiest thing that Mummy ever called anyone. She ventured a look at their tormentor.

He looked like a man in need of a lifebelt; Alice wasn't about to throw him one. A crowd of curious onlookers was beginning to form amongst the women shoppers.

'Trying to get her little girl to a lavvy and he stopped her, said she hadn't paid,' said one plump woman who saw her role in life as that of a Greek chorus.

'Shame, look at the poor little mite,' said another.

'Called him a Nazi,' said the first. The women began to nod in approval.

'I must attend to my daughter, now you have reduced her to this, come Dorothy,' said Alice as she went to exit, stage left, through the swing doors onto The Parade.

'Daisy,' muttered her daughter under her breath as she walked, stiff-legged, alongside her mother back down the road to the café, hating the way her knickers were sticking to her bottom and starting to feel very cold and clammy, as were her socks.

They left behind them a store detective who knew exactly what Alice had nicked, but who also knew he wasn't paid enough to deal with a hysterical child who had just wet itself, a brass-faced lifter who would have played the situation for all it was worth and a crowd of handbag-wielding women who looked set to mutiny. He was an old soldier, he'd been in the desert with Monty, and just then he wished he'd gone for one of those car-park jobs through the British Legion, like his friend Nobby.

Daisy stood dejectedly inside the ladies' lavatory. She

felt damp and thoroughly miserable. Her tears and her legs were all but dry, and very sticky. She doubted if anything in her life had ever been more dreadful.

'A little accident,' said Mummy and smiled knowingly to a woman drying her hands. The woman looked down at Daisy and smiled gently, said 'poor pet' and left, as tears began to well up again in Daisy's eyes.

'Come on now, don't make a meal of it, soon be over,' said Mummy, and she fished in her handbag and produced a large white handkerchief.

Daisy recognised it as one of her father's and her sense of grief began to rise. If Daddy were here, if Daddy was not ill, none of this would have happened. For some strange reason she began to feel angry with him, and at the same time guilty for feeling that way.

Her mother moved quickly and smoothly as though this was nothing more than a change of costume between scenes. She ran water into the washbasin, lathered up the dried piece of pink soap, washed her child's face and legs with her hands and wiped them dry on the handkerchief.

'Into the loo, darling.'

Once inside, off came Daisy's clothes so that she shivered. Alice produced one of the stolen vests and popped it over her head. It felt new, stiff and itchy.

'Good job I got you an extra large size. Hmm, should have got you some drawers while I was at it. You'll just have to go home without.'

Quickly dressed again, Daisy began to get warm, but felt strange without any knickers on. Mummy pulled a long length of stiff San Izal off the roll and bent down to attack Daisy's shoes. Out by the washbasins again, she produced a comb and tidied the girl's hair. Satisfied that Daisy was looking respectable, she turned her attention to her own hair, then produced her compact and lipstick.

Daisy just stood there, staring numbly up at her mother.

'Come on now, buck up.'

Daisy nodded.

Alice bent down to the child and looked her in the face.

'That was a very brave thing you did. I thought we were for the high jump there, no mistake. Once you'd peed your pants, though, he couldn't get rid of us fast enough.'

A big smile crossed Alice's face. 'If we ever get cornered again, you'll have to turn on the waterworks!' By now she was chuckling.

Daisy looked her mother straight in the eye, and came close to mastering the art of giving someone a filthy dirty look.

'I didn't do that on purpose and I will never do it again. I hope you get caught and go to prison for ever, even if I have to go and live with Gran.' She might as well have slapped Alice across the face.

The woman stood up slowly and then sank down onto a nearby chair, shaking. For what seemed for ever to the little girl, her mother was silent, but she didn't care. Alice reached over and took her hand. She tried to pull it away, but Alice held tight, pulled her daughter to her and gave her a kiss. Then absent-mindedly she wiped away the lipstick mark on Daisy's face with her forefinger.

'I know you're mad at me, you have every right to be. I do try, I really do, you'll never know how much.' She paused. 'Yes, you probably will know, but only when you're grown-up and have a little girl of your own, you'll know and you'll understand.'

Daisy stood stiff and dumb, wanting to hug her mother back, but she was too angry to move.

'You'll understand, and no doubt you'll still be

appalled, but my God, you'll roar with laughter. Come on, let's go and pick a lipstick for me. We'll even pay for it.'

Alice stood up and held out her hand for the little girl to take, and Daisy did so, reluctantly. Mummy held open the door into the café for Daisy and as they walked back onto the street, Daisy wondered if everyone could tell she had no knickers on.

Alice gave her daughter's hand a little squeeze and whispered, 'You will, you know, when you're grown-up. Understand, I mean.'

And, as usual, she was right.

Not even buying a lipstick, or being allowed to have a spray of Goya's Gardenia perfume from the smart lady in Frost's chemist's shop could put the shine back on the day for Daisy. For some reason she felt exhausted by it all. On the bus back to Lichfield she fell asleep, having relented enough to cuddle up close to her mother.

Alice hugged the little girl to her, and thanked God for their escape from the law that afternoon. She was more determined than ever to make sure that Malcie did not take the child with them.

She didn't want to go, but she had no choice; there was no other way they could make any money and stay together. She would never go back to working with George and she knew she was incapable of holding down a regular job.

Alice felt annoyed that Fred had agreed to Malcie's plan so readily, but then that was Fred all over. He always loved the idea of easy money.

As the bus lurched along the country road she looked out over hedges starting to fill with spring foliage and flowers, and the ploughed fields behind. In the distance, every so often, you could catch a glimpse of the Ladies

101

of the Vale, the three spires of Lichfield cathedral. They were a landmark for miles around, though they were now being challenged by the new television mast being built at Hints.

She stroked the sleeping child and felt bitterly ashamed at what she had put her through, but at the same time couldn't help but smile at the absurdity of the scene in British Home Stores.

Poor kid, having a pair of wasters like Fred and me for parents, but what other option was there? Cooking and cleaning and waiting on hand and foot like our Betty does and our mother before her so that a man gives you a roof over your head, bread on the table and respectability on the street. What for? A turkey and a bottle of sherry from his boss at Christmas and a week in a caravan in Towyn every summer to look forward to? Not for me, thought Alice. I tried it with Caroline's father and it nearly killed me, a slow choking death of lying to fit in with the other families on the avenue, pretending to be something I'm not and don't want to be, but everyone else thinks I should be. The only role I ever played that I didn't enjoy and the reviews were lousy.

So I bolted. So what? The first divorce in the family.

She smiled to herself, remembering the scene as she turned up back home with a suitcase and Caroline and announced she had left her husband for a job with the rep company in Lichfield. Mam had the screaming hysterics and locked her in the bedroom, despatched Dad over the hill on his bike to get the priest from Whittington and Caroline was set on her knees in the front parlour with her rosary while the house was sprinkled with holy water.

All the good times, all the curtain calls, the parties at the Horse and Jockey, the Chevrolet car, her fur coat and weekends in Brighton flooded back to Alice and reassured her.

102

Yes, times are tough right now, but up until this Fred has seen me right, she thought, and she clung to the hope he would see them right again.

Daisy stirred in her arms and asked sleepily, 'Are we there yet?' Alice shook her head and the child drifted back to sleep. Alice deeply regretted what had happened to her little daughter that afternoon. She admitted to herself that she also regretted her estrangement from her older daughter, who had chosen to stay with her father and had taken an instant dislike to Fred. Helped by my mother and Betty, no doubt, she thought.

Now Caroline lived over seventy miles away, with a husband of her own, providing a roof over her head, bread on the table and respectability on the street.

It made Alice feel so very weary: dear God, she prayed, don't women ever get a chance on their own, to be themselves? But then, God's a bloody man, isn't he?

By the time the bus trundled into its place at the bus station it was packed with people on their way home from work. A weary Alice and Daisy made their way up Bird Street past the Minster Pool and the Cathedral Close before they got to Mr Pickup's three-storey house.

Daisy and Mummy were nearing the end of their baked beans on toast when Aunt Ruth arrived with a flushed Nana Rosen in tow.

The old lady's eyes were sparkling as much as the paste jewels in the brooch she wore pinned to the lapel of her old blue coat. Nana had only recently plucked up the courage to go into a pub with her daughter and was beginning to enjoy the experience; she had discovered port and lemon. In amongst the early-evening customers in the public bar of the Old Crown on Bore Street, she had found a friendliness and gaiety which reminded her of the cafés of Vienna in her youth.

103

Two glasses of port later, she was pink-cheeked, glassy-eyed, nostalgic and ready to hug anyone who crossed her slightly blurred line of vision.

Daisy had little enough time to put down her knife and fork, let alone to prepare for one of Nana's all-embracing, vice-like demonstrations of affection.

'Darlinnnnnk!' The port-fuelled hug managed to take in both Daisy and the chair back. Daisy submerged, fearful for her life, as Nana set about strangling both her and her vowel sounds.

'Vot is this you are eating?' said the old lady as the hug went on.

'Beans,' Daisy managed to mutter from the depths of the onslaught.

'Beans, schmeans, vat is this for a little girl's tea?' Nana began to relax her grip and Daisy started to feel a slight return of blood to her limbs.

Ruth had a gentle grin on her face at the sight of her partially inebriated mother. She enjoyed seeing her have a good time, it had taken years of persuasion to get the old girl to set foot inside a pub.

'Let the child go already Mother, she's turning blue!' Then, turning to Alice, 'That film's on at the Regal tonight, I thought we'd go.'

Alice was gathering up the tea things from the table, and beginning the washing-up.

'Which film?' she said over her shoulder as she stood at the sink.

'You know, the one with Rachel Roberts in. The banned one.'

'The what?'

'With that good-looking young boy, Albert Finish.'

'Finney,' Alice corrected, up to her elbows in Marigold gloves and washing-up. 'Albert Finney.'

'Him.' Ruth got her Old Holborn tin out and set to work. '*Saturday Night and Sunday Morning*. It's an X. It's been banned in Varvik, you know. It's supposed to be on the bone.'

Alice paused while she translated her friend. 'Near the knuckle, rude you mean.'

'Yes, it was censored. They won't show it in the Varverikershire.'

'Warwickshire,' said Alice.

'What I said already. So we're going. That's why I brought my mother, she can stay with Dorothy.'

'Daisy,' the little girl gasped as she recovered from Nana's hug and now had to fend off a cheek-pinching session.

'Your name is Dorothy, do try and remember that,' Alice corrected automatically.

'Daisy I like better already,' her daughter replied. Nana Rosen's syntax was infectious; you could catch it from a hug.

'Daisy, schmaisy,' Alice said, the virus having reached as far as the sink. 'All I ask is that you try to remember that deep down inside, you really are a Dorothy. Hold onto that fact, no matter what happens.'

Daisy, head on one side, examined her mother, who was currently hanging up her Marigold gloves and applying hand cream. Alice, realising she was being scrutinised, crossed the kitchen and kissed her daughter's head.

Daisy looked up at her mother and said, 'We both have to remember.'

Alice was shocked by the child's sudden flash of insight and covered up her surprise by giving her another big kiss.

Nana couldn't help but notice and it sobered her up;

she cast her mind back. Often it was children who knew and could face up to things while their parents just lied to themselves when swamped with the atrocities life can inflict. They worked hard at deluding themselves and all those around them that everything was fine. Sometimes the truth needs children.

Once Mummy and Aunt Ruth were out of the door and on their way to the Regal, Daisy and Nana got ready to enjoy themselves. Nana dug deep into the small shopping bag that passed as her handbag and produced her purse and a big bag of Maltesers. She fed the electricity meter, then turned the electric fire up to full blast and popped a couple of sweeties into Daisy's mouth.

'So what is happening to those two poor men in Scotland?' she asked, 'get the book and tell me.'

Daisy went and got her library book, sat down opposite the old lady and turned to chapter nineteen of *Kidnapped*, wishing only ever so slightly that one day Mummy or Nana would have the luxury of television.

'"The House of Fear,"' she began as Nana settled back to enjoy herself. Her spoken English was serviceable but her reading was only enough to allow her to get by in shops and catching buses. Ruth often brought her German papers if she went to Birmingham, and sometimes on the rare trips to London she came back with a new book or second-hand magazine; besides which, Nana's eyesight was starting to fade. Having Daisy read to her was a great pleasure, and she was soon lost in the adventure of Alan Breck and David Balfour who had now reached Appin, Colin Campbell of Glenure having been killed.

I wish he was alive again! It's all very fine to blow and boast beforehand; but now it's done, Alan; and who's to bear the wyte of it? The accident fell out in Appin – mind

106

ye that, Alan; it's Appin that must pay; and I am a man that has a family.

Daisy paused after James of the Glens' words. 'It says here, Nana, that wyte means blame.' Nana understood about retribution: from a corner of her mind came a lorry full of storm troopers pulling up in the street, the men jumping out, shouting. Boots and guns. People trying to get indoors, get away, hide, as men and boys were rounded up in reprisal for a shooting.

Nana nodded to Daisy. 'Those Redcoats they were like the,' she paused, not wanting to say such a terrible word to a little girl who had been born after these events and would – please God – never know their like in her lifetime.

'Those Redcoats, there will always be soldiers like them, *liebling*, go on with the story.'

With a pause for a glass of milk, Daisy and Nana were dining with Alan and David on collops in Cluny's Cage with the hidden chieftain himself by the time Daisy started to yawn and find her eyes beginning to droop.

Nana helped the little girl get ready for bed. After the tooth-brushing came the ritual brushing of her hair and Nana thought back dreamily to the days when she used to sit and brush little Ruth's hair.

As she tucked Daisy in, the girl whispered, 'The Redcoats were Nazis, weren't they?'

Nana nodded.

'Mummy called a man a Nazi today, after I wet my knickers.' Nana's wrinkled forehead swallowed her eyebrows in surprise. She sat down and listened as the day's events came tumbling out.

By the time Daisy finished her story she was so tired

she was all but asleep, and the old woman just sat and stroked her hair, and made soothing noises that Daisy should forget about the whole incident because everything was all right. But inside Nana wished she were a little younger and stronger so she could shake Alice till her teeth rattled.

She didn't condemn the woman, far from it, but she just wished, sometimes, that she could shake some common sense into her.

Chapter 10

Graham's Party

The blue party frock hung on the back of the door on its satin-padded, frilly hanger and condemned Daisy.

Every tuck, every gather, each flounce and piece of decorative braid sneered at her for her plain, straight hair and serious eyes, accusing her of not being pretty enough. Someone who giggled with other little girls, shone at charades and always won pass the parcel should wear me, it said.

Daisy viewed the dress as a condemned man might look through his cell windows at the gallows, as she braved the chipped enamel bath down the corridor from their rooms.

The impending doom of Graham's party stretched out before her.

'Up we come darling.' Mummy wrapped the towel round her and pulled out the plug. Daisy didn't hang about. The water went out of the bath at Mr Pickup's with an obscene gurgling belch, which would suck you right out as well if it got a chance.

After the quiet cosiness of the bathroom at the Horse and Jockey this was a cold and threatening place where you didn't linger. Daisy wasn't sure which was worse:

the indignity of standing in the sink in their room or the horrors of the bathroom which also boasted a beady-eyed spider lurking in the corner and a snarling gas geyser.

Daisy gave a shiver and her mother set to work, towelling vigorously.

'Wrapped up tight like an Indian papoose,' laughed Mummy as she tucked the bath towel round her daughter and began rubbing Daisy's hair with another. By the time she had finished Alice noticed a rosy glow in her daughter's cheeks and had to admit to herself that it made a change. She always looks so pale and solemn, Alice thought.

She produced a box of dusting powder and a big green swansdown puff, and looked on as Daisy smothered herself. They both disappeared into a cloud of Woolworth's finest Devon Violets.

Clean vest, clean knickers; white lacy socks and then the dress.

'Arms in the air!'

Mummy dropped the dress over her head and turned her round, pulling it into place and fastening the hooks and eyes down the back.

Daisy was imprisoned inside her godmother's vision of the perfect party frock, and she knew there would be no time off for good conduct. In a dress like this good conduct was compulsory. So was playing kiss chase, musical chairs, salmon-paste sandwiches with crusts cut off and giving your Granny a kiss like a good little girl. Daisy longed to take to the heather like Alan and David in *Kidnapped*.

'Perfect. Now all you need is a smile. Come on, darling, you can do it. It's going to be a lovely party, think of it as an adventure. You'll enjoy yourself.' Alice took one look at her daughter's face and wondered why she was putting her through this ritual hell.

'Smile.'

A thin muscle movement trembled across Daisy's face like a pale sun trying to break through a winter sky.

Alice decided, for once, that honesty was the best policy: 'Think of it as a play, a performance. I'll be playing the mummy who loves going along to visit Aunt Betty and Gran and doesn't mind the horrible things they say to her, and you'll be the little girl who loves going along to parties and playing games.'

Daisy eyed her mother doubtfully.

'I will if you will, darling,' said Mummy.

'OK,' said Daisy.

The bus journey to Whittington was agony for Daisy, the stiff layers of net petticoat sandpapered her bottom and she squirmed in her seat. As they passed the Horse and Jockey she spotted the kennels were full of empty crates and part of the wire was torn.

'Daddy'll have to get that fixed or we'll have dogs all over the place,' Daisy pointed out to her mother.

All Alice could manage was a silent nod. News from the hospital was not good when she telephoned that morning.

Am I being a coward by not telling her we are never going back there, or how seriously ill her father is? No, Alice decided. Why bother her little head with more worries, she always looks anxious enough as it is. Alice could see the coming party etched on Daisy's face.

They got off the bus at the corner by the Dog Inn and from out of a brown paper carrier bag Mummy produced Graham's present, *The Boys' Book of Science* wrapped up in Scottie-dog paper, and handed it to Daisy. They set off up the village street towards Aunt Betty's house, with Daisy walking as slowly as possible, eyes fixed on the

111

jaunty little dogs, trying not to look at the approaching front door with balloons tied to the knocker.

'What a lovely day for a party,' said Mummy with false cheerfulness to another mother escorting a soap-polished boy, 'my, doesn't he look a smart little chap.'

Daisy knew her mother was acting, and decided she had better join in as all four walked up the garden path.

Inside it was as bad as the playground with no hope of the class bell to rescue her. Gran was there, as was Aunt Betty, doing what she did best: providing the perfect setting for her perfect son. This party would keep her in conversation until his summer triumphs at the school sports day. Daisy kissed them both, said 'thank you for inviting me' and was pointed in the direction of Graham.

Admiring friends, all with hair damped and combed into place, all wearing clip-on bow ties, surrounded him. Graham's tie was tartan. The girls huddled behind, giggling with the excitement of it all.

'Happy birthday, Graham,' said Daisy and gave him a kiss as she handed him the present. Big mistake.

'Urg, she kissed you!' yelled one of the boys, and girls squealed in delighted horror. Graham took the present as he wiped the kiss off his cheek and turned to his friend to open it. Daisy was left, as usual, on the outside, not sure what to do next.

Alice watched as Daisy's cheeks flushed with embarrassment and felt the pain just as badly. Looking across the room her heart sank as she realised she was in for a rough time herself. There in the corner was George, with Vi helping to prepare some simple props on a tray.

'Hello Vi, how's your mother's legs, darling?'

George looked as though he had just been shot. Vi looked flustered.

'Much better, can't complain.'

112

'Just going to entertain the . . .' George petered out.

'That's right, Uncle George, the kiddies' friend,' said Alice sweetly, then as Vi moved away to collect something, she said softly, 'only mind you steer clear of my kid, right?'

George fled, shedding playing cards from his sleeve as he went.

'Hello Mother.' Alice's ears told her that she was in for a far, far rougher time than Daisy. She turned round to face her older daughter, who was standing with her arms folded defensively across her chest.

Alice went to hug her, but the arms unfolded fast enough to fend her off, and Caroline's head turned so that Alice only managed to brush the cheek of the younger, petite version of herself.

Alice soldiered on. 'It's good to see you, how are you?' The words fell flat, lame.

'I'm find, thank you. We've come down to see Trevor's parents, and I've just popped over to help with the party.' The words in return were cold, prepared and said without feeling.

Daisy slowly edged away from the other children, and turned to seek the security of her mother. Instead she froze at the sight of her older half-sister and her mother together. Daisy's worst fears were confirmed: it was a plot, Caroline was here. Were they going to make her go home with Caroline? Daisy began to feel a cold fear creep into her stomach, swamping her usual dread of parties.

Caroline turned and headed for the kitchen and the security of Gran and Betty's approval.

Alice was left wishing life had a script for the right words when you really needed them. She did not know her older daughter did not hate her, but hated the self-

113

pride which had stopped her hugging her mother and telling her she longed to have Alice and all her laughter and adventures back in her life.

The children were herded into a semicircle and sat cross-legged to watch Uncle George. Aunt Betty had swallowed her distaste for Alice's theatrical friends and asked him to perform; in the Whittington one-upmanship stakes of birthday parties Betty knew she had beaten every other mother, by having a professional magician.

Daisy was unimpressed as all those around her ooed and aahed. Shorn of his white tie and tails, the spotlight and Mummy in her sequins and feathers, he looked sad and worn out.

Besides, there was another conjuring act in progress which Daisy wanted to keep her eye on, that of her mother and Caroline. Daisy had taken her usual place, tucked away at the back, trying to make herself invisible. She wriggled back on her bottom a bit more, leaned over to give the door leading into the kitchen a nudge and looked through the crack at Mummy, Caroline, Gran and Aunt Betty all gathered round the kitchen table making sandwiches. Were they talking about her?

She saw Caroline pick up a tray of jellies in wax-paper dishes and hurry off into the balloons, streamers and paper tablecloths in the dining room.

'Caroline's here.' Gran, like so many adults, stated the obvious and managed to make it sound like an accusation.

'Kind of her to help, they're going back tonight.' Betty tried to make conversation.

Alice knew she should come out with something bright and witty like she usually did in self-defence, but only managed to nod and pick up a butter knife. 'I'll help you out with the sandwiches.'

'Betty and I have been thinking.' Gran's idea of a party

frock would have made Aunt Zita weep, Daisy noticed. The same black came out for all occasions: weddings, birthdays and funerals; a mink tie, a string of crystal beads and a God-fearing hat accompanied each event respectively.

'You can't go on like this, Alice, there's little Dorothy to think of.'

'Daisy,' muttered the little girl to herself as she strained to hear above the noise of the partygoers joining in with Uncle George and Aunt Vi.

Alice was cornered and she knew it. 'You've been doing a lot of thinking, Mother.'

'Don't be flippant with me my girl, it's a disgrace.' Gran was buttering fiercely. 'When was the last time that child went to school? What sort of life has she got, in that dump of a digs, you just go gallivanting off and leave her with anyone.'

'I do not, Dorothy is always looked after properly. Just you look out there, she's the best-dressed kid here.' God knows which production Zita nicked the material from though, she added inwardly.

'Last night you were seen coming out of the Regal, Mrs Barnes told me,' Betty challenged, ever ready to get revenge for all those kicked knees.

'My word, Mrs Barnes going to see an X film like that. It's been banned in Warwickshire, you know. She'll have to go to confession.'

'Mind your lip,' Gran was beginning to lose her temper. 'You were there with that, that,' she spat out the words, 'Fred's bit on the side. Have you no shame? Who was looking after your daughter?'

'Ruth's mother. They caught the last bus home.'

'You're always round with them.'

'They've been kind to me, and they've offered me a

hand when things are rough and that's more than I can say for you and Betty. All you have ever done is harp on.'

Gran tried to steer the conversation back on course: 'Betty and I have been thinking.'

'Sounds like it.' Alice fought the urge to grab her daughter and bolt away on the next bus back to Lichfield.

'We've been thinking and we have had a word with your Caroline.'

'Yes Mum.' Caroline stood in the doorway, curling her fingers up and tugging at the ends of her sleeves; a move Alice remembered she did as a child, when anxious.

'We think Dorothy would be best if she went and stayed with Caroline and Trevor until you get yourself on your feet again.'

Sitting at her listening post Daisy turned to stone, horrified. She felt the same panic-stricken urge to run as her mother.

'That's what you think?' Alice, like her daughter, stood like stone.

They nodded.

'I don't mind, Mum, really.' Caroline tugged at her sleeves, hoping her mother would agree. Taking the child would be one way back, to make it up between them. She wanted to run to her mother and say come and stay with me and we'll have fun again and adventures like we used to when I was little.

'Trevor and I are hoping to start a family. I'm at home all the time now, I haven't bothered looking for work after my last job finished and I—'

'You haven't spoken to me properly in years, not a word. You never acknowledged I married Fred and you've made a point of never speaking to your sister and now you tell me you don't mind really?'

116

Caroline managed a nod.

'We just thought . . . ' Betty realised she'd been buttering the same piece of bread for the last ten minutes.

Alice looked at her sister straight in the eye, and then her mother. 'It's not thought. It's spite.'

Alice tried to think back, to remember what had bred such animosity between herself and her sister. She could not; it seemed as if it had always been there, growing with the years from childhood jealousies to imagined adult slights.

Daisy lost the rest of the conversation as twenty children stopped sitting still and paying attention and let their excitement rip.

George and Vi quickly packed up the tray of props and bustled into the kitchen. George took a sideways look at Alice's expression, sensed the tension and feared she had been telling them about that night at the Hippodrome.

'I'll not bother with an encore, we'll be off.' They fled.

Betty, one of nature's party organisers, shot into action, relieved that the scene in the kitchen had ended.

'Come on children, tea's ready!' They stampeded into the dining room.

Aunt Betty was soon presiding over the tea table, relishing every moment, and the other women ferried in food.

Cabbage hedgehogs bristled with little cold sausages on sticks, which all the boys pounced on first. Bowls had been filled full of potato crisps, their blue-wax paper twists of salt prudently removed.

Daisy believed food was food, no matter where, and joined in. The condemned child decided to eat a hearty meal before the execution of party games.

The noise subsided slightly while they ate; Caroline went over to Alice.

'Mum, can I have a word?'

Alice, still seething, just looked at her, one eyebrow raised.

'Not here, outside.' Alice nodded and followed her daughter into the kitchen. Daisy went to slide off her stool and follow, but Gran intercepted her. Daisy started to panic; for once she forgot about food and strained to see her mother and sister through the window as they stood in the garden.

Alice wasn't sure what was coming next. She and Caroline stood facing each other; Caroline tugged her sleeves down, twisting her fingers nervously around the cuffs. Alice remembered the same pose the night Caroline had burst into tears of rage and anger and told her she wanted to go and live with her father, that she was ashamed that her mother had left and the girls at the Friary taunted her about their divorce.

Alice could see her other daughter through the window, her face strained and anxious, watching them intently.

'Mum,' Caroline began suddenly and Alice braced herself for a wave of Caroline's anger.

It never came; wordlessly Caroline folded into her mother's arms and started to sob quietly. Alice held her close and kissed and kissed her.

Daisy watched from the dining room and wondered what it all meant.

She was relieved to see Mummy and Caroline arrive in time for the birthday cake. They followed Aunt Betty into the room as she started to sing 'Happy birthday to you' and everyone joined in as the cake was placed in front of a very smug-looking Graham.

'Don't blow the candles out yet dear,' his mother ordered as she reached for a camera from the sideboard;

another perfect moment to put into her photograph album with a caption written neatly underneath. The bulb in the big circular flashgun on top popped in a flash of light and Graham was exhorted to blow out the candles, which he did, showering the cake with a mouthful of sausage-roll pastry. Daisy decided no matter now tempting the white icing with its blue swirls and writing might look, she would forgo having a piece.

The children left the debris of the table and headed back into the parlour where the gramophone waited to play a selection of kiddies' favourites and the furniture was set for musical chairs. Off they went, skipping round to 'The Runaway Train', which came to a strangled halt as the needle was yanked off the record and everyone made a dive for the chairs.

Daisy paused long enough for the chair nearest her to be occupied by a boy with a triumphant grin, and she retired gracefully to stand by her mother and sister. She stared up at Caroline, hardly knowing her or what to say. Caroline just felt the same and returned the same awkward smile.

Mummy gave Daisy a knowing look. 'Took a dive, huh?' Daisy nodded. There were some things in life best avoided and musical chairs was one of them.

'Never mind, Dorothy,' said Caroline, who shyly bent down to kiss Daisy on the cheek.

'Daisy,' she confided, 'I like being Daisy.'

'OK then, Daisy it is.'

Daisy could feel questions beginning to grow, and opened her mouth to ask Caroline why she had never lived with Mummy and Daddy, or if she had ever had adventures in shops with Mummy.

Alice watched as the thoughts began to form and, just as her younger daughter opened her mouth to speak, said,

'Look, it's pass the parcel, in you go,' and gave Daisy a shove towards the centre of the room. Alice felt a bit heartless as she did so, but right now maintaining the fragile, newly formed peace with her older daughter was more important.

Daisy sat down in the circle of children and gave her mother a betrayed look. A little girl won the prize of a bar of Fry's Five Boys chocolate, then Aunt Betty announced, 'Charades', and Daisy felt a desperate move was called for.

'I feel sick,' she declared.

Betty was a veteran of children's parties and knew it would only take one vomiter to trigger a whole house full of excited little stomachs. She smoothly extracted Daisy from the mass of children and steered her back towards Alice.

'She's got a poorly tum, poor dear, better sit this one out.' Trust Alice's bloody kid, she thought to herself sourly; if Alice doesn't ruin something for me, then her girl does.

Mummy gave Daisy another knowing look. 'Must be the excitement of it all, she does so love parties.'

Daisy tried to give a sincerely tummy-aching nod of agreement, pleased with how successful her move had been.

'Poor little pet,' said Caroline as she lifted Daisy up onto her knee and gave her a cuddle.

To Alice's surprise and delight, Daisy let her, and cuddled back. The three sat on the edge of the room and slowly became oblivious of the noisy party going on around them. By the time the games had reached Oranges and Lemons Alice could have wept with joy.

A knock at the door saw Betty leave the fray and return with a young man who wore the look of suppressed terror only a man can have when faced with a children's party and the fear he will be asked to join in.

Trevor had come to collect his wife and terror was replaced with disbelief when he saw her sitting with her mother and what could only be her half-sister; not only was their colouring the same, but their features had a vague similarity and their brown eyes were identical.

Alice and Daisy walked Caroline out to the waiting Ford Prefect. There were hugs all round and Alice was so thrilled she even kissed Trevor on the cheek and went as far as calling him 'darling'.

'We're expected back at Huddlesford or we'd have given you a lift back to Lichfield,' said Caroline. She bent down to Daisy. 'One day you'll have to come and visit us in Manchester. Would you like that?'

Daisy felt it would be diplomatic to nod. While some kind of blood link had made her accept Caroline without question, she felt decidedly unsure about her husband. From the way he stood, holding open his car door, anxious to get away, Daisy realised he felt the same.

Alice and Daisy stood and waved goodbye, oblivious to Gran now joining in the farewells. Alice felt an almost intoxicated joy that the last wound of her first marriage was on its way to becoming healed.

'It would be for the best you know, Manchester,' Gran said darkly and returned inside.

Determined that nothing her mother or sister might say would ruin what had turned into an unexpectedly monumental day, Alice took Daisy back into the party. Once there she collected their coats and murmured that Daisy was feeling so poorly they had better catch the next bus back to Lichfield.

'I hope it isn't catching,' Alice hinted, turning an imaginary upset into an infectious ailment. 'There's something going round.'

This had the right effect: Betty was not going to insist they stay.

Daisy performed her thank-you-for-having-me-it-was-a-nice-party speech with a false sincerity her mother had to admire and they were on their way to the bus stop. Daisy was clutching a balloon, a paper-napkin-wrapped piece of Graham's birthday cake and a colouring book by way of consolation for missing the rest of the fun. Alice gave her daughter a shrewd look.

'I feel sick,' she mimicked.

'I hope it isn't catching,' Daisy replied.

They were still feeling smug about how clever they were when the bus reached Cherry Orchard on the edge of the city and a slight old man sat down on the seat in front of them.

'Hello Alice, how's Fred getting on?' He had been an occasional visitor to the Horse and Jockey.

After Alice thanked him for his enquiry and gave him a safe 'Improving slowly', he decided to strike up a conversation.

'Went over to Aldridge on Monday afternoon for little Johnny Atkin's funeral.'

Alice replied she didn't know he had died. Death and funerals were not subjects she wanted Daisy to dwell on; they were things that had never entered the child's life before now. Alice knew, barring a miracle, they soon would.

'Eighty-four years old he was,' he continued, 'and only forty-four inches high. Would you believe it, not much taller than you, me duck.'

Daisy was fascinated, not by the idea of death but that a man could be that old, and that tiny.

'Dwarf,' the man explained. 'Came from Tipton way.

During the Great War he used to work on the munitions at Witton. Made him foreman, they did. Used to stand on a big box and tell all the women what to do.'

The bus carried on on its way. Across Birmingham Road by the railway station was the old St Michael's Hospital, which wore its tall, narrow chimneys on the outside; the man pointed for Daisy to see. 'That's where he was, for what must have been, oh, I'd say the last eighteen years or so. Took him in there when he couldn't manage on his own any more. Too old. Had a little cot in the corner of the ward. I used to go and visit an old chap in there, and I always used to stop by his cot and say hello to Little Johnny, you always got a cheery word.'

Daisy was absorbed with the idea of a grown man who was so small he was shorter than her; so old he was eighty-four, ten times older than her, but still slept in a cot. Alice said goodbye to the man as they climbed down the bus steps opposite the Friary School. Daisy's head was still spinning from the story and she nearly forgot her booty from the party.

She held out her neatly wrapped piece of birthday cake to the man. 'Please would you like a piece of Graham's birthday cake.'

Tears of delight all but appeared in his eyes. He thanked her, said repeated goodbyes to them both and set off down towards Sandford Street, across the park.

Alice wondered what had prompted Daisy to part with a big piece of cake, because she knew how preoccupied the child was with food and that this had increased recently when they lived hand to mouth. She put it down to the tale of Little Johnny Atkin capturing her imagination.

Daisy watched the man disappear with her piece of cake, and wished that Graham hadn't had his mouth full of sausage roll when he'd blown the candles out.

As they walked back to Mr Pickup's, Daisy asked if they could stop outside Bradshaw's on Bird Street. She looked longingly in the shop window at the record players, radios and televisions. Daisy had seen some television, and as much as she really wanted one, what she longed for was a radiogram like the one Aunt Betty had. You could switch the radio on *and* play records on it. When Daddy came home from hospital they could get one. The one with Pye written on the side looked the nicest.

She felt her mother's hand tighten on her shoulder and looked up.

There was the grey man who had visited Daddy at the hospital. He tipped his hat politely to Mummy.

'Alice,' he said by way of greeting. His grey raincoat was open and he wore a grey suit underneath. Even his tie was drab. Daisy eyed him up and down; unlike Uncle Malcie this one didn't look as though he'd ever give you a threepenny bit, let alone half-a-crown, so she turned her attention back to the shop window.

'That's Mrs Smedley to you, copper.'

'Charmed to see you again, too, I'm sure. No Malcie today?'

'Why should there be?'

'You seem to be seeing a lot of him, you and Ruthie.'

'Who Miss Rosen and I associate with is none of your business.'

Daisy looked up, slightly interested. Mummy was starting to enunciate.

'Keep it that way. It might become my business, if what I hear about Big Malcie and some funny money is right.'

He took a step closer to Alice and lowered his voice.

124

'Watch yourself, Alice. I always had plenty of time for your Fred. He never crossed the line, though I know he bloody well leaned over it often enough. But Malcie? Now he's a different story, remember that. A nasty piece of work.'

He tipped his hat again and walked on.

Shaking slightly, Mummy clasped Daisy's hand firmly in her own and marched them off up Beacon Street without a word, and before Daisy had time to decide on which colour Dansette portable with an automatic record-changing arm she was going to have in her bedroom.

Chapter 11

Ruth Sets off for Rhyl

Nana Rosen's kitchen was in chaos, and Daisy found it very upsetting indeed. This was a place where she could expect warmth, lots of food, baking, and comfort. Today it was full of clothes waiting to be ironed. A big suitcase sat in the middle of the kitchen table with its lid open, like a baby cuckoo in a nest of robins, out of place and demanding to be fed.

The whole thing was so unsettling that Mr Bloum had fled for the furthest corner of the garden, unnerved and seeking the sanctuary of planting out radishes. He hadn't even appeared for elevenses, as he did usually if Daisy and Alice were there.

Baking was out of the question; Daisy had to put all hope out of her mind of scraping clean a mixing bowl with her finger, and she was finding it difficult to concentrate on a piece of yesterday's sponge cake. Nana was so flustered she hadn't even given her a glass of milk.

'Blue dress, blue dress, where did I put it, Mother?'

Aunt Ruth was going round in circles. Mummy was perched on the edge of the old armchair, looking almost as wild-eyed as Nana, but nowhere near as frantic as her friend.

'When did you hear?' she asked, as Ruth reappeared to throw some nylons into the hungry-looking case.

'Last night, I was in the bar at Dave's and Derek phoned up, asked if I was there and he told me then. I rang up like he said and got it there and then.'

Aunt Ruth was off to Rhyl to replace a dancer in a show who had run off with a trumpet player.

'Good of Derek to suggest you,' said Mummy. Ruth paused. 'Yes wasn't it, bless the darlink. It's the first decent piece of work I've had in months.'

Derek hadn't said how many women he'd tried before her, and Ruth's pride hadn't allowed her to ask.

'So far avay!' wailed Nana Rosen, who was stricken by the idea of her daughter working in a foreign country, despite assurances from both Ruth and Alice that Rhyl was only a change of trains at Crewe away.

'It's work Momma, and we need the money, though I hate to leave you all. Especially now, with Fred so . . .' Ruth was not so frantic as to forget the truth of Fred's condition was not to be discussed in front of Daisy. They had been to see him the day before and he was so ill he could barely hug Daisy or take any notice of her.

That to Alice was the most terrifying part of his decline. Fred lived for Daisy's visits, was this a sign of his impending death?

The ward sister had taken Alice to one side, just before they left. What she said had not been good: the cancer was spreading.

'So far!' Nana sat clutching her apron in despair. Daisy felt slightly indignant that a second piece of cake hadn't been placed automatically in front of her as she finished the first. Things must be bad.

'Cheer up Nana, it's the seaside.' Daisy remembered wistfully the summer holidays with dogs running round barking on the beach and giant sandcastles with paper flags stuck on top of bucket-moulded turrets.

'We could go and visit Aunt Ruth, go to the seaside,' she said hopefully.

'Go so far!' Nana rang out like a tragic opera. The idea of her daughter going was bad enough, that someone should make her leave the security of her kitchen and go as well was unspeakable.

'Uncle Malcie would take us,' Daisy assured her. In recent weeks she had got used to the idea of being driven around in the smart red Jaguar. These visits were punctuated, often as not, with half-crowns which were all building up nicely in her savings. Her dream of actually having thirty bob of her own was not as wild as she first thought.

'Will Derek still be there?' Mummy asked, as she leaned over the ironing board, checked to see the iron was warm enough and set to work on one of Ruth's blouses.

'No, he says he'll be in Chester by the time I get there,' said Ruth as she frantically folded clothes into the case, 'his *Hay Fever* is going really well. Had some good write-ups. You should have gone with them.'

'Just as well I didn't.'

Ruth crossed the room and rubbed her friend reassuringly on the arm. 'Suppose so.'

'So far avay!' Nana lamented, and to Daisy's relief the old woman absent-mindedly picked up her plate and returned it in front of her with a massive doorstep of cake. Worry had dented Nana's portions. Mummy took one look at the size of the piece Daisy was trying to get into her mouth, rolled her eyes in horror, and handed the child a fork.

'Will you be all right?' Ruth asked Alice.

'Course we will. We'll come down and keep Nana company, won't we?'

Daisy, mouth full to the point of choking, looked at Nana and nodded agreement reassuringly.

'So far! Vot time is Malcie coming to take you avay?'

Nana had thawed slightly in the face of Malcie's rides home in the Jaguar with her shopping bags in the boot while she sat in the back like a duchess, fivers gently pressed into her hand and the presentation of bottles of Harvey's Bristol Cream.

Each time he entered the house he was sat down in the best chair in the front parlour, and presented with a plate of cake. It worried Ruth. She had heard stories so terrible she had not told them to Alice: how he could take a man's face off with a blade without thinking, of Post Office van raids where he left men's heads smashed in with a pickaxe handle. Yet he could sit by the fire in her mother's front parlour, plate of cake balanced on his knee, and graciously accept a second cup of tea while telling her about running barefoot as a child at his grandfather's croft house which had a roof made of turf. Like he was two people, Ruth thought.

'Malcie said he'd come at half past twelve. The train doesn't go until after half one,' said Ruth. She attempted to close the case, but it refused to fasten. In the end they called Mr Bloum in from the garden and he fought the catches while Ruth and Daisy knelt on top.

Nana produced a paper bag full of greaseproof-paper-wrapped sandwiches and cake. In the delay between packing and Malcie's arrival the paper bag grew into a butcher's brown paper carrier bag with a tin full of biscuits and a whole cake added, along with half a pound of cheese and a packet of 99 tea from the Co-op.

'You don't know what the food will be like!' Nana

129

warned, as she folded up a half a bag of sugar and added it to the provisions.

Ruth knew better than to stop her mother; this was her way of saying goodbye, even if it was only for twelve days. In Nana's life too many people had gone out to work in the morning or stepped out to go shopping or to the theatre and never been seen again.

'Who else is on the bill?' Alice asked, trying to bring an air of normality to the kitchen. Though if I'm the one trying to keep things calm then it must be bad, she thought.

'Usual stuff. Magician, couple of comics, and a vent act. The top of the bill changes, depending on who they can get. Think it's Acker Bilk one night.'

Mummy looked impressed, Daisy pricked up her ears.

'Who is the ventriloquist?' Daisy held her breath. What if it was him, what if it was the best man in the world after Daddy? What if he was there with Aunt Ruth in Wales and she didn't get to see him? Would she ever see him again? A panic started to rise in Daisy's stomach.

'Don't know,' said Ruth, who had a pretty shrewd idea who Daisy hoped it would be. She leaned forward and whispered in the child's ear, 'If it's him, I'll let you know. Promise.'

Malcie arrived early, which pleased Ruth because it prevented her mother from slicing up a ham she had in the larder to add to the carrier bag, which was about to burst its string handles.

As Malcie carried the case to the car Ruth turned and hugged Nana, whose wailing was quietly changing to weeping. Ruth held her close.

'You'll be fine. I'll be back before you know it. You never get upset when I go to London and that's further away.'

130

'But it isn't Vales, it isn't foreign!' Nothing anyone could do would reassure Nana geographically.

Ruth said her goodbyes to her mother at the garden gate. She could not bear the idea of parting at the railway station, she had said goodbye to her father at one and never seen him again.

Daisy and Alice rode with them to Trent Valley station. Daisy was excited to see all the sheep and cows crammed into the steel pens at the trackside. Ruth found they brought to the surface a whole range of emotions and memories of the day she and her mother were herded onto a train like cattle. She stamped on the memory. It belonged to another world, another lifetime. Still the echoes remained and made her farewell to Alice more tearful and trembling than she had thought possible.

'I'll send postcards, with a phone number on where you can call me. With an address. Send me a telegram if anything should, you know, I mean Fred. Or send it to the theatre. Oh Alice, take care of yourselves and him.'

They watched and waved the train out of sight. Malcie was surprised to find himself affected by Alice and Ruth's battle to fight back their tears. He felt protective; it was his duty to take care of them.

He felt he had inherited them from Fred: one of the worst actresses who ever walked on a stage, an ageing dancer with an accent that stripped paint, an old woman who fussed, a gardener who once lived in a mansion with servants and now hid in a potting shed and a child who was probably the sanest of the bunch.

He started out doing a favour for a dying man while looking out for his own dodgy cash. Now he found himself thinking about them and wanting to be with them more and more, and caring for them. He knew Ruth and Alice were wary of him, for they knew his reputation, but the others simply accepted him and liked him.

'Ach, I'm going bloody soft,' he said to Daisy. She didn't understand, but she had the sense to nod solemnly.

They drove back into Lichfield and Malcie treated Alice and Daisy to a mixed grill at the Swan Hotel. Daisy's feet barely touched the floor as she sat in the sedate dining room, white damask napkin under her chin, suitably impressed that her lamb cutlet had a paper frill around the end, and her glass of lemonade had ice cubes and a slice of real lemon.

Outside the city was starting to prepare for its biggest day of the year: the Whitsun Bower. 'Will you take us to the Bower, Uncle Malcie? It's ever so good. They have bands and a Bower Queen and a procession and horses and a fair.'

'Uncle Malcie might be busy, he might have to go to work,' said Alice, who was beginning to feel uneasy about the hold the big Glaswegian now seemed to have on Daisy's affections.

He certainly hadn't replaced Fred in her daughter's eyes, no one could ever do that, but Daisy now assumed he would be part of their day-to-day lives. Alice had to admit his money certainly was, and he would want paying back soon. However he never laid a finger on her or Ruth so he didn't expect payment of *that* kind, but Alice knew Malcie was not the sort of person who did anything for anyone without expecting something in return.

Malcie felt secretly pleased the child wanted him to join in her fun. He thought back a couple of years to when he'd seen Fred and Alice out with the child: a proper family enjoying a day together. Something he'd never had with that cow Celia who hadn't given him a child but upped and ran off with a Yank from the base at Holy Loch.

132

Little did Daisy realise she had got one over on Big Malcie MacFadyen, something people rarely did and lived to walk without a limp. Daisy was thinking not so much of his company but more along the lines of the endless supply of change there seemed to be in his pockets to buy rides and massive pink candyfloss sticks. Daisy reasoned her pleas for him to come to the Bower would have one of two results: he would go and spend money on her, or he would say he couldn't and give her some money to spend. She'd be a winner either way.

'Course I'll come with you, ma wee girl,' he said.

Daisy squealed with delight at the success of her plan. It might require half a dozen polis to take him in, and big hard men at that, but the job had been done just as efficiently by an eight-year-old with a trickle of gravy dripping down her chin.

Chapter 12

Bent Money at the Bower

It was the best Bower ever, the *Lichfield Mercury* said so; and few would have disagreed. In the early summer of 1961 Harold Macmillan was proved right: they'd never had it so good.

The Fifties with their post-war gloom of rationing and making-do had gone. Memories of the Blitz and official telegrams that regretted to inform were fading as fast the bomb sites were being built on every day; there were jobs for all, money in pockets and plenty of things to spend it on.

There was the Bower, for a start. Fifty thousand people crammed the streets of the city, to have a good time in the sunshine. Special trains were run from Birmingham, Wolverhampton, Burton and Derby, buses and coaches flowed in all morning and cars had to be abandoned as far away as the Shoulder of Mutton as the streets filled.

Little did the crowds who watched the Courte of Arraye outside the Guildhall that morning know or care, but they were taking part in the best Bower of the twentieth century. Peace and prosperity, two things that occasionally went missing between 1900 and the Millennium, were at their height, and the fellowship created by the hardships of war had not dwindled into selfishness.

No subsequent Bower quite captured that spirit of ordinary people of goodwill having fun and enjoying themselves in a leisurely, knees-up, no need to rush, plenty for everyone, ain't life grand kind of way.

For Daisy, like every child who walked through the packed streets, it was a second Christmas. The excited expectation had given way to the day itself, and the Bower lived up to all its promises.

The fair and the sideshows spilled through the streets. Balloon-sellers stood on street corners, there were shakers of tissue-paper streamers to buy, every shop was decorated, and every face was smiling. There was colour and music everywhere. It was a crowded fairyland where magic made sure everyone had a good time.

The ritual boiled-egg breakfast was bolted. Daisy could hardly eat, it was Bower Day. Even Mr Pickup looked cheerful. Daisy fidgeted on the doorstep, waiting for Uncle Malcie to arrive. Every so often a decorated lorry with people in fancy dress went past, or someone in costume on their way to the start of the procession at Greenhill. Daisy thought she would burst if Uncle Malcie didn't arrive soon.

In the midst of her excitement she remembered Nana and Mr Bloum; they had said they wouldn't be coming. They didn't like crowds, Mummy said. Daisy couldn't comprehend why anyone would choose to miss the Bower, but she promised to win a coconut for Nana to make a cake with and for Mr Bloum to hang the other half in a tree for the birds to eat. She would, too, if only Uncle Malcie would arrive.

Mr Pickup joined her and they sat on the front step watching all the world go by, Bower Day even managed to make Mr Pickup seem cheerful. Most of the people from the Dimbles seemed to have walked down Beacon Street on their way to the Bower, everyone in their best clothes: little boys in white shirts and grey shorts held up with coloured snake belts; little girls with summer dresses and ribbons in their hair, mums and dads with pushchairs. Though there was not a cloud in the sky, raincoats were still cautiously folded over arms and would become burdens by the end of the day.

Daisy spotted Uncle Malcie coming up the road, shortly after he crossed the entrance to the Cathedral Close. It was hard not to see him, he was so tall with his gingery-red hair, walking straight-backed, his impressive deportment the only thing that National Service had given him: they did a lot of drilling at the Colchester glasshouse.

Mr Pickup seemed to melt into the background when the big man arrived; he had that effect on some people. Daisy ran to him in delight and they walked up the last part of the hill together. Alice met them at the top of the stairs, wearing a watercolour cotton dress, a fine straw hat and carrying a small basket containing cardigans for herself and Daisy. Together they set off towards the Bower.

It was a battle to walk through the town centre and up Greenhill where the procession was assembling. On the way Malcie dug into his pocket and bought Daisy not one, but four balloons and she held onto their knotted strings in amazement. They stopped at Garrett's shop to buy some sausage rolls and cakes to eat later. Daisy was pleased to note that these sausage rolls, unlike Aunt Betty's, were more sausage than meat.

Each time they went into a shop Uncle Malcie produced a five-pound note and apologised for not having any change.

136

They looked round the floats and the procession and then decided to go back down to the Guildhall to watch the official start.

Daisy thought Pauline Sneyd the Bower Queen had a dress as beautiful as anything Aunt Zita ever made. Everyone cheered as she was crowned and Mr Richards the mayor kissed her as well.

Old Mr Salloway, the alderman from the jewellery shop, presented the prizes for the best floats and fancy dress.

The noise and the excitement of it all nearly swept Daisy off her feet: no sooner had the Staffordshire's band and drums gone by than the silver band from the colliery at Cannock Chase came, then the Sea Cadets playing their kazoos.

Mummy and Malcie kept handing her pennies to give to collectors in fancy dress, or to throw to people on the back of floats: George and the Dragon, a tulip field made of paper flowers and children in Dutch costumes, and there was even some pretending to be the statue of Dr Johnson from the Market Square. He had to clamber down in a hurry when the procession reached the railway bridge and his seat proved too high to go underneath.

Not only was this Bower the best, Daisy decided, but also it was the first one she had ever seen from a perch above the crowd. Malcie had picked her up, as though she was as light as a feather to give her a ride, and he stood with her on his shoulders for the entire length of the procession. Her own father would never have had that kind of physical strength, his illness had been creeping on ever since Daisy was a baby.

There was a lull as the procession ended, and they chose to stay in the city rather than go to the events in Beacon Park.

Uncle Malcie seemed impatient, Daisy thought, as she and Mummy went on the gallopers. They sat side by side on painted horses and hung on tightly as the world spun round. He stood by Mummy and condescended to wave back to Daisy as she went round on a smaller roundabout.

'No Malcie, she's too little and it's too rough,' said Alice when they got to the dodgems, something Daisy had never even been allowed to consider before.

'Oh please Mummy.' This was new and exciting territory for Daisy. She had heard Graham boasting about his dad taking him on the dodgems.

'No, certainly not.'

But Malcie just picked her up and dropped her down into a dodgem car, and climbed in beside her. When they set off, Daisy was terrified, but pride would not let her burst into tears, she had begged for this. She clung tightly to Malcie as cars crashed into them, and then tighter still, burying her face in his side, as he went in pursuit of other cars to crash into, or rear-ended them.

Daisy's world was spinning slightly and her teeth ached from clenching them as she walked unsteadily from the ride.

The sideshows succumbed to Uncle Malcie's skills, and Daisy had her arms full of his winnings of Nana's coconut, a doll with a squint, a teddy bear and two goldfish in bags which ended up taking possession of the po under the bed.

The latter meant trips down the corridor in the middle of the night, until the time Mummy forgot. That Clem and Cleo were still alive the next morning qualified them for an honourable discharge, Mummy said. Daisy walked carefully down to Minster Pool clutching the po tightly to her chest. Intent on not spilling a drop and oblivious to the looks from passers-by, she gave them their freedom.

'Close your eyes and hold out your hands,' said Uncle Malcie.

Daisy obeyed and was rewarded with cupped palms overflowing with copper, threepenny bits and the odd sixpence here and there.

'You and your mummy go and enjoy yourself on the fair, I've got some work to do.'

Alice gave a nod to Malcie and, despite Daisy's pleas for him to stay, he left to pay a visit to Alderman Salloway's jewellery shop on Bore Street, and then Worthington's on the corner of Market Street.

At the first he bought an expensive gold watch, then at Worthington's he looked over a selection of gold bracelets and bought two. He was so impressed at the sight of a tray of rings, he said, that he picked out a nice diamond to surprise his wife with at Christmas. The salesman beamed with delight and opened the door for him when he left.

In each shop Malcie paid with crisp new five-pound notes, peeling them out from under a paper band from Martin's Bank which was the only genuine article in his wallet.

A little further down Bird Street he paused outside Bradshaw's to admire the same televisions and radiograms that Daisy had coveted, before going in and treating himself to the best portable radio in the shop.

He considered trying to find Alice and the child again, but thought not; it would be impossible in this throng.

So he decided to call it a day, and, drunk on his own adrenalin from pulling off a good con, he walked leisurely back down Friars Alley, through the park and onto the Walsall Road where he'd left his car near Christ Church. He'd some nice stuff to fence and some real notes in change, and he had thoroughly enjoyed himself

139

treating Alice and her wee girl at the fair.

When Alice declared it was time to go home Daisy all but mutinied, she was so intoxicated with the excitement of the day. That was an indication to Alice, if one was needed, that her daughter had had enough.

'It's not fair,' she whined, full of sweets and candyfloss and laden with her many prizes.

'It's getting late,' said Alice, whose feet were beginning to hurt. Her head was starting to spin from all the noise and the rides Malcie's money had bought.

'I know. I want to see it when it's dark.' Daisy had never seen the fair at night and the thought of it thrilled her, it would be like a firework display with people and music and noise.

'Nope, come on, time for home,' said Alice, as she fastened her hand about Daisy's and started back down Levetts Fields.

Daisy's sulking dissolved by the time they got to Conduit Street, for there were too many exciting things going on around her to let her stay sullen.

The pubs were starting to spill drunks out onto the street, all full of the good-natured spirit of the day. Daisy watched in fascinated horror as two men staggered off the pavement by the old Corn Exchange and sank to their knees in the gutter, roaring with laughter.

'It's like VE day all over again,' said Alice to herself as she steered Daisy towards the quieter Dam Street and up to the Close.

Walking past the cathedral, the Bower became a distant roar and the singing of blackbirds on branches became the loudest noise in the late afternoon.

Alice's high heels made her sway across the cobbles, holding Daisy tightly by the hand. Students from the theological college, still in costume from their tableaux in the Bower procession, were moving some of the scenery from the back of the lorry which had carried them, dressed improbably as beatniks. One or two of them gave Alice a sly glance as she walked by.

As they left the Close and turned to go up the hill Alice swore to herself silently and came to a sudden stop. Coming towards them was the man dressed in grey. As polite as ever, he tipped his hat.

'Good afternoon Alice.' Daisy remembered him as the man who had visited Daddy in hospital. He had ignored her then, he ignored her outside Bradshaw's shop, and he ignored her now.

'Mr MacCallum.' Alice didn't bother with a greeting.

'How fortuitous we should meet. Your landlord said you'd gone to the fair.' He liked fortuitous, he'd watched *No Hiding Place* on his sister's telly and Inspector Lockhart had used the word.

Bleeding filth, Alice thought, he would go round to our digs, wouldn't he? Just what I need.

'Oh?' she said innocently, none of her thoughts showing on her face. She knew that with this one it was best if you let him do all the talking, because he fancied himself. Give him enough time and he'd answer his own questions.

'Yes. It appears that Salloway's have had some counterfeit money passed on them this afternoon.' He couldn't contain himself well enough to play the cat and mouse of the television detective and his prey. 'Where's Malcie?'

Alice knew better than to try 'Who? Oh him?' or 'Never seen him', because MacCallum would have heard from old man Pickup that a big Scotsman with ginger hair had called for them.

'He just popped round to see me this morning, asked if

141

I needed a lift to see Fred in hospital, he walked us down into the city out of politeness and that was the last we saw of him.'

Daisy looked at her mother. She was telling a really big fib. Uncle Malcie had been with them all day; he'd let her sit on his shoulders. He'd bought rides and sandwiches for lunch and candyfloss and toffee apples and more rides and won a coconut for Nana and two goldfish they'd called Clem and Cleo. She'd had a go on the dodgems with him, even though Mummy said no. In fact Daisy was so full of it all she was bursting to tell someone.

The grey little detective fixed Alice with a look. 'Not since this morning?'

'No,' said Alice and imperceptibly tightened her grip on Daisy's hand as she felt the little girl fidget with the desire to tell him all about her wonderful day out with her Uncle Malcie.

'Tell him I was asking for him.' He touched his hat and walked off in the direction of Minster Pool, totally unaware he had been questioning the wrong Smedley. Daisy would never be a stool pigeon, but just then she'd have happily sung like a canary.

Alice sagged slightly as she watched him go, and turned to her daughter. 'Good girl.'

'Why?'

'Because you didn't tell him about Uncle Malcie.'

'Why?'

'Never mind. Come on, I'm sure there's some of that pork pie from Garrett's left in the bottom of the basket, we can have it for tea. I'm gasping for a cup.'

'Why did you tell that man a big fib?'

'I didn't tell him a big fib, I just didn't tell him everything. There's a difference.'

'Like between a big fib and a little fib? That was a little fib?'

'Yes. You can fib like buggery— Like a big fib, with his sort, darling. Come on; let's get back to Mr Pickup's. Aren't your feet killing you? Mine are.'

Daisy was impressed. While Mummy did do a lot of fibbing, she usually admitted it afterwards; but this was the first time Mummy had told her she could run amok with the truth with any particular person.

Daisy was chasing crumbs from the melting golden pastry of her pork pie round her plate and Alice was sitting with her stockinged feet up on the table with a second cup of tea and a cigarette when Mr Pickup knocked on the door.

'Mrs Smedley, can I have a word?'

It was the tone of voice usually associated with rent arrears, even though they were paid up and in advance.

Alice put her cigarette in the ashtray, winced slightly as she slipped her shoes back on, and opened the door a crack.

'I had the police here this afternoon, asking about you. I tell you, I don't want any trouble, see; this is not that sort of a house. He was asking about your—' The words fancy man or even ponce were forming in their landlord's mind, but he remembered just how big a bloke Malcie was and the word 'friend' came out instead.

Alice opened the door wide and smiled brightly. 'I know, dear Mac, what a darling, we bumped into him walking home.' Here she dropped her voice slightly. 'You see he's in the,' she looked up and down the corridor for dramatic effect to make sure they were not overheard, 'the same lodge as my husband, and called round to see if we were all right. It's so kind of them to help a woman on her own with a child, isn't it? I told

143

him, when we met, that you were taking such good care of us here.'

Mr Pickup paused. 'He was asking if that Scotch bloke had been here.'

Alice dropped to conspiracy level again. 'You see they're in the same, er, you know, line of business as it were.' Well, that was near enough to pass for one of Daisy's little fibs, Alice thought.

Mr Pickup reckoned the big man looked mean enough to be a copper. 'Oh yes, right you are.' He disappeared.

Alice closed the door behind her. Leaned on it and gave a theatrical sigh.

'Things are getting a big warm round here, aren't they darling?'

Daisy had now wiped the plate clean with her finger. She looked up. 'I know, it's nearly summer. My lettuces will be ready soon.'

Chapter 13

To the North

Nana had not really grasped the idea of the long-distance telephone call: she thought she had to shout to make her voice travel all that way. Though she had been wealthy enough in Vienna to have a telephone in her own home, she had never had to use one since her arrival in England. The idea terrified her.

Ruth's picture postcard of the sea front at Rhyl arrived with the address of her digs and the backstage number at the theatre, with instructions to try and reach her at 11 am each day.

While Ruth was pacing up and down during her break, anxiously watching the phone and trying to stop others using it, Alice was armed with a purse full of change and attempting to place a trunk call. Daisy put all her weight against the door of the call box to keep it open while Nana paced up and down outside, like her daughter miles away.

'Hello, yes, hello, Ruth? Yes? Ruth! Darling, wonderful to hear you, let me try to put some more money in . . . Ruth!'

'Is it Ruth, is she there?' Nana was not just beside the call box, she was beside herself.

'Yes, darling, we're all fine, yes. Fred's doing a lot better. Malcie took us to see him yesterday. The doctor said he was pleased, hang on, let me put some more money in. Are you all right? Really? Incredible! Yes she's here, hang on darling.'

Mummy turned and gestured to the old woman to come into the box. It was a squeeze as Nana got in and Alice got out. Nana and her voice more than filled the space.

'Hello, darlink, I can hear you! You can hear me!' So could most of Staffordshire. 'Are you vell? Vot is the food like? Are they treating you good, darlink?'

Nana managed to grasp the idea that she had to stop talking to let Ruth reply. In Rhyl Ruth resorted to bellowing back down the telephone to her mother.

'You speak,' Nana gave the handset back to Alice who immediately fed more money in. Nana looked dazed and told Daisy, 'I spoke to Ruth.'

'Listen, we'll be going with Malcie soon. Don't know when, soon. Probably before you get back. I'll leave Aunt Maggie's address with your mother. She's said we can stay with her when we're there, it'll look better. We've got to, that MacCallum's been round again, it's getting too close, I think he knows. Even questioned old Pickup. It's getting a big dodgy. Look, the money's running out, talk till we're cut off. We miss you darling, Fred sends his love. Yes, I'll tell him. What? Yes, bye-bye.'

Back at Nana's house they needed fortifying after the walk to and from the telephone box at the Whittington road end and making the actual call. Nana decided they should all have big cups of hot chocolate and large pieces of cake.

They discussed the call and the conclusion was that Ruth was having a good time, the show was a success, the people were nice, she was eating properly but the cooking was nowhere near as good as Nana's and she would be back home next Tuesday.

Daisy was disappointed that she hadn't been able to talk to her aunt. She had wanted to ask if the ventriloquist was who she hoped it would be.

After the excitement of making the call, the day fell flat, but they had Malcie to look forward to. For once Alice and Daisy were to see Fred during the evening visiting hour. They spent the afternoon helping Nana to give Ruth's bedroom a spring clean, turning the heavy feather mattress, putting the blankets and eiderdown on the line to air, scrubbing paintwork, polishing the dressing table and wardrobe and rehanging the freshly washed curtains. If Nana didn't have her daughter at home to look after she could fuss over her belongings instead.

The hospital was a completely different place by night. It even looked friendly from the outside, all its windows full of light. The corridors did not echo so frighteningly with fewer people around, and as Daisy entered Daddy's ward each bed was a pool of light from the lamps above.

Alice's relief was almost tangible when she saw her husband. His terrifying decline seemed to have halted, and tonight she thought he even looked slightly better. The paper-thin pallor of his skin had lessened; his bones seemed as though they were actually covered with warm, living flesh again.

Daisy noticed none of this; all she knew was that she was seeing her daddy again. Nurses turned a blind eye to the child curled up on top of the bed hugging him closely. Strict signs forbade patients to sit on beds, but Daisy was the best tonic Fred got every visiting day.

Without Ruth, Malcie took it upon himself to occupy

147

Daisy at the end of the visit, to give Alice and Fred some time alone. He marched her down to the foyer and bought her a bar of chocolate and stood by her side as she ate. Daisy tried to make conversation with him, something that she had discovered he didn't seem good at, unless he was talking to a grown-up. Tonight he seemed to feel even less like talking, he looked as though he was thinking about something else, not her. Daisy took the opportunity to ask for another chocolate bar, something Aunt Ruth would never have agreed to. She slipped it into her pocket to give some to Mummy when they got back to Mr Pickup's.

In the ward, Alice held on tightly to Fred's hand. She told him he looked better. 'Less ill, you mean, not better.' They sat in silence, holding hands.

'I've not been a very good husband, have I.' He had been working on this speech for days, and even so it had started to come out wrong.

'Don't say that.'

'I haven't. I know I haven't. You try to hide it, but I know how hard things are for you and Dorothy.' His eyes began to fill with tears. 'I'm sorry, you know. I tried. I can't bear to think of what's going to happen, when I'm ... There isn't even any insurance, apart from what'll bury me. Oh Alice.' He covered his eyes with a frighteningly thin hand and fought to keep a sob from turning into a racking cough.

Alice swallowed tears of her own.

'Oh Fred, being with you, having the Jockey, Dorothy, everything. I couldn't have been happier, I couldn't be.'

'What now though, what happens ... when?' His inevitable death hung between them, they both knew it was a matter of time, but neither could bring themselves to say; this current respite was a small bonus, but it did give Alice a chance to hope. He might recover, doctors aren't always right, she thought.

'Don't worry, we'll manage, haven't we always? Gran and Betty go on, but they won't see us go without and there's Ruth and Nana and . . . '

'Ruth. You know, Alice, there aren't many women who would have done what you have, put up with their husband . . . you know.' Even now he was embarrassed to talk about it.

'What's there to put up with? I love you, I love Ruth. She's my best friend, we're like two peas in a pod.'

'I know. I think that's why it happened. She'd come in the Jockey and you and her'd get to talking and going off to auditions and things and when it happened that night, it was wrong. I know that, but I couldn't just drop her afterwards and I couldn't have a bit on the side, it would have wronged you both and I'm to blame. I'm sorry.'

'What for? For falling in love? Christ, Fred, it's like one of Daisy's big fibs or little fibs.'

'Dorothy, her name is Dorothy.'

'I know, but she's got into her head she's a Daisy and if that's some kind of fib to herself then let her get on with it for now. Good God, we all lie to ourselves, she's just started younger than most. She must have inherited a talent for it from us.'

Fred smiled to himself at the thought. It did seem to be the one thing they were both good at.

'It's either a big fib or a little fib to her. If you'd just had it up against a wall one night with Ruth then dumped her, I would never have forgiven you. Have you any idea of what she's been through? In that camp? We got drunk one night at the Jockey after closing, when you were out at a licensed victuallers' do. She let her hair down and she began to tell me. Dear God.' The memory came to

149

Alice, as fresh and as raw. 'Dear God, no one should have to live through that, no one. She'd been hurt enough, more than enough. If you'd dumped her, or if the pair of you had carried on behind my back, then it would have been one of Daisy's big fibs. The minute you'd done it, I knew, I knew from the look of the pair of you. I was bloody mad, I can tell you.'

'You were? You never said.'

'I know. I didn't want to lose you or my best friend. I was mad because you'd put me in that position.'

'You never said.'

'I know. She'd been through so much, why couldn't I let her be happy? I had you. I had a wedding ring, a daughter. What had she got, apart from a tattoo on her arm and a head full of nightmares? So we all took part in a little fib, so what, what harm has it done? Like Daisy says: big fibs or little fibs.'

'Dorothy, her name is Dorothy, do try to remember that.'

'You pick what you call yourself, big fibber or little fibber or downright bloody liar. Don't worry about us, Fred. Don't. I'll always land on my feet, and your daughter, whatever she wants to be called, will always be fine because she can spot a big fib or a little fib a mile off.'

Fred lay back against the pillows, exhausted, but happier than he had been in a long time. 'Alice, you are the best thing, the best thing I have ever . . . you and Daisy.' He opened his eyes. 'Dear God, even I'm calling her it now.'

Alice stood up to go as the handbell was rung to end visiting time. She leaned over her husband and gently kissed his cheek. 'Don't worry about it love, it's only a little fib.'

Malcie saw Alice wipe away tears with the back of her

hand as she came out of the sister's office and walked down the long corridor towards them, and pretended he hadn't.

'Right Malcie. This job. The nurse said Fred has stabilised, I don't want to be away from him for too long, so what about it and when?'

He was all but taken aback by her directness, but when cornered Alice always came out fighting, and what the ward sister had told her about Fred had backed her into the hardest corner of all.

'Quick in, quick out, that way no one spots us, polis or the big boys. Two days to get up there, three days to hit the shops, two days back, overnight if you like.'

'Fine. Then what?'

'Nice little earner for you, no questions asked.' Until the next time, he thought to himself, partly because he knew a good idea when he had one and partly because he couldn't bear the thought of not seeing them all again.

'Suits me. When?'

'Tomorrow?'

'Fine, pick me up at Nana's. Though how she'll manage with another goodbye within a week I'll never know.'

'Avay to Scotland! Vot for?' Nana looked panic-stricken. If it wasn't bad enough that Ruth was in a foreign country, now Alice and Ruth were leaving her and going abroad to Scotland. She had kept clutching at her apron at Ruth's departure, now she was almost chewing it in horror.

'Just for a few days,' Daisy heard her mummy soothe. 'Malcie has got to go to Glasgow on business so Daisy and I are going to hitch a ride with him so we can go and visit my Aunt Maggie in Paisley.' This was the propa-

151

ganda she had given out to Betty and Gran when she paved the way for their journey, though it had taken some fancy footwork, even by Alice's standards, to dissuade Gran from coming along to see her sister as well.

Daisy sat on the step stool in the corner of the kitchen and shared in Nana's turmoil. The night before, when they had returned to Mr Pickup's after visiting Daddy, Mummy had started to pack. A very worried little girl had sat up in bed and watched her.

'It's going to be an adventure,' Mummy assured her. Daisy thought back to their last adventure in Sutton Coldfield, and did not feel at all heartened.

'What about Daddy?'

'Don't worry, darling, it's only a few days and it will give Daddy a nice rest so that he'll be all the better to see us.' Alice used the words to convince herself as well, but they didn't work.

Breakfast had only been a jam doorstep and the last of the milk, while watching her mother throw a final few things into the case. At the sight of Alice and child leaving with a suitcase, Mr Pickup was pacified with another week's rent and the promise of a tin of short-bread. Now Daisy sat silently, watching the grown-ups.

Mr Bloum hovered outside the back door, on the pretence of filling pots with bedding plants, because he was so concerned by Nana's distress. His own emotional radar did not like things one bit. He knew something was wrong, he knew Alice didn't want to go, and that worried him.

What has she got herself into this time, he wondered, as he jabbed at the soil with his trowel. What on earth is she thinking of?

Malcie's arrival did something to ease the tension. He came with a bottle of sherry for Nana and a promise of a good malt for Mr Bloum on his return. Then came the moment when he lifted the case, opened the Jaguar's boot, and Nana dissolved into grief.

'So far avay, both of you, it's not natural! Take care darlinks, take care of the little vone.' Daisy discovered there was something more suffocating than one of Nana's hugs when the old lady clutched her to her side in terror.

Mr Bloum went so far as to shake Malcie by the hand. 'Have a safe journey.' He didn't let go of the hand but fixed Malcie with a look straight in the eye. 'Take good care of them.' Then he disappeared to the depths of the vegetable garden and sought solace by turning over the compost heap, worrying the soil with his big garden fork.

They set off for Lichfield, Daisy and Mummy in the back, looking out at the fields and playing the game of only counting brown cows, which they played on long journeys with Daddy. They didn't go through the city centre and up Beacon Street past Mr Pickup's, but went by the big roundabout with the Bowling Green pub, and onto the wide western road which cut through the fields at the back of Christ Church, where Malcie pointed out the road sign.

'To the north,' he said, 'that's where we're going.' Daisy looked out of the window: sure enough there was the sign and it was even written in white on the road. She looked out of the rear window and watched it disappear.

The big car ate its way north along the A6 with as few stops as possible. Malcie was in a hurry, and Alice didn't mind, she wanted this over with as soon as possible.

Mummy was right, Daisy thought. This is an adventure. They were going places she had never been before. Her late night and the disturbance of Mummy starting to pack meant that after lunch she spent a good part of the afternoon sleeping snuggled up against her mother.

She woke up when the car stopped.

'Are we there yet?'

'No darling, we've just stopped because Uncle Malcie has got to do something.'

The big man gave Alice a nod and set off. Daisy watched him go.

'Let's go for a walk, this is Kendal. You've been here before,' Mummy said.

'Have I?'

'Yes, once when you were a very little baby.' The idea that she could have been somewhere before, but was such a baby that she couldn't remember, always fascinated Daisy.

They walked until they came to a bridge over a river and Alice held Daisy up to look over the parapet. The river was wide and shallow, with long green streamers of weeds floating out in the current.

The bridge, like the houses, was different. Instead of Lichfield's orderly Georgian red brick or stuccoed fronts, all the shops and houses and even the church were built with grey stone blocks, aged with soot and grime.

'Daisy, darling.' Mummy approached the subject sideways.

'Yes?'

'Can I let you in on a secret?'

Daisy was all ears.

'It's just that I don't think Uncle Malcie likes to be called Uncle Malcie.'

'Really?' What a strange sort of secret.

'You know how you like to be Daisy, and not Dorothy.'

'Yes.'

'Well, Uncle Malcie doesn't like being called Uncle Malcie one bit. I think, in fact I know, he likes being

154

called Uncle, just Uncle. He doesn't like the Malcie bit.'

The child had a look of consternation. 'You and Aunt Ruth call him Malcie.'

'Yes, I know. He likes Malcie on its own and he likes Uncle on its own, but he doesn't like the two together, you know.'

'He'd never said.'

'I think he was too shy.' Oh Lord, Alice thought, what a big fib.

'Oh.'

'So do you think you could just call him Uncle? It's very important. I mean, darling, look how you get upset when people call you Dorothy. Getting your name right is important, isn't it?'

Daisy nodded, she understood exactly. They walked back to the parked car and saw Uncle Malcie putting some boxes in the boot. 'Hello, where have you been?' He ruffled her hair, seeming pleased.

'We've seen a river with funny long green weedy stuff in, Uncle,' said Daisy. Above her head the two adults exchanged looks.

'Good girl,' said Malcie, pleased the message had got home. When you're six foot four inches tall with a broad Glaswegian accent and ginger-red hair you tend to stick in people's memory, and when you're passing counterfeit money in shops, it doesn't help at all if there's a little someone alongside you telling people what your name is as well.

He turned to Alice. 'Nice jewellers top end of this street, good plain solid silver cups and trophies, get your-self a first prize and two runners-up. Watchmakers round the corner just after that, buy your old dad a gold watch.' He winked at Alice and turned to Daisy. 'Do you know what's special about Kendal?'

'No, Uncle.' He smiled. 'It has special sweeties all of its own. Called Kendal mint cake. Let's you and me go and get some to eat on our long journey north, while Mummy goes and does some shopping.'

'Uncle.'

'Yes?'

'I thought Granddad was dead.'

'I bet he'd still like a watch, though.'

Penrith was like Kendal with its grey buildings, only the streets were narrower. Uncle Malcie parked the Jaguar and went off on his own, while Mummy and Daisy went for another walk. This time they went into a market hall, which seemed dim after the brightness of the street outside. Daisy saw some china ducks in a shop window that she thought were beautiful, all glistening green feathers, far smarter than the actual ducks she saw on the side of the Minster Pool.

'Well, I suppose it is a little bit of a fib,' Mummy told her. 'I mean, darling, you wouldn't want drab ducks like the real ones sitting on your mantelpiece, now would you?'

Uncle Malcie returned and he and Daisy sat in the car while Mummy said she was just going to pop out to the shops for a couple of things. Before she left she produced a book for Daisy to read. She seemed to be gone a long time. Uncle Malcie got out of the car and began to walk up and down, then round the car, then up and down again.

Daisy opened the car door to go to him.

'Back in the car. Now,' he barked so sharply that the child shot back in again, wondering what she had done to upset him. She wished her mother were there.

When Mummy finally appeared the big man walked up

the street to meet her, took hold of her arm and marched her back to the car, putting her packages into the boot and all but shoving her into the back seat. He drove off in a hurry.

'What kept you?' Daisy saw he was as sharp with Mummy as he had been with her. Why? She didn't understand.

'I was chatting to the woman.'

'What? What did I tell you? Quick in, quick out, minimum of talk.'

'She just wanted to talk. When I started looking she kept on about her boy winning cups for his running. I couldn't stop her. It would have seemed too rude to walk out.'

'Well don't. Remember that.'

They drove in silence. For some reason Mummy kept holding her tightly to her. Daisy started to wriggle, but she didn't speak. Uncle Malcie didn't seem to want to. Daisy wished she was at Nana's, in fact she even wished she were at Mr Pickup's having beans on toast, anywhere but here. The friendly Uncle Malcie of Bower Day had disappeared.

'When are we going home?'

'Soon,' said her mother, kissing the top of her head, 'soon.'

Uncle Malcie thawed as they drove on. It was exciting when he stopped the car by a sign at the side of the road.

'See that? What does it say?'

'Scotland,' she told him. A big smile grew across his face, the first decent smile from him she had seen since Kendal. 'That's right, now you come here.'

She stood with one leg either side of the sign. 'You're in both countries now,' he laughed.

They drove on until they reached a hotel in a town

called Lockerbie. A man came out to meet them, shook Uncle Malcie by the hand, and the pair of them walked away, in conversation.

'He's an old friend of your uncle's,' Mummy said. Daisy looked at him. He seemed nice: tall, but not as tall as Uncle Malcie, and a bit fatter.

It was like old times with Daddy when they went on holiday, Daisy thought. They sat in the dining room and a waitress brought them their dinner, with mashed potatoes and gravy, which really impressed Daisy. It was almost as good as the Sunday dinners Mummy used to cook at the Horse and Jockey.

The bedroom was exciting too. It had two beds in, and Daisy quite liked the novelty of sleeping in her own bed, something she hadn't done since they moved to Mr Pickup's and she had always had to share a big bed with Mummy. But when Mummy turned out the light she felt frightened on her own, in a strange room with different noises from the cars going by outside. She wished she could snuggle up to her mother.

Breakfast was new, too. Instead of her usual egg and soldiers or Nana's porridge, she had a bowl of cornflakes, and decided they tasted better when Mummy sprinkled sugar on the top.

Uncle Malcie seemed in a better mood when he joined them, and ate his way through a big plate of bacon, eggs and fried bread. Mummy just had a cup of tea, a cigarette and a worried expression.

Sitting in the car again, watching the road go by was beginning to be boring, but, before she knew it, Daisy had something new to look at. Big hills, nearly mountains in size, and fast little rivers soon punctuated the landscape. It was unlike anywhere the child had seen before.

Lunch was big plates of sandwiches at a roadside café,

158

and all too soon the houses seemed to be getting closer together, then there were streets, and soon Daisy was in a city bigger and darker than Birmingham.

The streets were full of cars and people. She felt glad she was sitting in the safety of the big red car, next to her mother. The city seemed ready to burst with people; the buildings were so dark and tall that daylight was only a patch above them. Then suddenly it opened into a big square with a statue of a man on a horse, which made Daisy feel much better.

Uncle Malcie decided they should go shopping again. It was all getting a bit boring and a bit like hard work to Daisy. He marched them through the streets, and kept going into jeweller's shops. Daisy's feet were beginning to ache, they had walked so far, and she felt frightened of all the people walking round them so intent on getting to where they were going, they bumped into and jostled her, no matter how tightly she held onto Mummy's hand.

Uncle Malcie bought more watches and so many cups Daisy thought he must have been starting his own gymkhana. She had seen a table full of gleaming cups at Canwell Show, and decided that he must be aiming for something like that.

Occasionally he bought Mummy a string of pearls. She admired several, but always bought the ones which were most expensive, and Uncle Malcie would laugh a little about that and give a sort of 'Women, huh?' look to the assistant as he peeled off the notes from his wallet.

Daisy just sat on a chair in the corner in every shop and didn't say anything, like Mummy had told her. The first few shops had been exciting, she looked at all the beautiful canteens of silver cutlery and candlesticks, and hairbrushes and hand mirrors in the display cases. Now Daisy was bored stiff. She seemed to have been sitting

159

for ever, first in the car and now in the shops, and when she wasn't sitting she was walking for miles.

At one stage she stopped in the street, on the point of mutiny. Mummy bent down to her. 'Darling, I know it's horrid and boring, but be a good girl, please, it won't be long now, promise.'

Uncle Malcie or Uncle, as he now preferred, stood a few paces away, scowling. Daisy wondered why he was so angry, and Mummy was so anxious. It was all getting to be too much. She wanted to go home, but home was more than a day's drive away and that worried her.

As they walked out of one shop where they had bought yet another gold watch for him and a nice string of pearls for Mummy, Uncle Malcie suddenly decided to smile.

'Time to stop work,' he said, 'back to the car.'

Daisy just hoped they were going back to the car for good. They had made several return trips to put their shopping in the boot throughout the day. Each time she had hoped they would get in and drive away from the noise, dirt and crowds, but each time Uncle Malcie just carefully locked the boot and they had set off again.

This time it wasn't a false alarm.

As they drove along streets which seemed so choked with people they spilled off the pavements, Daisy got her old Uncle Malcie back. He couldn't stop smiling, just like on Bower Day.

'Nice bit of work that, Alice.'

'Do you think it was all right?' Mummy sounded as though she was asking Daddy or Aunt Ruth after a performance.

Malcie nodded. 'Aye. I think I did the right thing. I would have stood out too much in Birmingham, but on a busy Saturday afternoon on Sauchiehall Street, Mr Good Businessman treating himself and his wife, with a nice polite wee girl sitting patiently in the corner, they couldn't sell us enough.' He turned to Daisy. 'You were a nice polite wee girl, weren't you? Good girl.'

Daisy wasn't quite sure what he was on about, but he seemed happy enough, so she smiled back at him.

'What time did you say you'd get there?' he asked.

'I just said late afternoon,' Mummy said.

'Right, I'll drop you and the kid off and go and deliver the stuff. I'll pick you up on Monday morning about ten. We've done better than I thought today, we'll hit Carlisle on the way back and drive on. Should have you back in Lichfield in the early hours.'

Daisy noticed that her mother looked relieved and wondered why.

Chapter 14

Aunt Maggie's

The Jaguar went round the big circle slowly, with Mummy peering out of the window.

'They all look the same, it's that one. Yes, that one there.'

They stopped and Uncle Malcie got out, and opened the door for them.

'Here we are darling, Auntie Maggie's, or rather Great-Aunt Maggie's, for you.'

'Great-Aunt?' It was something Daisy had not heard of before.

'Yes, you remember? Gran's sister, she came down to visit, though you were still quite little, I suppose. It must have been, oh, three years ago.'

Daisy couldn't remember.

She looked round. The circle of road had big tall houses all around it, in crescents. Each one had a massive doorway, every house looked the same.

'It's a very big house,' said Daisy, impressed.

Mummy laughed. 'No darling, it isn't all Aunt Maggie's house. They are flats, she lives in one at the top of the stairs.'

Mummy led the way in through the big door, to a

162

corridor dimly lit by a window at the top of the stairs. There were lots of stairs, each landing with doors on either side. They seemed to climb for ever.

'Third floor, that's us.' Mummy checked the numbers and knocked on a door. Uncle Malcie stood a little way back, holding the suitcase, smiling, looking happier than Daisy had seen him since they set off from Lichfield on the road marked to the north.

Another Gran opened the door. 'Come along in,' she held the door open, 'and this will be Fred's girl.' She sounded like Uncle Malcie but she was just like Gran, only plumper and without the constant disapproval. Daisy was impressed that this version of Gran actually smiled.

Mummy launched into an explanation.

'This is Mr MacFadyen, a business friend of Fred's. He very kindly brought us up with him.'

'I've got to see some work up here and then I'll be going back Monday morning, so Alice asked if I could bring her and the bairn. Now you're here I'll be off. Monday morning about ten, then,' he said, adding his part of the story.

Aunt Maggie insisted he stayed for tea. Uncle Malcie accepted, and, to his and Daisy's satisfaction, they discovered that Aunt Maggie shared Nana's approach to teatime and home baking.

Aunt Maggie poured the tea and then returned from the kitchen with a glass for Uncle Malcie. 'You'll have a dram, to thank you for bringing them.' Malcie raised his eyebrows slightly at the amount of whisky in the gl
Aunt Maggie's hospitality went far beyon
Widowhood had dried Gran up into a
proval, but in her sister's case it
being married to a dour Scottis
She was determined to enjoy hei

163

As the scones and cake disappeared and Uncle Malcie emptied his glass, things got a lot jollier.

Aunt Maggie didn't seem to mind that Alice had gone on the stage, the way Gran did. Mummy started to tell her some stories and they all laughed. Aunt Maggie roared with laughter when Alice told her about all the dresses Aunt Zita had made for Daisy, and admired the little dress and jacket she was wearing. It was a revelation to Daisy that someone could look so like Gran, could have even more holy pictures, a Jesus on the cross with a red and gold heart, and a Mary in a blue dress with a baby Jesus, and yet be so happy.

'Mind you, Alice, if you think you can go on the stage you try the Empire, the Glasgow Empire.' By now Aunt Maggie had a glass with a wee dram of her own.

Uncle Malcie, finishing his second large glass, laughed as well.

'There's many a fine English act died before. They're tough, really tough.'

Alice was laughing along, and told them she'd heard all the stories.

Malcie got to his feet reluctantly and perhaps a little unsteadily. They walked to the top of the stairs to say goodbye to him.

'You take care of yourselves, I'll see you Monday.' He paused and reached for his wallet. 'Here, that's for yourself,' he gave Aunt Maggie two five-pound notes. 'Treat yourselves.'

He went down the stairs, walking in less of a straight line than usual, waving to them.

Daisy heard the powerful engine of the Jaguar rev loudly as he set off.

'That's a good man, Alice, you and he?' Aunt Maggie ed.

'You sly old fox! No!'

'Likes you, likes the girl, good friend of Fred's you say? Well many's the widow who's married a good friend.'

'I'm not a widow yet, Maggie, and not . . .' Mummy gestured towards Daisy.

'Aye, you're right, you're right, sorry dear, but think on. He'd take care of you and it's a tough life on your own, with a bairn, I should know.'

The old woman put a kindly arm round Mummy's shoulder and led her back into the flat.

Daisy hardly heard what they said, because she was on another planet, literally.

As the grown-ups had sat round chatting, she had become bored. It was all a bit much, really. She had trudged round shop after shop, sat in the car again, and now they were talking away. By the side of the sofa was a pile of newspapers and she nudged it idly with her foot. The top paper moved and underneath was something coloured. She picked it up. She had never seen anything like it before, it was incredible, it was marvellous, and in fact it really was marvellous. It had written on the front, *Marvel Comics proudly presents*. She was lost to a world of red and yellow and blue and drawings like she had never seen before, where strange people fought villains and beat them up with punches that went 'zap' 'pow' and 'splat' in capital letters.

'What have you got there darling?' Daisy didn't hear and Alice had to repeat herself.

Wordlessly Daisy showed her, anxious to get back to the next page. She had had annuals at Christmas time with drawings in, but this! This was something totally, totally wonderful.

Aunt Maggie looked over her shoulder.

'One of Iain's comic book things, there's dozens of them. He left them behind when he joined up. Young Michael was supposed to come round and get them.' She paused to proudly produce a photograph of a grandson in his dashing uniform, with kilt and red and white checked band on his glengarry.

'There's a big box, I think, in the bedroom you're in. Would you like to read them?'

Daisy nodded. There were more, this wasn't the only wonderful one of its kind in the whole world.

Daisy was lost for the rest of the evening. She only stopped reading long enough to sit at the table, and eat the ham salad Aunt Maggie put in front of her. The table was full of her best china for visitors. The pickled onions and beetroot sat in fancy glass dishes with a special fork to pick them out. The trifle afterwards was served in glass bowls, and had so much sherry in it the fumes made Daisy's eyes water.

She helped clear the table afterwards like Mummy said and then she disappeared into the bedroom, to sit on top of the faded blue candlewick bedspread, with its bunch of red roses at the centre, and read and read. She only stopped to get undressed, brush her teeth and kiss Aunt Maggie goodnight.

'I'm not sure you should be reading those, they'll give you nightmares,' Mummy said as she tucked her in. Daisy hardly heard. When Mummy went through to the parlour to talk to Aunt Maggie, look over old photographs and reminisce, Daisy turned the bedside light back on and began to read again, mesmerised.

She was still reading when Mummy came in to go to bed, but she didn't get told off for once.

Mummy fell against the wall slightly while getting undressed, rebounded off the wardrobe and ended up on

166

the bed beside her with such a plop that Daisy was almost bounced out. She stopped reading. This was even more interesting than the comics were.

Mummy managed to get her head through the neck of her nightie at her second attempt before manoeuvring the blankets back and climbing into bed beside Daisy.

Daisy submerged under the ensuing hug. Nana must have been giving lessons.

'I'd forgotten how much your Aunt Maggie likes a dram,' said Mummy and fell asleep. It was the first time Daisy ever recalled hearing her mother snore.

Chapter 15

All Hell

'Get up, get up out of that bed you lying, stinking slut!'
All hell broke loose in the bedroom as Aunt Maggie
descended like the wrath of God and flung back the
curtains. 'Get up and get out of my home this instant, you
cheating, stinking . . . whore!'

Mummy and Daisy woke and sat bolt upright. Daisy,
confused from deep sleep to wide awake, couldn't think
where she was, neither could Alice as the morning light
and a hangover hit her.

'Get out, do you hear? The shame of it all, the bloody
shame!' Aunt Maggie slammed the door behind her.

A look of horror was enamelled on Alice's features.
'Stay here,' she gasped at Daisy and shot out of the door
after her aunt.

Daisy tried to get the world into focus, a world that had
suddenly become a very frightening place. She tiptoed to the
door and pulled it open a crack and heard the two women
shouting, or rather heard the old woman shouting as she
stormed from room to room, with a frantic-looking Mummy
following behind her, wrapping her nightdress about her.

'Never! Never have I been so ashamed! What have you
brought on me?'

'For God's sake what's wrong?'

The old woman came to a halt and turned to face Mummy. The friendly aunt of yesterday had vanished. From what Daisy could see Gran's grim face had replaced her; or rather a face more furious than she had ever seen on her own grandmother.

'Wrong, you ask me what's wrong? I'll tell you. You and that fancy man of yours. Never, never in my life did I expect my own flesh and blood. Your mother's right, there is something wrong with you. How could you be so, so, wicked!'

'What have I done?'

'Done? I'll tell you. I put one of those bloody fivers in the plate at Mass. Jesus Mary and Joseph, the priest called me over after. Told me it was false. Counterfeit! Bloody counterfeit. Said, "Mrs MacKay this isn't legal tender," said it was counterfeit.'

Mummy stopped looking frantic and started looking as though she had just been hit with a sandbag.

'Counterfeit?'

'Yes, that's your game is it? Bloody criminal counterfeit. Well I'm telling you now, lady, get out of my house this bloody instant. You and that child of yours. Get! Father said it was serious, said he'd have to call the police. Go on, get out before you bring any more shame down on my head.'

'But where can we go?'

'I don't know and I don't care. Get out before I have the law here around my neck.'

Mummy bolted for the bedroom, nearly knocking Daisy over from her vantage point. A cold fear gripped Daisy's entire body. She had never seen her mother look so frightened, not even in the shop when the man caught them in Sutton Coldfield.

'Mummy?'

'Not now darling,' Mummy threw their case onto the bed. 'Come on, time to get dressed, we're going.'

'Mummy?'

'Don't just stand there darling.' Mummy was peeling her nightdress off, struggling into her bra, pulling a dress on, hitching it to get at her suspenders and putting on her stockings.

'Mummy!' Tears began to well up in Daisy's eyes. She was too frightened to move.

The sight of her terrified daughter made Alice stop.

'Look darling, quick scene-change. Into costume and off we go. Come on, put your clothes on.' Alice started to grab some clothes for the girl.

'But I haven't had a wash.'

'Well you'll just have to go dirty for once. It won't matter. Come on now.'

'What about breakfast?' Even in a crisis such as this, Daisy's stomach demanded its rights.

'Bugger breakfast. Come on!'

It was the fastest she had ever dressed in her life.

As they frenziedly threw their clothes into their case they could hear Aunt Maggie storming about in the next room, ranting away to herself furiously. Mummy stopped long enough to straighten Daisy's clothing and brush her hair.

'There, got everything? Off we go ... Hang on a minute.'

Daisy stood still, her heart pounding as her mother went to the door.

'Just stay there, darling. I'll be back in a minute.'

A bewildered Daisy sat on the bed and listened as her mother went out and tried her aunt again. 'Look Maggie, there must be some mistake. There is lots of that sort of stuff around, Malcie must have got it by mistake.'

'Mistake! I'll give you bloody mistake, thinking you can come here and, and . . .'

Daisy heard a slap. Mummy shot back into the bedroom, a red patch starting to spread across her cheek.

'Come on darling, exit stage left, pursued by a bear.'

Alice slung her handbag over her arm, hoisted the case and grabbed Daisy with her spare hand, steering them out of the bedroom and across the hall.

'Bye-bye Aun-' Daisy began, but Alice decided her aunt was in no mood for goodbyes and pushed her daughter out of the front door.

They didn't stop for three streets, until Alice found a bench they could sink onto with relief.

'Well darling,' Alice began to rebuild her bravado, 'what a morning, all hell broke loose!'

'All hell,' Daisy agreed with her. She was so numb she wasn't quite sure how she felt, but all hell seemed to sum things up. The morning sunshine was bright but not very warm, and she huddled up close to her mother.

'What are we going to do?'

Alice opened her handbag and lit a cigarette. 'Not too sure really, darling.'

'What about Uncle?'

'Malcie?'

'Yes, you said I had only to call him Uncle.'

Alice smiled. 'From now on darling you can call him anything you want. I don't know, darling, I don't know where he is. God, I can't even warn him, he'll turn up there tomorrow, and get an earful of that.'

Despite their situation, Alice slowly began to smile. 'Serve him right, no more than he bloody well deserves. In the meantime we had better see about getting ourselves sorted out.'

171

She opened her purse. It contained only a few pounds of real money and several of Malcie's infamous fivers.

Alice held one of them up to the light. 'Trust a bloody priest to be the only one to spot it.'

'Spot what?'

'Never mind. Come on, there's only one place to go at a time like this.'

'Where?'

'The theatre.'

Thanks to the advice of a woman in a newsagent's shop, where Alice had bought more cigarettes and a bar of chocolate to stop Daisy's pleas for breakfast, Alice got them onto a bus headed for the city centre.

Daisy was amazed at the transformation of the place. Saturday's crowds were gone; she only saw a few people, pigeons and a man sweeping up the litter. The streets seemed friendlier now there was more room.

Alice stopped twice and asked directions. Each time Daisy did not understand what the people said, they talked so funnily, like Uncle Malcie, but more so.

At Central Station, with its massive blackened glass roof, Alice asked about the cost of tickets to Birmingham. They hadn't got enough real money and Alice was too frightened by the morning's events to risk using Malcie's notes.

They sat in the station café, and Daisy began to feel better after a glass of milk and a bacon sandwich, while Alice chain-smoked and thought out loud what they could do next.

'We can't stay here on the station all night,' she said. The thought filled Daisy with terror. She wondered what Superman or Batman would do. She wished she had one of the comics with her now. Life seemed so easy in the comic books, there was an answer for every crisis, but in the warmth of the station café, with a full stomach, Daisy's confidence in her mother remained intact.

Alice was fumbling in her handbag for a comb for Daisy's hair when she gave a low squeal of delight, and produced a blue velvet box.

'The answer to our prayers! The last one I did yesterday. I forgot to give them to Malcie!' She showed the box to Daisy, secretly, under the table. It contained a necklace with three strands of pearls, fastened with a gold clasp in the shape of a bow. 'They cost thirty guineas!' She shut the case and dropped it back in her handbag. 'Saved!'

'Will the man let us buy a ticket with them, instead of money?'

'No, but I'm sure I can find someone who will. Like I said there is only one place to go at a time like this, the theatre.'

Even the stage door of the Glasgow Empire looked frightening. Alice took a deep breath and walked in.

Once inside they both felt better; they were back on their own home ground. The look, the smell, the sounds of scenery being changed and hoisted onto trolleys reassured them both.

'What do you want?' The man in the stage-door manager's glass-walled little office did not sound welcoming.

'Stay there darling, don't move, I'll be back.' Alice left Daisy sitting on their case as she walked over.

From what Daisy could hear, it wasn't that big a fib. Alice told him she was in show business herself, which was true. Her man had left them in the lurch and she had to get herself and her daughter back to Birmingham, little fib: Uncle Malcie hadn't left them, so much as Aunt Maggie had kicked them out.

173

They needed to find some good digs for the night; once again this was true. She needed some money, true. Here the man started to look defensive, thinking Alice was going to try and sponge off him.

At this point Daisy decided it was time to turn on her melter, the one she used to best effect on ticket collectors. Alice told him that before he left, her man had given her these, and produced the pearls with a flourish from her handbag. He could see what quality they were, they had cost thirty guineas: they might have been worth that, but Alice had not paid for them. She hoped to get twenty pounds for them.

Daisy could see that the man looked at Mummy like he'd heard it all before, and no doubt he had. He turned to Daisy, who gave him her melting spaniel-eyed smile.

He wrote down the address of some good theatrical digs, run by a nice lady who used to be on the halls herself.

'Wait here, I'll go and see a man who might be interested in yer pearls.' Daisy liked the way his broad accent managed to get more 'rrr's into the word pearls.

Alice came back over to Daisy and gave her an encouraging hug. In every theatre in the land there is always someone, or someone who knows someone, who can buy whatever you've got to sell. Sometimes money doesn't even change hands.

One of the sparkies who had been setting lights between shows appeared. He ran Alice's pearls between his fingers, held them up to the light, rubbed them against his teeth.

'Ten,' he said.

'You would see my child starve? Twenty.' Daisy listened as Mummy got into her stride, it was like a visit to Aunt Edie's.

'How do I know they're not knocked off? Ten.'

Alice fished in her purse and produced the receipt.

174

'There, paid in cash.' She didn't go into details about what kind of cash. 'Seventeen.'

He looked at the receipt, which said thirty-one pounds and ten shillings. 'Twelve.'

Alice rolled her eyes. 'I need the cash today, fifteen.'

They shook on the deal and he produced a wad from his pocket. Daisy watched as he counted off the notes. Just as when they visited Aunt Edie, Mummy didn't bother to hang around. She thanked the doorman, Daisy gave him a big smile and they left.

By the time they got to the digs they both felt tired, dirty, hungry and thoroughly miserable. It had been only hours since Aunt Maggie had ripped them awake and thrown them out, but to both of them it seemed like days.

Alice rang the doorbell; the woman who answered did not bat an eyelid.

'Was on the halls myself, years ago, dearie,' she told Alice as she showed them to a small attic room with a rag rug and fraying oilcloth. 'Soprano. My brother accompanied me sometimes, violin and musical saw.'

Alice thanked her; she just nodded and didn't ask questions. They'd paid in advance.

An evening meal was included in the price. They spent the afternoon curled up on the bed together, catching up on their sleep. Daisy listened to her mother's story about the time that she and Aunt Ruth had been in a panto, *Dick Whittington*. Ruth played the cat but her tail kept falling off because Aunt Zita hadn't made the costumes.

At dinner time Alice went through the door first, Daisy followed and there he was, sitting at the table with a napkin on his lap.

Chapter 16

The Most Wonderful Man in the World, after Daddy

Daisy was struck dumb with shyness; her mouth dried and glued her vocal cords together.

'Come on darling, say hello.' Alice pulled out a chair and motioned for Daisy to sit. The girl waded to the table through a tide of her own disbelief. It was *him*.

Alice smiled and said hello to the other guests, two pale men, a young woman with dyed blonde hair and a lacquered perm.

'Hello Albert, how the devil are you.'

He looked at her vaguely; he recognised Alice, but couldn't place her.

Alice helped him out while a dumbstruck Daisy looked on. 'Alice Smedley, sometimes worked with George Benedict.'

He registered dim recollection. 'Yes, Alice. Doesn't your husband keep a pub somewhere?' He had a London accent, well spoken but the occasional Cockney crept in.

'That's right, Horse and Jockey at Freeford, just outside Lichfield. Last time I saw you must be eighteen months ago, you were at Birmingham.'

'Yes, though it would be nearer the two-year mark. Who's this?' He turned to Daisy, who could hardly look at the dapper man with his slicked dark hair and trim moustache. It was him, the best ventriloquist ever and the most wonderful man in the world, after Daddy.

Alice smiled, 'This is my little girl, Dorothy, and she isn't normally this shy, are you darling?'

Daisy managed a nod, but only just.

'Do you remember Mr Saveen, darling, he does a vent act? You remember? You sat in the stalls with your daddy and watched him at Birmingham.'

Daisy nodded again, blushed and managed to croak, 'Yes.'

Two plates of soup were put in front of them but Daisy's appetite had vanished; she bent over her bowl, and tried to look at Saveen at the same time.

Alice set about her own soup and wondered what was wrong. Then it hit her. Daisy was a fan! Alice had seen it before, she had never experienced it first-hand, but she had been around enough big, top-of-the-bill acts to know it. Daisy was star-struck! She watched in amused disbelief.

As the soup plates were cleared, Daisy risked looking up. Alice smiled. 'You know, Albert, Daisy has always been a big fan of vent acts. Haven't you, darling?'

'Yes.' Daisy was beginning to find her voice.

'Really.' He smiled at her, not really wanting the bother of having to make dinner-table small talk with a difficult-looking child.

Daisy took a big breath and managed to ask him the most important question of all, 'Is your dog with you?'

'No, I'm afraid that he doesn't like long journeys and stopping in digs, so he has stayed behind at home in his nice warm basket with a big bone.'

Daisy nodded solemnly. 'We had a dog like that. It got car sick, Daddy wouldn't let it come with us.'

'Quite right,' said Saveen, and he turned to the meat and over-boiled two veg.

It all became clear to Alice: Daisy was smitten by the damned dog! She knew her daughter loved dogs, she had fussed over the few spaniels Fred kept at the back of the pub. Alice tried to remember Saveen's act. He made a point of using animals, as well as the traditional dummies. She recalled a parrot in the act, but the thing that brought the house down was the dog, some sort of terrier. He didn't use it a lot, but when he did, he brought it on just before the end of the act, briefly, and it would 'say' a few words. It was always a winner.

It only accounted for minutes of his act, but it had completely captured her daughter's imagination, and her heart. Alice couldn't help but sit through the rest of the meal with a huge smile on her face.

It was a fairly subdued table; the two boys had just finished a turn in rep in Dundee and were up for an audition in Glasgow the next day. The blonde-dye job was the receiving end of a knife-throwing act and was waiting for 'her Lionel' to join her. He had gone home to see his old Mum who was poorly. Sickness must be an occupational hazard for the mothers of variety acts, Alice thought.

'Not her legs, is it?' she asked conversationally.

By the end of the meal Alice was beginning to ache with tiredness. She helped her daughter down from her seat. 'Come on Daisy, up you get.'

'What did you say?' Albert Saveen looked startled.

'Daisy, that's my daughter's nickname. He real name is Dorothy.'

'I like Daisy,' said the girl and she blushed.

'I like Daisy too,' said Saveen. 'In fact, shall I tell you something?'

178

Daisy had gone back to the nodding-only stage of shyness.

'I have a little girl called Daisy May, she helps me on stage. She sits on my knee and talks to me.' He laughed, and broke into the song from his act, '*Daisy May, people say she'll marry me some day, And from the way she sighs and looks into my eyes, I somehow think that Daisy may.*'

Alice tucked her little girl into bed and kissed her. 'I'll not be long behind you, I don't know about you, darling, but I'm exhausted.' Daisy nodded back at her and snuggled down under the covers to get warm, waiting for the moment when her mother got into bed and she could cuddle up to her warmth and reassurance. Alice sat on the end of the bed and worked Pond's cold cream into her face.

So that was where Daisy had come from. Big fibs and little fibs like her daughter said, and when life had worked its worst and she had lost her home and her father to a hospital bed, Dorothy had decided to tell herself a big fib. She would become someone else, someone who didn't mind the pain and the uncertainty of having her perfectly normal, happy life turned into a hell of cheap digs, scrounged meals, missed schooling and staying one step ahead of the rent man through her mother's crazy schemes.

She became a little wooden girl who had a wonderful talking dog.

Alice climbed into the bed and they hugged together. 'Night night, sleep tight.'

'Mind the bugs don't bite,' came the muffled reply from under the covers. That just might be a possibility in these digs, Alice decided.

179

She lay there and stroked her daughter's hair, feeling as though her heart would burst. Poor kid, she thought, adults can turn to drink to blot out their misery, children have only their imagination.

Chapter 17

Going Home

Daisy liked trains, especially when they had tickets for them, and didn't have to listen out for the ticket collector as a prelude to hiding in the lavatory. She liked the coloured pictures in their frames and the mirrors above the seats, the way you could walk down the corridor and look at the people in each compartment, like you were looking in through house windows into people's homes. It appealed to her natural curiosity.

They were sitting in a compartment to themselves, either side of the window, enjoying the view and each with the benefit of a large boarding-house breakfast inside her.

Daisy's moods were a barometer of her mother's, and the child was content because her mother was. Alice found she could relax for the first time in forty-eight hours. Aunt Maggie was behind them, Malcie was out of the way, she had paid for the ride, had some money in her purse and nothing to worry about apart from changing trains. Gran's undoubted fury when Aunt Maggie's news reached her, Malcie's reaction to their flight and what happened next could all wait; it was all suspended in time. In the meantime she intended to enjoy the journey.

There was nothing to do, nothing she could do, except talk to her daughter and play games with her: I spy, counting the cows in the fields, guessing the names of the people who walked down the corridor and what they did.

A middle-aged woman wearing a squashy hat went past. 'Vera, a schoolteacher,' said Daisy. 'No, Joyce, a lady who works in a baker's shop going to visit her daughter,' guessed Alice. They waved to people waiting at level crossings, and went to the buffet car for tea and little packets of biscuits in cellophane.

By the afternoon they had shared the compartment with a handful of people, no one staying very long, but each providing brief entertainment and snippets of conversation. Now they felt drowsy, the noise of the wheels lulled them. Daisy's head dropped and she drifted in and out of sleep, reliving meeting Saveen. To her disappointment they had not seen him at breakfast.

Alice dozed, determined not to rerun the horror film of Sunday morning with Aunt Maggie, and instead began to think about good things: meeting up with Ruth, hearing all her gossip from the show in Rhyl, and seeing Fred.

Alice dared herself to be optimistic. He could never work again, that was for sure, but they might be able to apply for that National Assistance; perhaps even get a council house. One of those at Botany Bay, near Nana, would be nice, or down in Whittington. Daisy could start going back to school. Hell, no, Dorothy could go back to school, her real daughter could. Perhaps they could even get a dog. She'd ask Bob, who used to go in the Jockey. He kept labradors and some spaniels, mainly as gun dogs. Not a big dog, but there was always a spare pup somewhere. She smiled in her half-sleep at the thought of Dorothy's face when the dog arrived. Dorothy. Daisy would have to go. There would be no need for her when Fred came home.

The train clanked, rolled and slowed its way into Birmingham New Street, and amidst the confusion of rebuilding the station and the Bull Ring, they made their way to the lower level and the train for Lichfield.

The slow train plodded its way from the city centre to the suburbs, and when Blake Street station and the open fields arrived the scenery outside the carriage was like an old friend welcoming them back home.

By the time they got off the train at Lichfield City, walked down the tall flight of steps with elegant iron roof arches soaring above, and made their way out onto St John Street, early evening peace had descended on the city. The shops and offices had all closed and pub doors were just beginning to open.

The lights were still on in the doll's-house-shaped GPO building by Minster Pool; Daisy could see the shapes of people bustling about behind the frosted glass. Up they walked towards Mr Pickup's and passed a crocodile of girls from Westgate, the Friary School's boarding house, being herded off somewhere in their red and white and house-colour striped dresses and grey blazers by the indomitable Miss McGuiness. Daisy wasn't too sure if she wanted to follow Mummy and Caroline, if she ended up somewhere like that. Being an ordinary pupil sounded exciting, being a boarder looked even less entertaining than a weekend at Gran's. Crossing the end of Gaia Lane was Daisy's own private sign that they were nearly at Mr Pickup's front door. As unwelcoming as their digs were, they were both glad to be there after a long day's journey.

'Damn, I meant to pick up a pint of milk for tea,' said Alice as she let herself into their room, 'never mind, just have to drink it black.'

Daisy remembered with a jolt: 'We promised to get Mr Pickup a tin of shortbread! And we haven't got a present for Nana either!'

'Never mind darling, I'm sure they won't mind really.'

But Mr Pickup was at the door, he walked into their room behind them without knocking and he looked as though he did mind.

'I've had the police round here.'

Daisy watched her mother freeze. 'When?' Alice gasped. Surely to God they couldn't have caught on to Malcie's spending spree so soon.

'Saturday. That bloke again, MacCallum. Same lodge as your husband? Don't make me bloody laugh. Wanted to know where you were and that man of yours, the big Scotch one.'

'He's no man of mine.' Suddenly Alice felt so tired. She didn't have a fight left in her, she didn't have the power to summon up any bravado, to brazen it out with the sour little man. 'What did you say?'

'Wouldn't you like to know.' But he couldn't stop himself from telling her; he had been brooding over it all, waiting for this moment.

'Told them you'd gone off with him, gone to Scotland, done a bunk for all I knew, for all I bloody care. Listen.' He came up close to Alice, firing his words into her face. 'I've had enough of you. This is a respectable house, this is. I have had enough. I want you and that kid of yours out of here. I want you out tonight, understand?'

Daisy stood frozen with disbelief and tiredness and looked on as something inside her mother snapped. Neither Daisy nor Mr Pickup heard it go, but he felt its force as Alice pushed him across the room and pinned him against the wall. Daisy was simultaneously impressed and amazed. She had never seen her mother attack

184

anyone before. The surprise of it all shook Daisy out of her sleepiness as Alice rallied for one last fight. She was not going to be thrown out on the street, not again.

'No, you understand this. You listen to me. I have had enough of you lurking about, making accusations. We have paid our rent up for another two weeks. Here we are and here we stay.'

'Oh yeah? One phone call, that's all it takes. Don't suppose you want the police to know you're here, do you?' He saw doubt and fear cross her face and knew he'd won as he pushed free from her hold. 'Out. Tonight. No messing.' He went to leave, and turned round in the doorway. 'And I had that hospital telephone here as well.'

'What? What did they say?' Alice was by his side, holding tightly to his sleeve.

'They said you should get in touch. Urgent.'

Terror overtook her. 'When did they call? What did they say? What were their actual words?'

He almost softened, seeing her in a state of real distress. 'I don't know, they said he'd taken a turn, you know, wasn't good.' He paused, and seemed to be weighing things up in his own mind.

'Look. I want you out, I don't want any trouble but I can see how you're fixed. Go and call them. Then come back here and get yourselves out. I've had enough of you, and your sort. You swan around here like you're Lady Muck. You are bad news, trouble. I'm sorry about your husband, but I don't want no more of you. You're out of here tonight.'

Alice stood immobile. Daisy just curled up on a chair in the corner trying to make herself very small, so the whole world would go away.

He took one look around the room. 'Out. Tonight. I'll

even give you your rent back.' His business sense got the better of any compassionate thoughts he might harbour. 'One week only, mind you.'.

To Daisy it seemed as though her mother stayed rooted to the spot for minutes after he had gone. Then Alice crossed the room and began to tear through her handbag for her purse, grabbed hold of Daisy's hand and pulled her out of the room, down the stairs and out onto the street.

Daisy almost stumbled and fell as her mother held on tightly to her hand and ran back down the street to the telephone box by the GPO building. She dialled the number she knew by heart and began frantically feeding pennies into the box, pressing button A when the call was answered.

She got through to the ward sister, told her who she was and asked what had happened to her husband.

Daisy was frightened. She held on tightly to her mother's waist in the confined space of the kiosk. She looked out through the grime-edged panes of glass at the small pool of light the box's bulb spilled onto the pavement in the dusk. People walked past. All she could hear was her mother's breathing, punctuated by the occasional soft sob, which Alice tried to stifle.

'Yes. Right. I'm sorry, I would have been in touch sooner but I have been away. I couldn't call. Sleeping? Right. Tomorrow then, first thing.' Alice put the handset down slowly. It was Daisy who remembered to press button B, and to scoop out the change. She held it up to her mother, who took it and automatically put it back into her purse.

Alice opened the door and went to step outside, but stopped in her tracks and turned back to the phone, fumbling for change again. She looked at the printed advertisement, framed behind glass above the telephone's black money box, 'Bates's Taxis, Lombard Street, Lichfield,' dialled the number and asked to be picked up in half an hour. This time, Alice remembered to press button B: there was no change.

They turned and slowly walked back towards Mr Pickup's and Daisy started to shiver. Alice rubbed her hand encouragingly across the little girl's shoulders.

By the entrance to the park next to the library, Alice sank down on a bench and pulled Daisy to her. She looked her in the face, stroked her hair and took a deep breath.

'Well, this is a to-do isn't it?' she started brightly. 'Listen darling. I've just spoken to the hospital, and I'm afraid that Daddy is very, very poorly. The sister there, she says he is fast asleep now, resting, but we had better go and see him tomorrow.' She thought how to phrase the next words. 'Because Daddy is so poorly and because Mr Pickup is very angry we are going to go and stay with Nana, for tonight. That'll be fun, won't it? She'll be pleased to see us, won't she? So we are going to go back and pack our bags and have a ride in a big taxi round to Nana's.'

She jumped up from the bench, gave a smile and reached for the little girl's hand. 'Come on, off we go, time for another adventure.'

Daisy was tired, she was hungry, and she was worried about Daddy being so poorly; the idea of an adventure did not appeal to her at all. She put her hand into her mother's, and it received, as always, a gentle squeeze of encouragement that somehow made things seem better, and together they set off back up the hill to Mr Pickup's.

Daisy helped her mother to pull the old trunk out from

187

under the bed. As they did so, it banged against the po. 'Well, that's one thing we won't mind saying goodbye to, isn't it?' said Alice, opening the wardrobe and dumping armfuls of its contents onto the bed. Then she swept up all their shoes and dumped them in the bottom of the trunk and set to work methodically folding the clothes and putting them in the trunk. Halfway through, she paused, crossed to the shelves by the sink, and found Daisy's silver eggcup, spoon and napkin ring, which she stowed carefully at the bottom of her handbag. The few groceries were put in a brown paper carrier bag.

'Darling, you just keep folding away like that. No, stop, come to think of it. Use this box, and put all your books and things in, anything round the room you can find. I'm just going to pop and have a little word with Mr Pickup.' Alice took up a cardboard box with 'Knight's Castile Soap' printed on the side, emptied the rubbish from it into the sink and handed it over.

'Be back in a jiffy, darling.'

Daisy felt strange on her own in the partly dismantled room, but did what her mummy had told her. Crayons, colouring books, and annuals were carefully put in the box, along with some magazines belonging to her mother. She found her school satchel buried underneath them and was tempted to leave it behind, but she remembered she liked her wooden pencil case with its painted flowers, and decided that it had all better come along.

The doors of the wardrobe stood open, its shelves yet to be emptied. It gave the room a strange unnerving air of uncertainty. She wished Mummy would hurry up.

Alice kicked Mr Pickup's door. She could hear his television inside. Perhaps I should have done more to get him on our side, charmed him, played the poor frightened woman, Alice thought, though she had to admit that some men were incapable of falling for her charm; usually those with no imagination.

She kicked the door again. He must have guessed it was her, it was doubtful if any of his other cowed tenants would have made such a noise. He opened the door a crack. Alice shoved her hardest and taken by surprise he fell back a couple of steps. She pushed into his room.

The furniture reflected its owner's taste and the standard of cleanliness matched his own personal hygiene or lack of it, but a new television, the largest Alice had ever seen, sat in the corner. A freshly opened bottle of White Horse whisky stood on a small table by a greasy, torn armchair. One single light bulb under a fraying shade on the high ceiling lit up the room.

'I've come for my money, you bastard.' Alice had good reason to leave Daisy behind in the room. Her previous tiredness had gone and in its place she had the raw nervous energy and inner anger of a cornered she-wolf protecting its cub, her fear for Fred translating itself into fury at the man she held responsible for many of her woes. This was going to get very nasty and the last person she wanted to witness it was her daughter.

Back in the half-empty room Daisy began to take fright at the idea of leaving what had become a place of security for her, even if she did not like it very much. She stopped packing and went to the door. She listened but could hear nothing, so she went halfway down the stairs until she could pick out her mother's voice. Mummy was shouting and that alarmed Daisy, because she could hear that her mother wasn't even bothering to project in her best stage voice.

This was out-and-out yelling, something Mummy said you should never do. Interested by this development, Daisy went further down the stairs until she could make

189

out the words. Then she sat on the stair and listened.

Mr Pickup had been startled by the fury of Alice's arrival.

'You've no right bursting in here, I'll—'

'I want my money and I want it now and I want two bloody weeks.'

'One week I said, one. One week, and if you aren't out of here I'm going to call the police.'

Alice's kick caught him on the knee, much to her fury, she'd been aiming for his groin, but her suit skirt was a slim-line pencil one. Daisy heard the yelp as, unseen by her, Alice hitched her skirt by the hips and went to try for another shot.

'I'm going to call the police, they'd like to know about you I'm sure, and what's more I can have you for assault.'

Alice only managed to get his knee again, must be years of practice aiming at our Betty, she thought. She stood and stared at him in a rage. Then a smile slowly began to creep across her face. It frightened him even more: he could see what Alice couldn't, that it was tinged with a look of near-insanity.

The smile continued, and Alice snatched up the whisky bottle, ready to throw while she tipped over the table. With the other hand she slowly undid the buttons of her suit jacket.

'Call the police, go on then, but,' she fastened her fingers around the top of the thin blouse underneath in a mime of ripping it open, 'before you pick up that receiver I'll yell bloody rape and tell them what a dirty old man you are, always rubbing up against me and trying to touch up my little girl. Don't think they'd like that, do you? That MacCallum may be one of the nastiest coppers I know, but he's a very moral man. Takes a dim view . . . of perverts like you.'

190

'You wouldn't bloody dare, I don't know what they want you for, but you wouldn't bloody dare, not the fix you're in.'

She might not have been the greatest actress ever to tread the boards, she might never have got beyond playing a maid or a guest at the ball, but there was one thing anyone who had ever seen Alice act would have admitted. She could project. Her scream brought a fine layer of dust drifting down like spring snow from the lampshade.

It went all the way to the stalls, or rather Daisy's seat on the stairs. Rather than terrify the child, it reassured her. She could tell Mummy was projecting, like she had showed her, and breathing from her diaphragm, so everything must be all right, Daisy reasoned.

Inside the room, Alice took another deep breath and went for an encore.

'You can have your money, you bitch.' He produced a roll of notes almost as greasy as he was. Alice held out her hand, still brandishing the whisky bottle in the other, while he counted out the cash.

Alice tried one last bluff. 'And our fifteen pounds deposit.'

'You never paid a—'

Her impassioned 'No' managed to get even higher up the scale. The echo was still playing off the walls as the two fives and five ones were added.

She put the whisky bottle down, folded the money carefully and buttoned up her jacket.

'Thank you, our taxi should be here any moment.'

On her way back upstairs Alice encountered Daisy.

'I thought I told you to stay in the room.'

'They were good screams, you really projected, it was better than the one you did in *The Ghost Train*.'

'Thank you darling, I was rather proud of them myself. Pity you couldn't see my exit, though.'

They met the worried face of the quiet man who lived on the floor below them, brought out onto the landing by Alice's screams.

'A mouse. I'd get the council in if I were you,' Alice smiled sweetly.

The taxi driver obviously had imagination. He not only managed to fit two suitcases, a trunk, a cardboard box and three overflowing carrier bags into his taxi, but he also found space for Alice's dressing-room screen and his two passengers. He even helped them carry it all downstairs.

Mr Pickup stood in the doorway and sourly watched them go.

Daisy gave her best smile. 'Bye-bye Mr Pickup, sorry we forgot to bring you any shortbread.'

Despite her day-to-day lamentations and exclamations, Nana Rosen never batted an eyelid when faced with a real crisis: she'd dealt with too many of them in her time.

She heard the taxi draw up, and was wondering who it could be when a sheepish Alice appeared at the back door.

'Can we stay the night?' She didn't need to ask the question.

Mr Bloum appeared and helped to unload the taxi, and paid the fare, despite Alice's protestations. Nana set about the more important matters in hand. She had adapted quickly to the English solution to any problem and brewed a pot of tea.

'Now, ven was the last time this little von had something to eat?'

Daisy was so tired, so confused by all that had

happened to her in a single day, she couldn't remember. This shocked Nana more than their unannounced arrival. A big glass of milk, a round of meat-paste sandwiches and a slab of cake later, Alice was undressing the girl and tucking her into Ruth's bed.

Thankfully the child sank into the feather mattress and looked around the spartan but friendly room, filled with a pool of warm light from the bedside lamp. A field of pretty tiny flowers covered the eiderdown, and her Aunt Ruth's belongings brought her a sense of order and security. An old top hat sat rakishly on top of the wardrobe, on the walls were framed photographs of Ruth with other show people, a picture backstage with Bob Monkhouse, Aunt Ruth in a feather headdress in a Tiller Girl-type dance troupe. On the table beside the bed, Mummy, Daddy and her aunt smiled back at her, champagne glasses raised, laughing. Alice leaned over her and gave her a gentle kiss. 'Night night, darling.'

Nana appeared with a hot-water bottle, popped it under the covers and leaned over her; Daisy braced herself, but instead of the usual heavy-handed hug came a kiss as gentle as her mother's. The light was switched off and both women stood, framed in the doorway by the light from the landing, and looked at her for what seemed like a long time. It was a vision of comfort as she drifted slowly off to sleep.

Downstairs Nana would hear no explanation from Alice until she too had eaten. Then she poured them each a hefty glass of Malcie's sherry and Alice began. The old woman didn't interrupt, she didn't judge, she merely sat and nodded. Unburdening her last few days lifted a weight from Alice's shoulders. Only when she had finished did she realise she was sobbing in a mixture of tiredness and despair. Nana leaned over the table, squeezed her hand in a gesture of compassion, and poured her another big glass of sherry.

'I must talk to Mr Bloum,' she said. 'There are no secrets in this house. He will know what you should do, darlink.'

Nana unhooked a cheap tin pocket torch from its place by the back door and set off down to the shed to confer with her lodger. Alice simply sat at the table, numb, and past thinking. What she needed right now was someone who could tell her what she should do. She wished Ruth were with her. No problem seemed too bad if Ruth was around. Compared to what Ruth has been through, what have I ever really had to suffer that hasn't been my own silly, stupid fault, she thought.

Nana and Mr Bloum came into the kitchen. Alice knew they had been talking for a while, but how long, she wasn't in any condition to tell. Tiredness and the effects of two large glasses of sherry were beginning to take their toll.

Mr Bloum sat down at the kitchen table with them. He looked serious. Alice tried to pay attention. He noticed how tired she was.

'We'll talk about it properly tomorrow, it is too late now and you are exhausted,' he said.

Nana looked back and forth at them and nodded.

'Yes, too tired.'

'But you mustn't worry, we will help you. You are like family to us. You have been very kind to Ruth, to us all. We love you and we love the little Dorothy. Even when she thinks she is a Daisy.' His English, as always, was deliberate. He seemed to think the words in his own language first of all and then translate them into English.

'You could stay here for ever, but it would be very crowded, so I think it is best if we find for you a house

194

of your own to rent. Perhaps from the council, or in the village.'

Alice sat and listened, she didn't think she could find the power to talk. She just nodded, and Nana continued to nod, Mr Bloum joined in. Like farmyard chickens round the table, came a crazy sleepy thought into Alice's head.

'You must not worry about money. We can help you out.'

Alice's fuddled brain began to stir. 'I couldn't, darlings, really. You're as strapped for cash as I am. Neither of you has a job and Ruth is finding it as difficult to get work as I am. No, I can't. Thank you for offering, but no.'

Nana gave a slow smile, and looked at Mr Bloum, as if for approval. 'Darlink, Mr Bloum has a job.'

Alice was stunned. 'He does?' She had only ever seen him in his garden. Come to think of it, the only time she had ever seen him leave the garden was to go to the gate to inspect Malcie's flash car.

Mr Bloum nodded. 'Yes I work.'

Alice's look of amazement stayed fixed on her face. Mr Bloum gave a glance and a nod to Nana to tell her she could explain.

'Darlink, Mr Bloum is a banker.'

Alice could feel a hysterical laugh start to rise in her throat, created from her tiredness, despair and the absurdity of it all. Mr Bloum in a pinstriped suit, bowler hat and umbrella hooked over his arm, pushing a wheelbarrow full of compost.

'Mr Bloum is a banker, darlink. He was a banker before the war came. When he does not garden he does the banking.'

Alice didn't think she could keep from laughing for much longer.

'The market, darlink. You know, up and down, the

195

stocks and shares. He is very good. Sometimes we have the crash, but not like the crash in Berlin before the Nazis. My God! Let me tell you! People needed a wheelbarrow full of notes just to buy their bread. Sometimes it goes up, sometimes it goes down.'

Nana looked to Mr Bloum to see if he approved of her explanation.

'I hope you would respect my privacy,' he said seriously. Alice could only join in with another nod.

He decided to add to Nana's somewhat simple version. 'I worked in my father's bank. After the war, after the camp when I came to England, and met Nana and Ruth, I did not know about anything. I had no contacts and there were too many people before me, all the favours were used up by the time I arrived.

'So the Government said, you live here, but you must work. Work in the mill or work in the mine. I work in the mine. It was not nice. I stayed only as long as I had to. Underground the heat and the noise, every day. I did not like the mines, but it meant I could stay and it meant I could make money. So I bought the newspaper, I studied the market. I bought the shares. Only small at first but I build it up.'

Nana cut in, 'Tell her about 1956.'

'That year, I made a big mistake, got too big for my boots as you say. Big mistake, lost a lot of money, but since then we have done fine I think, not too much, not too little, but enough, and enough to help you.'

Nana gave another nod, to encourage him to go on. 'I met Ruth at a dance and she invited me home to meet Nana. I went back to my lodgings and packed my case and came to live here, I made the garden. It's good to be out in the air all day making things grow, after the mines, and after—' There he stopped.

196

After being in the camp where the only thing that grew was death, Alice finished for him in her head. So that was what Mr Bloum did in his potting shed all day, he cross-pollinated the Stock Exchange.

'So you mustn't worry,' he told her, and then went back out to his shed again.

Before she climbed into bed alongside her daughter, Alice pulled the curtains back. She looked down the garden to where a tiny light from a hurricane lamp glowed in the shed's window, as the green-fingered financial wizard worked some figures out on the back of an old seed catalogue, planning for her future.

Chapter 18

The Chest Hospital

Daisy's face was a mask of hurt, 'But you said I could come!'

Mummy had never been to see Daddy without taking her along; the very idea shocked the child.

'No, I'm sorry darling but I'm afraid I have to go and see Daddy on my own today,' Alice hated every word she said, but she knew she was right. Daisy looked at her mother in horrified disbelief, tears beginning to form in the corners of her eyes, but Alice stood firm, even though inwardly she was beginning to crumble.

During the previous night, as Alice lay silent and unsleeping, stroking the sleeping child's hair, she had made one of the toughest decisions of her life; a life where some major turning points had been taken on instinct or the merest whim.

At breakfast, while Daisy lost herself in the delights of porridge and an egg in her silver cup, Alice had taken Nana on one side and told her of the decision: she wasn't going to take her daughter with her to the chest hospital. She didn't know what she was going to find when she got there, Alice reasoned, she dreaded to think how Fred would be.

'What if he is still unconscious, what if he's even . . . '
Alice couldn't finish.

'No you are right, you must face this alone I am afraid.' The old woman had reassured her it was a wise decision, as they whispered in the corner of the room.

Alice then steeled herself, broke the news, and watched as part of her daughter's world caved in.

'I know you'd like to come, but Daddy is very, very poorly. In fact he is probably going to be fast asleep, so it's a long way to go, isn't it, just to see him sleeping? So I want you to stay here and help Nana for me and say hello to Aunt Ruth when she gets back.'

Daisy sat at the kitchen table and stared at her mother, trying to work it all out; she could not understand why Alice would leave her behind.

'Even if Daddy didn't wake up, I could just look at him,' Daisy suggested.

'But it's a long way to go just to look,' Alice said gently.

'I don't mind.'

Alice was beginning to run out of reasons why Daisy should not go. Nana came to the rescue. 'Darlink, your daddy vould not know you vere there, and besides, poor Ruth, coming home on her own, and no Alice or Daisy to say hello. Think how sad she vould be.'

Alice saw Daisy's determination begin to falter, 'Yes darling, poor Ruth. She has had to be away for so long, she'll be so upset.'

'But what if Daddy is awake and I'm not there?'

'Well, I'll tell him, of course, that you were looking after Ruth and helping Nana. He would understand.'

'Really?'

'Of course, darling.'

Daisy grudgingly admitted that it would be mean if one

of them was not there to welcome Aunt Ruth when she got home.

'But you will tell Daddy that, and that I love him.'

Alice fought back the tears, 'Of course I will, darling.'

Daisy was scraping her porridge bowl clean as Alice put on Fred's old mac and Nana emptied all the change out of her purse and handed it to her.

'Where are you going?'

'I'm just popping over to the telephone to call the hospital and ask how Daddy is.'

'Wait for me.'

'No darling, you stay there and finish up the porridge for Nana.' Alice was not sure what the news would be, and if it was bad, she was not sure of her own reaction. She wanted the luxury of being able to break down, cry, sob or howl at the sky if need be. The constant attempt to keep her child reassured, safe and comforted was beginning to be as great a strain as watching her husband die.

'Let me come! Why won't you let me?' Daisy's voice was almost a wail. She couldn't understand why suddenly her mother was doing things without her. It had never happened before.

Alice understood the reason for her daughter's distress.

'Come on then, hurry up, let's get your cardigan.'

Hand in hand and in silence they walked along the lane, crossed the main road and made their way to the telephone box. They walked through the birdsong of a cool summer morning that promised to get hotter and dry up all the dew on the grass which soaked through the pattern of holes in Daisy's sandals.

Each of them was wrapped in her own thoughts. Daisy's were a jumble of longing to go and see Daddy, feeling guilty if she didn't and guilty if she did not stay to welcome Aunt Ruth. She was lost in a general confusion, which had been creeping up on her since Sunday after being thrown out by Aunt Maggie and everything that had happened since.

Alice was forcing herself along, dreading each step that took her nearer to the telephone, terrified of what the news might be.

Daisy insisted on coming into the box with her, and though part of her didn't want her in there, Alice found comfort in holding her daughter close as she made the call.

Back at the cottage, in the yard and out of earshot of Daisy, Alice held a whispered conference with Nana and Mr Bloum, 'No change, still very poorly and he hasn't come round. They advised me to get there as soon as possible.'

The three of them planned the best course of action, while Daisy innocently tucked into a glass of milk and a biscuit at the kitchen table.

Alice would not catch the bus, but use the old bicycle from the shed, go to Betty's house in Whittington and ask her to take her by car. Betty should be at home but if not, Alice would catch the bus from there to Lichfield.

Mr Bloum pumped up the tyres while Daisy looked on in silence.

'Better get these old tyres nice and hard,' he said, trying to coax her into conversation, but Daisy could only look on, mute in her misery. Mr Bloum was dreading the day ahead.

Daisy watched her mother get ready to leave and added another emotion to the jumble going round in her head, that of resentment. She had never seen Mummy ride a bike before, she didn't know that she could. Daisy felt left out.

201

'You will tell Daddy, won't you? You will tell him I love him and that I stayed behind so Aunt Ruth would not be upset.'

'Of course I will,' Alice hugged her daughter close and gave her a big kiss. Then she set off, handbag in the wicker basket, Fred's old mac threatening to tangle itself round the chain. She almost welcomed the ride: she had to concentrate so hard on pedalling and steering that all other thought was impossible.

Daisy stood and waved goodbye, feeling unsure and afraid. Nana's comforting hand rested gently on her shoulder. In the distance Alice risked turning in the saddle and giving one last wave. Daisy, Mr Bloum and Nana held their breath as the bicycle wobbled precariously and nearly came to grief. Then Alice went round the corner and out of sight.

The two adults heard Daisy sigh and moved swiftly to stem the flood of doubts and fears they saw on the child's face.

'Come along my dear, I think you will be delighted by de lettuce!' Mr Bloum sang out the words with forced jollity and, taking her by the hand, led Daisy into the vegetable garden.

Betty was at home. She took one look at her sister's face and realised something was wrong. Together they went to their mother's house in the next street, and death or its proximity united the three women temporarily. Any letter of condemnation from Aunt Maggie, if there was to be one, had not yet arrived and both her sister and mother accepted Alice's abbreviated version of the truth: she had returned from Scotland to find Fred's condition had worsened.

Without hesitation, Betty offered to take Alice to the

hospital. They didn't have much to say to each other on the journey. Alice was thankful for the ride and for the fact that her sister had not asked questions.

Betty knew that this was a crisis, possibly the end, and put all her energy and concentration into driving as quickly as she could. She was not a mean woman, rather she had been born with a heart less generous than her sister's. Alice loved the world and would call anyone darling at the drop of a hat, while Betty had a finite supply of affection. She saved it for her family and as the years went on she conserved the supply for Graham, her adored son. Betty could never get over the fact she had given birth to someone so wonderful.

At the hospital Alice found herself succumbing to Daisy's fear of the long corridor. It went on for ever, and, at the end of it, she didn't dare to think or to hope.

They saw the sister first and she offered little comfort, before taking them to a room off a side ward. The sight nearly brought Alice to her knees. Earlier in Fred's illness she thought he looked as though he was dissolving into the white sheets and pillowcases.

Now he had.

A grey-white waxen skeleton lay on its back in the bed. Only the slightest movement of the bedcover showed Fred was still breathing, that life still fought there. An obscenity of tubes went into and out of his body. Betty had to help Alice to the bedside chair. She stood behind her, holding onto her sister, to give her comfort and strength; all petty sisterly jealousies were wiped away in the awfulness of the moment.

Betty hadn't seen Fred for weeks; she hadn't been prepared for the sight of someone she knew reduced to this. She had managed to reach a comfortable, self-

203

centred middle age without ever seeing death up close before. Their own father had died suddenly of a stroke. Betty had seen him in his coffin, only for a moment, wearing his best suit and an expression no different from sleep. Before her on the hospital bed death was coming slowly, inch by inch, cell by cell, breath by breath. She could not cope. The loving hug and kiss Betty bestowed on her surprised Alice, who managed to bring herself to her senses long enough to thank her sister, and then she slipped her hand under Fred's thin arm without disturbing any of the tubes. She slid her hand down until her palm met his, closed her fingers gently, and waited.

Betty tore back down the corridor and out into the fresh air, back to life and the living, away from the hushed room and the hospital smell of disinfectant and floor polish.

She sat in her car for a while, the window open, listening to the blackbirds in the overgrown hospital garden, saying a prayer. Then she set off for home, still thinking her younger sister was a foolish godless idiot, only now she thought this with compassion instead of her usual anger. When Betty's husband arrived home that evening the warmth of her welcome and an unheard-of kiss surprised him. Seeing Fred dying had made Betty look beyond her usual hero-worship of her son and catch sight of her marriage once again.

The sight of two rows of plump green jewels of lettuce in Mr Bloum's garden impressed Daisy. These were her lettuces, she had helped to plant them. Now they were ready to be eaten. Mr Bloum showed her what to do. She stood with her feet either side of the row, felt around the bottom leaves until she reached the stem. It felt strange, but nice, the back of her hand against the warm soil, her hands full of cool crisp lettuce leaves.

'Now don't hold too tightly, or you'll break and bruise the leaves, but lift gently, pull and, there you are!'

The lettuce, root and all, came out of the fine soil easily. She held it in her hands triumphantly. This was hers, all her own doing. You put a tiny seed into the soil and this huge green plant appeared, drops of water sparkling like emeralds on its leaves! And what's more you could eat it afterwards.

Uncle George could make scarves and bunches of plastic flowers appear but here, by the magic of life, she had produced, from a single seed smaller than a grain of rice in Nana's rice pudding, a great, big, real lettuce. The thought of such magic, real magic, such power intoxicated her. If she put one tiny pea from her plate into the soil and watered it, and hoed it like Mr Bloum did, then she'd have a whole pea plant like he had, covered with pea pods you could pick and eat right there or cook with mint in a saucepan on the stove. It was intoxicating, she was drunk with the green-fingered Midas touch of the gardener. She was hooked for life.

She bore the lettuce in all its glory to the kitchen and proudly showed Nana what she had grown. The old woman's delight did not disappoint her. The small wooden stool was placed in front of the tall stone sink with a flourish. Daisy climbed up and turned on the tap to wash her lettuce leaf by leaf, picking off the occasional insect. She placed it in the colander to drain in time for lunch with a bottle of Heinz salad cream.

Ruth suspected something was wrong the minute she opened the door of the train. By the time she and her case

205

were on the platform she was convinced.

All the way from Rhyl she had been looking forward to arriving at Trent Valley station. Malcie and Alice would be back by then, and would be there with Daisy to meet her.

She imagined the look on Daisy's face as she handed over the funny little Welsh doll, with its long dark skirt and stovepipe black hat, which now sat at the top of a carrier bag full of presents.

Even if Malcie did not show up with the Jag, Alice and Daisy would be there. Alice would be roaring with laughter and telling dramatic tales of their expedition to Glasgow on the bus back home to where Nana had laid on chicken and dumplings, with baked apples to follow; with a table full of cakes, and endless pots of tea. She had been looking forward to her arrival, so the empty platform came as a shock.

She walked to the bus stop, lugging her case and parcels. She kept looking up Trent Valley road, hoping to see Alice come sprinting along, Daisy trailing behind, holding onto her hand, and trying to keep up.

They never appeared.

Ruth started to feel very nervous indeed. What had happened to them? Had they been caught? She decided to go to Mr Pickup's and see if they were back, but when the station bus got into the depot the bus for home was just setting off, and it would be another hour before the next one, so she ran for it instead.

The Midland Red buses on the country routes were not built for speed. They were the old ones, some of them pensioned off from the busier town and city routes. So were the drivers. These were buses which had earned the right to set their own pace, lumbering along, their drivers knowing exactly where each stop was, even if the sign had long blown down, or been overgrown by hedges or swamped by ivy. The longer the journey took the more certain Ruth became that she was going home to something wrong.

As she walked up the lane, the feeling got worse. By the time she was by the back door she was almost afraid to open it. Her mother had not taken up her usual vantage point on the back step to see the bus arrive at the main road and watch who got on and off.

Ruth set down her case and opened the back door. One look at her mother's face said it all.

Before Ruth and Nana could exchange a word an ecstatic Daisy had wrapped herself around Ruth's waist. Not only was Daisy pleased to see her, she was relieved, because Mummy had been right. Daisy had seen how upset Aunt Ruth was when she opened the back door; she almost looked as though she was going to burst into tears. That was because she thought Mummy and I weren't here, Daisy reasoned. Mummy had been right, like she always was.

'I stayed to be here when you got home, because Mummy said you'd be upset if I didn't because she had to go and see Daddy but she said I didn't better have to because he's asleep a lot.' Daisy's words of welcome, relief and explanation poured out in one long joyous burst.

Ruth hadn't understood half of it, but knew this was her cue. 'Darlink, how wonderful.' She embraced the little girl, lifting her up into her arms in a hug. Then she let her down and produced the doll.

Ruth's daydreams on the train came true in one regard, the doll was a success. It was a cheap souvenir-shop present, but it captured the child's imagination, because it danced. The doll's stiff skirts held a secret underneath: stiff bristles, which made the doll move around if Daisy placed it on a table and drummed her fingers alongside it.

Daisy gave a demonstration of the doll's skills and even though Ruth was torn apart with worry for her lover and her best friend, she played with the child.

'Darlink, go and show Mr Bloum the vonderful doll!' Nana could see the anguish her daughter was fighting to hide in front of the child and gently got Daisy out of the way.

In her own language, Nana was not some vague, syrupy-sounding old woman. Once she had embraced her daughter and reassured herself that Ruth had not been starved, and had placed food and coffee in front of her, she told her everything.

'So where is Alice now?'

'She has gone to the hospital, her sister has taken her in her car, I hope, or maybe by train.'

'Why didn't she take Daisy? How could she leave the child behind! It could be her last chance!' Ruth thought back to her own father snatched from her. 'Daisy must say goodbye to Fed.'

'Alice doesn't even know if Fred is going to be conscious, alive even. What should your last memory of your father be?' her mother reasoned. 'Do you remember a man who said goodbye I love you, or do you remember a dying body which cannot speak, which cannot move, which cannot show its love for you? No, Alice did the right thing I think.'

'But she should have the chance to say goodbye, to know it's the last time, to tell him.'

'At eight years old to tell him what?'

'To tell him she loves him.' Ruth broke into noisy sobs. She was not just crying for the man she loved,

208

dying in a hospital bed, she was crying for her own father. Nana knew this instinctively. Her arms enfolded her daughter, and a corner of her apron came up to wipe the tears and mascara. She held her daughter, a grown woman, as tightly as Alice held her own child.

'You must let the mother do what she knows is right for the child. As for you I say go upstairs, wash your face, change your dress, go and kiss Daisy and catch the next bus back to Lichfield.'

'What?'

'To get the train to the hospital. Alice will need you and you need to see Fred. For one so smart, Miss Fancy-Dancer who has been to Rhyl in a big show, sometimes I don't think you know anything.'

Alice had sat and watched a procession of nurses and doctors tend to her still-unconscious husband. Each flicker of an eyelid, twitch of a muscle by Fred she took as a sign for hope.

'He's very poorly and he's very heavily sedated,' one young nurse told her, 'why don't you just pop outside for a while, have a cup of tea and a cigarette. If there's any change, I'll let you know.'

Alice wouldn't move. She sat and cursed Malcie and blamed herself. Fred had looked so much better the last time she saw him, it gave her the confidence to go off and do Malcie's dirty work with him. If she'd stayed she could have had more time, they could have talked more, and what if this was her fault? With Ruth away in Rhyl he was left on his own, so alone, had something made him give up? It was all her fault.

She stayed by his side, but her mind ranged and raged all the way up the road to Glasgow and back down again.

*

209

Daisy stood shocked, stunned into disbelief as she saw Aunt Ruth go through the garden gate.

'Where is she going?'

Nana hugged her close. 'Darlink, I think Aunt Ruth was very worried that your mummy was on her own at the hospital and so she has gone to join her.'

'But she should have taken me,' the words almost came out as a moan. 'I want to go. I want my daddy!'

I want my daddy. Nana had heard those words in Yiddish, German, Polish, French, Belgian. She had heard her daughter cry the same words and they still cut her to her heart. Yet still she felt Alice had been right to leave the girl behind. That her father was going to die now seemed beyond doubt. Death is bad enough, thought Nana, as she held a now sobbing Daisy in her bear-like hug. At least she won't have to see it.

When Ruth entered the ward the sight of an empty bed where Fred had been punched her in the stomach with fear. She made her way to the sister's office, shaken.

'I don't think Mr Smedley can see another visitor, his wife is already with him, I'm afraid he's very poorly.'

Ruth was impatient. 'Dying, you mean.' The sister's lips pressed together into a thin line.

'Look, I'm sorry, I didn't mean that. I know how ill he is, I'm a . . . a close member of the family, you could say. He is very ill, I know. Alice is here for him, and I'm here for Alice if you see what I mean.' The sister remained tight-lipped.

'You must have seen her, you must have seen how badly she's taken this. She's lost her home, her job, now she's losing her husband. Can't you see how she is? I

210

will just sit there, quietly, by her side. She needs a friend.'

'Her sister was with her earlier.'

'That cow! You call that a friend,' Ruth's words burst out in her anxiety. To her surprise the sister's lips appeared again, smiling. She had been on duty during an earlier visit by Betty and come to more or less the same conclusion. On this ward, you saw death, and you saw grieving. If there was someone here to help with the strain of that grief, then she welcomed it and regulations could go to hell.

'Come with me, dear.' She led Ruth to the room.

Ruth took one look and nearly turned and fled.

A thousand upon a thousand corpses rose up from their stinking open grave and raped her memory. The stench of death and floors awash with the dysentery of the dying clung to her nose and face, she swallowed rising bile and stood in horror as the safety of the years tore from her, right back to Belsen.

She swayed, and the sister stood by to catch her, surprised the woman should react that way, but then, she reasoned, some people weren't used to the sight of death.

Alice looked up, saw her friend and read in an instant what was wrong. The two women helped Ruth into the chair; the sister went to get a glass of water for her. Alice hugged her close and whispered in her ear, 'Thank you for coming darling, I know what's going through your mind, thank you for being brave enough to do this for Fred. I always knew that, well, you fancied him something rotten, but I know now, I truly understand darling, how much you love him. He always knew you did, you know.'

Ruth's eyes came back into focus and she looked at her friend, who had just driven away her demons by admit-

211

ting that she shared her husband's love; something she did unselfishly. Alice pulled up another chair and they sat down to wait.

They waited in silence hoping he would waken just long enough for them to tell him how much they loved him. Or perhaps there would be a miracle and he would waken long enough to tell them he loved them. But the miracle never happened.

Chapter 19

Gran Steps In

After death comes the paperwork. Fred died in the early evening, just as the lights began to come on, the lamps in the hospital grounds bleeding the dusk with their yellow glow. He just left. One minute he had been breathing softly, then Alice and Ruth realised that he wasn't and they called for a nurse who gently confirmed he was dead.

Then the hospital, which had seemed up until now only concerned with keeping people alive, flicked a switch and the process for dealing with death clicked smoothly into place.

They were ushered out of the room, and two nurses began dismantling all the hateful apparatus around Fred, preparing him for the mortuary, for the undertaker. Suddenly he was just something to be disposed of, and so were the two women. Not unkindly, but efficiently.

In the sister's office questions were asked, forms filled, signatures needed, belongings returned. Gone. Alice's husband was some copies of forms in her hand, a bag of belongings and a body laid out. Over. The night staff would come on, the bed would be stripped and another patient would appear, another drama of living or dying for another family to enact.

After years of decline, of hopes raised and dashed, of visiting days and anxiously asking the doctor, that was it. Alice walked down the corridor in disbelief. How could everything around her seem so normal, so ordinary, while her life had fallen apart? Nothing could be the same again, but the train still took them back to Lichfield, the bus still crawled out of the depot. The Horse and Jockey was still standing by the roadside at Freeford.

The sight of Alice and Fred's old home as they went past on the bus tore at Alice and Ruth's hearts.

Never ever again would Fred Smedley, shirtsleeves rolled to the elbow, go round the tables collecting glasses, calling out to their customers, 'Time gentlemen, please! Come on drink up, haven't you got homes to go to?' while Dorothy slept upstairs, and Alice and Ruth laughed in the corner calling out 'Night all,' as people left. Sometimes Ruth got a lift home, other times Fred drove her and didn't come back until late into the next morning, while Alice slept secure in her home, her daughter, her husband and her best friend.

They sat numbly as the bus carried on its way. Thoughts wouldn't form. It wasn't until Alice climbed down the steps at the Whittington road end that the words formed in her mind: 'What the hell happens next?' She couldn't answer the question.

As they opened the back door Nana looked up at them and tears filled her eyes. They didn't have to tell her. She sat them down, poured cups of tea, called Mr Bloum in from his shed and the two women went over their day.

Then with incredible weariness they undressed and went to bed. Ruth climbed in beside her mother and lay dry-eyed alongside her throughout the night; it hurt too much to cry.

Alice managed to get into bed with Daisy without waking her. In the morning she would have to tell her.

Alice tried to rehearse the scene in her mind but the words wouldn't come. In the end she and Ruth took the girl into the front parlour and, sitting on Alice's knee, she was told a child's version of the truth, that Daddy had been so ill that he went off to sleep, and never would wake up again. He was dead, but he wasn't poorly any more and he could run and play with the dogs like he used to, now, in heaven.

Daisy stopped clinging to her mother long enough to ask, 'Do dogs go to heaven?'

'Of course they do, darling.'

'That's all right then.' When the last old dog had died, all thin, his eyes milked over with cataracts, they had buried him in the field behind the pub. What happened to him next had always worried Daisy.

'Daddy just got old and ill, like Goldie,' Daisy told her mother.

'Yes darling.'

The implication of her father's death just hadn't, or wouldn't, sink in. The child took it at face value, no sobbing, and no grief. The two women were amazed. Alice thought she hadn't explained properly. Neither realised that for something this big to be understood by such a little girl it would take a long time to seep in, slowly filling her up with a dreadful sadness which wouldn't break for years, and when it did neither of them was with her. That would be Daisy's real tragedy.

Nana started baking ferociously, and enlisted Daisy's help. Mr Bloum stayed in his shed, Ruth sat on an upturned bucket in the yard, smoking and staring out into space. Alice set off to tell her mother and sister. She got as far as the gate when a sobbing Daisy appeared and threw herself around her mother's waist.

'Don't leave me!' Alice had hoped to break the news alone, to have some time to herself during her walk to Whittington, along the wooded road by the large Victorian houses for the officers at Whittington Barracks. She wanted some time she could be on her own to gather her thoughts, to let some of her sadness out in tears; but she took one look at her daughter's anguished face and realised that the child had to go with her.

They arrived at Betty's shortly after the morning post brought a furious Gran to the doorstep brandishing Aunt Maggie's letter, and its contents were used as a stick to beat Alice.

A disgruntled Daisy was all but shoved out into the back garden by Gran and ordered to play. She inspected the hutches and Graham's pet rabbits twitched their noses at her forlornly. Daisy tried to find a dandelion in Aunt Betty's pristine garden, and had to content herself with picking grass to push through the wire. She wondered if rabbits went to heaven too, she hoped so or the dogs would have nothing to chase. The thought of heaven and dogs made her think of Daddy who was now dead. It made her want her mummy so she set off towards the house.

Daisy could hear the shouting before she opened the back door, so quietly she pushed the door open and stood in the porch, listening to the commotion in the kitchen.

'Your husband was lying dying and you went gallivanting off all over the country, breaking the law!' Gran was building up a head of steam. Betty just sat silently, still shaken by the sight of Fred; she didn't approve of her sister, but the idea of widowhood had overwhelmed her.

'And what's more you took little Dorothy with you!'

Daisy, the child in the narrow porch thought to herself as she listened, not really understanding the words, but knowing they were bad. She slowly picked some flaking paint from the wall.

'Mum, it was one counterfeit note, there must be hundreds of those things all over the country, Malcie must have just picked one of them up by accident and given it to Aunt Maggie, in all honesty. Before I knew where I was she had dumped us on the street, she didn't know or care what was going to happen to us.'

Part of the old Alice which had been buried by Fred's death surfaced; the situation yearned for her sense of the dramatic. 'We could have had our throats slit in the gutter for all she cared.'

Gran did not buy Alice's version. 'The shame of it, your own aunt, and having the priest come up to her afterwards. She'll never be able to hold her head up again.'

'That's all you're worried about, isn't it? What some bloody priest thinks?'

'You watch your mouth, lady. And another thing, what happened to that Malcie? Your Aunt Maggie was going to give him a piece of her mind, I can tell you, but he never turned up for you. You'd have been left high and dry in Glasgow, with Dorothy.'

Alice digested the news about Malcie; what the hell could have happened to him?

'Where did you stay last night, anyway?'

'With Ruth and Nana, Mum.'

'Them again. Always hanging about with them, with your husband's bit on the side. What is it with you, Alice? Have you no pride? Why didn't you come here, you should be with your family at a time like this, and so should your daughter.'

217

'Why, so you can tell me what a failure and slut I am? Do you know why I haven't brought Dorothy to see you before now? Because she is scared stiff of you.'

Gran stopped short, affronted, but Alice had the bit between her teeth. 'You treat her just like you treated me, you can't speak to her unless it's to tell her off. I'd rather she was with someone who actually liked her, who likes me. It's Betty and me all over again. I could never do right and Betty could never do wrong, and now it's the same with our kids. Graham's a little wonder and all you can do is go for Dorothy.'

'Don't be ridiculous, our Alice,' Betty found her voice.

'Am I? Look at you, you're the same. You've just turned into Mum, you're as sour as she is.'

'You're hysterical.' Her sister decided the truce was over.

'And you're just plain nasty, unless it's your precious son.'

'At least Graham isn't bonkers like your daughter. Going round pretending she's called Daisy. Head full of nonsense and you put it there. The child's almost off her head. When was the last time she went to school? You are a disgrace to this family and you're not fit to bring up a child.'

When Betty paused for breath Gran moved in. 'What are you going to do? Get a job, get a house? No, you'll go off somewhere in some play and drag that poor child along with you, filling her head full of nonsense and making her as bad as you are. Well, I'm not going to stand for it.'

'What has it got to do with you anyway?'

Gran's indignation spilled over. 'Do? When my daughter makes a fool of herself hanging around with her husband's whore, when she gets chucked out of digs . . .'

218

'How did you hear about that?'

'How didn't I, you mean. You're the talk of Lichield, getting chucked out of somewhere like Pickup's and hanging around with gangsters.'

'Gangster, Malcie? Hah!' Alice had to concede to herself that her mother had a point there, what the hell had happened to Malcie? 'Don't be ridiculous, Mother.'

'Ridiculous? Well I've had it with standing by. I'll tell you what you are going to do, my girl.'

'What?'

'You are going to come and live with me, there are jobs going at Gill's Cables, and that daughter of yours is going to school. Fred Smedley was a fool, God rest his soul, I know I shouldn't speak ill of the dead, but that's the truth. He was as big a fool as you are. He just indulged you. Actress? Don't make me laugh, you just hang about with low life and think you're someone important. Well it's over; I will not stand by and see you turn your daughter into as big a failure as you are. You are coming to live with me.'

'And if I don't?'

'I am going to court and I am going to get custody of that child. Do you think you'd get to keep her? With that MacCallum after you? That'll look good in court.'

Alice stopped as if slapped. 'MacCallum? What do you know about him?'

'I know he's come round to my house, asking about you and that big Malcie.'

Alice looked at her mother, horrified. 'When?'

'Weeks ago. Told me I should give you a damn good talking-to and get you out of there before you got yourself into any trouble. Imagine how that would sound in court? You are coming back home and you are going to put all this nonsense out of your head, and your daughter's.'

Alice slumped into a chair. Her husband had been dead for less than a day, she had been verbally assaulted by her mother, she had no home, no job, no money and she didn't know what to do next.

In the porch Daisy simply froze. She had absorbed more bad news in the last twenty-four hours than she could cope with. A numb child stood and listened and none of the words made sense, they were just angry, bitter sounds.

Seeing that she had had the desired effect on Alice and sensing victory, Gran was prepared to soften. 'Admit it, Alice, what life are you giving that child? She's a bright little thing, but she's going to turn out as bad as you, if you don't do something about it.'

'Bad? Do you really think I'm bad?'

'No, no mother ever thinks her children are bad. I don't mean bad, wicked, I mean bad, as in failure. Look at yourself, you had a good husband and nice home, a lovely daughter like Caroline and what did you do? You ran off.'

'I loved Fred.' Alice could feel tears start to rise at the thought of him.

'No one's saying you didn't,' said Betty, 'but the least you can do is admit that, well let's face it Alice, you've never been what anyone would call orthodox, now have you?'

Gran started up again. 'If Dorothy goes back to school, makes some nice friends with the little girls in the village, gets a normal life, she's smart enough to go to the Friary. She could become anything, a nurse or a teacher.'

That's the height of your ambition, isn't it, thought Alice.

'Let's be blunt, Alice,' said Betty.

'You mean you haven't been?'

Her sister was exasperated. 'To put it bluntly, look at yourself. Do you want her to end up like you?' Dear God, no, thought Alice.

They'd won.

Magnanimous in her victory, Gran conceded that Alice and Dorothy should spend the night at Nana's and move in with her the following day.

A subdued Daisy had gone inside when Aunt Betty called, and made polite conversation about Graham's rabbits. Alice had a pretty shrewd idea that the child had been eavesdropping.

As they walked back to Nana's house Alice tried to get her daughter to talk about her father. The fact Daisy hadn't cried was troubling Alice, it was like watching water build up behind a dam, knowing it would have to burst. Right now Fred's death was too new, too big, and too dreadful for Daisy to absorb. Alice decided to stop pressing the child about her father, convinced that in time her grief would surface; but she thought she had better break the other news, that they were to move in with Gran.

Daisy did not like the idea. Her response was more dramatic than her reaction to the news of her father's death. While that was too much for the child to accept, she could visualise quite easily the kind of hell living with her grandmother would involve.

She burst into tears. Her grandmother terrified her and, what was worse, Mummy was now suggesting she go back to school as well.

'But you said I didn't have to go!'

'Only while Daddy was ill, darling.'

'I hate her! She hates me!'

'Of course she doesn't. What gives you that idea?'

221

'She doesn't like me, she always tells me off, she never says anything nice. Why can't we go back to the Horse and Jockey?'

'Because another family live there now.' The child didn't seem able to grasp this, that someone else could move into her home. Alice held her close and decided it was time for a big fib.

'Darling, we'll only go and live with Gran for a little time, until we can get a house of our own in the village. But it will mean that Mummy goes to work to get some money for it, so you'll have to go to school and after school stay with Gran or Aunt Betty until I get home.'

'No,' the word came out as a wailing sound. The world was suddenly slipping away from under Daisy's feet. 'Why can't we stay here with Nana?'

'Because kind as Nana is, we can't make her go on sharing her bed with Aunt Ruth, now can we? We must give Aunt Ruth her bed back.'

'We could sleep in the shed!' Daisy was clutching at straws now.

Alice smiled and held her daughter close, wishing she could move heaven and earth to make things better for her and worried that there was still no sign of tears or grief for her father.

Alice broke the news to Ruth and Nana as they sat round the kitchen table. Daisy was helping Mr Bloum grow things; she had been so impressed with her lettuce.

'Gill's Cables?' Ruth looked horrified. 'Work in an office? You'll die of boredom, darling.'

Alice admitted she was so unqualified she would be lucky to get a job on the production line of the factory.

'And if I don't my mother is quite prepared to drag me through the courts to get custody of Daisy. Hell,

222

we'd better get used to calling her Dorothy again.' Alice had told them about MacCallum's visit and its implied threat.

This worried Nana. She had a fear of anything to do with the police; the Gestapo had seen to that and nothing anyone could say or do would make her change her mind. She was frightened to walk past the Whittington bobby, proud owner of a vegetable garden as good as Mr Bloum's and a sit-up-and-beg bike. He had said hello to her once and what nice weather they were having, and she had stayed awake all night, fully dressed, in fear of a visit.

'It would be good that the child is going to school, and you would be near enough to visit,' said Nana, who could see some of Gran's reasoning. The old lady held education as something sacred, and the fact Daisy had missed so much school worried her.

'A little stability in life can be a good thing,' she added, 'Look at Ruth now, if the war had not stopped her schooling she would have gone on to university, to music college, she would have been famous.'

Ruth scoffed, quietly proud of her mother's faith in her.

'You would darlink, don't ever doubt it. So Daisy does not like the school, but she must go. Education lifts us, it gets us out of the mire, it gives us hope, it makes us.' Nana was quoting her late husband's words. 'Where there is no education, no hope, you get Nazis. You know what my husband said was the greatest defence against people like them? The school bench and the library ticket. Without learning, without books we have nothing.'

Daisy should go to school, Alice conceded. 'It's just that she was so unhappy when Fred was ill and we lost the Horse and Jockey. She hated Mr Pickup's, God, perhaps I should have moved in with Mum then, but the idea of it . . .'

By evening the sky had unfolded into a wonderful sunset, and it was mild enough to sit out and watch the colours spread across the sky. The three women sat as Daisy and Mr Bloum carried out an inspection tour of the garden.

'You could pick some of your lettuces and take them to your grandmother tomorrow,' Mr Bloum told her, 'and some of the radishes and perhaps a nice bunch of flowers.'

Daisy looked doubtful. 'She doesn't like me.'

'Of course she does.'

'That's what Mummy says, but if she does like me, why is she so horrid to me all the time?'

'Do you remember when we planted the lettuces?'

'Yes.'

'Do you remember that even though you said you didn't like your gran you were going to give her a lettuce?'

'Yes,' Daisy scuffed at the soil with her sandal.

'Then we decided that you really did like your gran, but didn't know it, or you wouldn't have wanted her to be left out. Now.' Here he paused while he bent down to pull out a weed. 'I think you gran thinks the same way. She likes you, but I think she doesn't realise she does. She must like you or she wouldn't have knitted that cardigan and she wouldn't want you to go and live with her. Perhaps she's lonely, have you thought of that?'

Little fib there, Mr Bloum thought to himself, and he felt guilty. Like Alice, he looked at the little girl and wondered why she hadn't really cried yet. He decided to probe gently.

'I must say I was very sorry to hear your father died. He was a good man.'

'Thank you, yes he was.' The words didn't sound like a child's, they sounded like an adult's. Perhaps the grandmother is right, perhaps she needs to be around other children, he thought.

'You must miss him.'

Daisy nodded. 'The dogs have gone, the Horse and Jockey has gone, Mr Pickup's has gone, Daddy's gone.' Her words sounded a hundred years old, and Mr Bloum could only think back to his own experience and those children he saw around him in the refugee camps. Sometimes, he thought, the sadness goes down so deep that it stays buried until people start to mine it. When it reaches the surface it can be diamonds of compassion and humanity to help other people; or just a slag heap of hatred, self-abuse and pity that corrodes and destroys all it touches. He made a vow in his heart that he would help Daisy go panning for gold.

A subdued Daisy sat up in bed that night, watching as Mummy folded clothes back into the trunk. Her mother noticed the quietness and wondered why the tears still hadn't come.

'Do you think Gran really likes me?'

'Of course she does darling, really.'

'You aren't fibbing?'

'Of course not.'

'Not even a little fib?'

'Certainly not.'

Alice tucked her daughter in, and kissed her goodnight, and watched until she drifted off to sleep, relieved that she was starting to soften towards the idea of her grandmother. But it would have been a big fib if I said I was looking forward to this, she told herself. Alice closed the bedroom door behind her, and turned to go down the stairs, only to meet an ashen-faced Ruth coming up.

'It's Malcie.'

Chapter 20

Malcie's Proposal

The sharp-suited big man had gone: in his place was a hunched figure, his shirt covered in blood, his face a mass of yellow and green bruising. One eye was closed to a slit in the purple melon that had become its socket. His hair was sticky with congealed blood and a dirty rag bandage kept the fingers of his right hand together.

Nana was frozen to the spot, petrified that such violence had returned to her life. Alice began to shake with shock; it was all too much to take in, coming so soon after Fred's death.

'I'll get Mr Bloum.' Ruth bolted out of the back door. Alice and Nana recovered themselves enough to help him to a chair. As Alice tried to settle him he flinched, his ribs had been broken. He could manage to rest on the chair, propped against the table. Alice looked at his fingers, covered in blood. He stank.

Nana brought a mug of water but his mouth was so swollen he could barely sip. She was feeding him water from a teaspoon when Ruth and Mr Bloum came back.

Suddenly they heard Daisy coming down the stairs. Despite the pain, Malcie forced himself upright and Mr Bloum helped him out into the yard.

'Uncle Malcie's car is outside!' Daisy couldn't wait to see him, but her mummy stood blocking her way.

'I know darling, I know, but he and Mr Bloum are in the garden. They're looking at the plants.' Alice caught her daughter up in her arms and carried her back into the bedroom.

'But I could go too. I could put my dressing gown on and my sandals so my slippers wouldn't get wet.'

'No, it's far too late for that. Bedtime.'

'Owww,' Daisy spilled out the strangled vowels that translate into it's-not-fair in any language, as she was firmly tucked back into bed. Alice pulled the covers so tight that the child was all but pinned down.

'Never mind what's fair or not. I want you to stay in bed, understand. You'll see Uncle Malcie again. You must stay here.'

Alice headed back downstairs. By now they had Malcie by the sink. Ruth was propping him up while Mr Bloum took off his jacket and shirt. Nana was wringing out a cloth.

It was left to Alice to ask the question, 'What the hell happened to you?'

He could hardly speak. 'I bumped into some people I shouldn't have.'

Ruth remembered that Fred had told her Malcie had had to leave Glasgow in a hurry. She hadn't asked any more then, she had no intention of doing so now.

'This is no good,' said Alice. 'We'll have to get him upstairs in the bathroom. I'll go up and stay with Daisy, she's all excited that he's here, she can't see him like this.'

Because I don't want my daughter to see something this terrible and I don't want her to let slip about any of this to Gran or our Betty, she thought.

A disgruntled Daisy sat in bed and watched her mother continue to pack, sulking that she hadn't been allowed to see her Uncle Malcie. Alice kept up a bright string of conversation, to prevent her daughter from hearing anything, as Ruth and Mr Bloum helped him upstairs. Downstairs Nana set to work washing his clothes and sponging his suit.

When Alice was convinced Daisy was asleep and would not waken, she went to the bathroom, where she saw Mr Bloum bandaging Malcie's ribs. The horrific bruising on his face extended to most of his body. Behind the men was a bathtub of bloody water. Malcie was startled when he saw her. Mr Bloum, safety pin between his teeth, waved at her to go away.

In the bedroom Daisy opened her eyes and sat up excitedly. She had acted better than Mummy ever could, she had acted being asleep and it had fooled Mummy. In a flurry of delight at the thought of Uncle Malcie and some extra pocket money, she wriggled into her dressing gown and sandals and gently opened the door. She was so thrilled at the thought of going outside into the garden and surprising Mr Bloum and Malcie that she did not hear the noise from the bathroom.

Daisy tiptoed down the stairs and heard her mother join the other two women in the kitchen. Nana was making some porridge, and Ruth was attacking a shirt with a scrubbing brush and a bar of Sunlight soap.

'Do we know what happened?' Alice asked, still shaken.

'After he dropped you off he went to somewhere he used to go, I think,' said Ruth. 'He can't really talk, I think he got kicked in the throat. There was someone there who knew him and who knew some people who had a grudge, so he went and told them Malcie was back.

They jumped him, when he left a bar, and beat him up and kicked him badly. Told him if he didn't leave then he would be dead. I think one of them stood on his hand too.'

Nana winced.

'That would be the Saturday night. He says he managed to crawl back to the car, but couldn't make it inside. Oh Alice, they just left him there in an alley, no one came near him. He was unconscious until the Monday morning, he thinks. He wasn't sure. It took him a while to come round again. He couldn't remember where your aunt lived, and he couldn't ask anyone for help.

'He says he just kept passing out. He lost track of time. When he could sit upright he drove down here. He must have been out cold for over a day and then delirious for a while after. He said he had to keep stopping on the roadside if he thought he was going to pass out.'

Daisy didn't bother to listen to what they were talking about. She was too busy trying to figure out how to get into the garden. She would never be able to sneak through the kitchen without being noticed, and she could not undo the big bolt on the front door. To go back upstairs to bed would be to admit defeat, so she went into the parlour.

She tried to hide at the far end of the room when the door opened and Mr Bloum came in, with Uncle Malcie leaning on him for support. As Mr Bloum eased him onto the sofa he looked up and saw Daisy.

'Alice!' He turned to the kitchen and called warily.

Alice came in, took one look at Daisy and crossed the room in a flash, scooping up the child.

'I thought I told you to stay in bed.' Daisy was surprised at the anger in her mother's voice.

230

'What did you do Uncle Malcie, fall over in the garden?'

'Aye, something like that.'

'Come on, bed, now.' Alice was reaching breaking point. Fred's death, her ordeal with her mother and the arrival of a broken and battered Malcie was just too much. Daisy wriggled in her arms, and whined to be allowed to stay. Alice, exhausted, put her down. Nana realised Daisy was too excited to be sent upstairs, and did not really understand what had happened, so she took her in her arms and kept the child distracted. If they made a point of sending her to bed this would be something she would remember, dwell on and possibly describe to someone else.

'Come and sit over here and help me sort out my knitting needles, darlink,' Nana took her to the back of the room, but as she kept Daisy occupied the old woman followed what was happening with a watchful and worried eye.

Mr Bloum's pyjamas hardly covered Malcie. He lay on the sofa, wrapped in blankets, looking better for being clean, and provided with bowls of porridge and plenty of tepid water. He could now manage to hold a mug.

'You should really be in hospital,' Ruth said, 'you could have broken something.'

'No. No hospital,' he croaked.

While Nana and Daisy sorted bobbins of darning wool, Alice told Malcie her part of the story, and that she didn't know if her aunt had told the police, but MacCallum had called at Mr Pickup's and at her mother's.

'He'll be looking for me, I had better be going.'

Nana wouldn't hear of it, even though the thought of the police coming made her sick inside with worry.

'You must keep drinking, slowly,' said Mr Bloum,

handing him another mug, 'the dehydration is probably the most dangerous thing.' He knew what he was talking about, and Nana and Ruth agreed. They had seen enough people who had suffered beatings.

'How on earth did you manage to get back?' Alice asked.

'Took my time, only time I was really worried was when I had to go to a petrol station. The man came out and filled up the car, looked in the window, and nearly died of fright when he saw me. I shoved some money at him and drove off. Went and parked up a lane afterwards, in case he called the polis.'

Nana, one eye on Daisy, sat shaking her head in sorrow. She had thought he was what Ruth called a bit flash, but she had not realised he was a criminal.

He started to cough, wincing in pain. Alice was reminded of Fred's dreadful coughing bouts, and it cut like a knife.

They had told Malcie about Fred and he had been genuinely sorry.

'If there's anything I can do to help,' he managed to say. Alice resorted to one of her famous dirty looks. As far as she was concerned he had done enough.

'They got everything, all the stuff from the car,' said Malcie. 'Even the spare cash. I don't know why they didn't take the car as well.' What he didn't remember was there had been three of them, and he had inflicted nearly as much damage as they had before he finally went down.

'You will stay here tonight,' said Mr Bloum. Alice looked at him, once again amazed by the quiet gardener who was also a banker, and, from the look of Malcie now, also knew a great deal about doctoring.

It was decided that Malcie should sleep on the sofa,

propped up with cushions to ease the pain of his ribs.

'Where will you go?' Despite the fact he was a crook and he could bring the police to their door, Ruth was genuinely concerned.

'South, probably to Brighton, there's a couple of boys owe me a favour down there. I'll rest up for a while.' Alice thought he sounded like a character in a bad Western.

Nana watched while the excitement of finding Uncle Malcie slowly wore off, and Daisy began to drop with tiredness. When she was sure the child was asleep, Alice picked her up and carried her to bed. This time she was sure she was fast asleep.

It was decided that Mr Bloum would get up early, wake Malcie and help him dress. Nana and Ruth would prepare breakfast and some food for the journey. Alice was to stay in bed with Daisy until he had gone. The child had already seen too much.

'How is the wee girl doing?' Malcie asked.

Alice told him she was worried Daisy hadn't understood that her father was dead; she hadn't cried.

'She is a bright thing, she understands in her own way.' For once Alice had to admit that Malcie had said something smart.

Malcie was left suitably propped up with a drink of water by his side and a bowl of cold porridge if he could manage to eat. They said goodnight and went to leave him; he called Alice back.

'I'm sorry.' Few people had heard Malcie MacFadyen say that. Alice just shrugged.

'Alice, Fred was a good man. I know you love him, but the child needs a father and I'm asking you to marry me.'

233

It was the equivalent of knocking Alice to the floor and giving her a kicking.

'Marry? Malcie, Fred hasn't even been buried.'

'I know, I know, but listen. You'll never manage on your own. There's Daisy to consider.'

'Dorothy,' said Alice, 'I think it's time she became Dorothy again and joined the real world. My mother gave me a talking-to, Malcie, and though it chokes me to say it, she is probably right. She's a clever little girl, she deserves more in life than a fool like me for a mother.'

'I'd look after you both.'

'Oh yeah? Until the next time someone catches up with you and gives you a kicking, or a copper like MacCallum manages to nail you and then what? No, Malcie, you're a good man at heart, but you're not for me.' And you're certainly bloody not for my daughter, she added inwardly.

He shifted position, trying to get comfortable, closing his eyes against the pain. 'Pity. You and Daisy, Ruth, her mam, even that, what's 'is name? Bloum. He knows how to patch someone up, no question. All of you, this summer, I've had a good time with you all, made me welcome, not many have done that.'

She smiled and patted his hand, still with traces of dried blood around his nails. 'After the war, Ruth said they took her and Nana and put them in another camp, a displaced persons' camp. That's what we all are: them, me, you, we're displaced persons. We don't quite fit in where we are. That's why you felt so at home, Malcie; you're one of us, displaced.'

He reached a finger out to stroke her arm gently, the only gesture he was physically capable of. 'Displaced,' he agreed.

*

In the morning Daisy was heartbroken that Uncle Malcie hadn't stayed long enough to say goodbye, and that he hadn't even thought to leave her half a crown. That today was the day they moved to Gran's just added to her unhappiness.

She said goodbye solemnly. 'I'll come and visit you,' she promised Nana, 'and I'll come and help you in the garden,' she told Mr Bloum after he helped her pick one of her lettuces and some flowers for Gran.

Alice told Ruth and Nana about Malcie's proposal.

'File that one under lucky escape, darling,' Ruth said. Nana told Mr Bloum later, when she took him his elevenses. He was shocked at the idea but in a way heartened; the Alice he thought he knew would have married Malcie like a shot, but this new incarnation had sat still long enough and thought things through and decided to do something sensible for once.

The house seemed quiet, strange, without Alice and the child. Ruth sat in the kitchen, darning her dancing cardigan and brooding over the loss of Fred, and what could turn into the loss of her friend. She doubted if she could ever arrive at Gran's house and whisk Alice away to the races or the cinema or to give her moral support when she went to an audition. And was Alice serious about getting a job at Gill's Cables? Ruth rolled herself a cigarette, and thought things over.

She had come to her decision by teatime, when all three sat down to a table which seemed lost without Alice and Daisy.

'Alice's mother is right,' she told her stunned audience. 'Let's face it, neither of us are spring chickens. That last job in Rhyl I went on? I hate to admit it but it nearly killed me, keeping up with girls half my age. If Alice goes for a job at Gill's Cables, I'm going too.

235

We'll keep each other company and it will be a laugh.'

Nana could only open and close her mouth in amazement. Mr Bloum wondered if British industry was ready for Alice and Ruth.

Chapter 21

Aftermath

Even before Betty had helped her carry the old trunk upstairs, Alice knew that moving back to her mother's had been a big mistake. She remembered why she had married Caroline's father in the first place; it was to get away from home.

The first five minutes had been fine; Gran had accepted the flowers and lettuce, and kissed the child. Then she turned to Betty and said, 'Look at the lovely flowers Dorothy picked for me.'

'Daisy, I like being Daisy,' the words had come out automatically.

'Well, we'll have none of that nonsense here, madam. Dorothy you were christened and if it is good enough for the good Lord, then it's good enough for you.'

Daisy turned to her mother, her look appealing for help. Alice tried to soothe things. 'Why don't you run along upstairs and see what a lovely bedroom Gran has got ready for you, your very own room again.' She shooed the little girl towards the stairs.

'Honestly Mum, does it really matter what she calls herself? Lots of kids have imaginary friends. There's no harm in it.'

'I'm not having that nonsense in this house.'

Alice followed her daughter upstairs, her lips pressed in a thin line.

At the top of the stairs Daisy hovered on the threshold of her bedroom, not wanting to go in.

'What's the matter, darling?'

The crucifix above her bed terrified the child. A man dying in agony, blood dripping from his hands and feet and his crown of thorns. Alice was reminded of the dried blood matting Malcie's hair together.

'It's horrid, he's all cut,' said Daisy. They hadn't realised Gran had come up the stairs behind them.

'That's what comes of marrying a Protestant,' she snapped at her daughter. We have got to get out of here, thought Alice; we have got to escape.

For Daisy, even for Dorothy, the worst was yet to come. 'The undertaker's coming round this afternoon, like you asked,' Gran told Alice, pausing and making a determined effort to try and understand her daughter. God knows she has just been widowed, and we seem to have got off on the wrong foot, but there is no right one with her and her daughter, she thought.

'The headmistress says that Dorothy can go along in this afternoon, so that she can see her and make a start. I think it's for the best that she isn't in the house, when . . .'

The thought of the undertaker stopped Alice in her tracks. She could only stand and nod dumbly.

School. Not just school but a new one. Daisy wasn't prepared for this; she just stood in horror and looked at her mother.

'But you said . . .'

'Come on darling, be brave, it's for the best.'

Gran's scrambled-egg lunch stuck in her throat. There was no cake like Nana's, no big hugs and being called

238

darlink, no creamy glass of milk. When she asked to get down Gran whisked her off to the bathroom, scrubbed her with a flannel, combed her hair till Daisy expected to see blood dripping down her face and produced her satchel.

They were walking down the street towards the playground before a word of protest could form.

Alice sat in her mother's front parlour and stared back at another dying Jesus, and listened to the man talk about coffins.

That night Alice and her daughter lay in separate rooms and longed to be together in the same bed, cuddled up for security and love in a world which had suddenly grown very cold.

The battle lines were drawn at breakfast.

'She shouldn't go, she's too young.'

'Mum, I want her there. She wasn't in the hospital when . . . when it happened, and I want her to have her own chance to say goodbye.'

'She only started school yesterday, what will they think, her going missing right away.'

'I don't care what anyone thinks, I want my daughter by my side when I bury her father.'

Daisy looked on, eyes wide, as her mother was almost at her gran's throat.

Alice had been dreading this day without having to go through this. 'Tomorrow you can begin telling me how everything I do is wrong again, but for today, today . . .' Alice's words dried up. Daisy stuck her spoon into Gran's unforgiving porridge and longed to be at Nana's.

Gran, affronted, but conceding, got up and began clearing the breakfast table.

Daisy was stunned. She had never seen her mother like this before; it was the most dreadful thing in an ever-increasing list.

'What's today?'

Alice lifted her up onto her knee. 'Darling, you know that Daddy has died. Today we say goodbye at his funeral, when we bury him. Or rather the undertaker does. We go along to church, sing some hymns, say our prayers and watch Daddy's coffin be buried, and we say goodbye.'

'Daddy is inside the coffin?'

'Yes.'

'On his own?'

'Yes.'

'Do we see him?'

'No, we just see his nice coffin in the church and then it goes into the grave . . .'

'Like Granddad's? Do we put flowers on it like Gran does?'

'That's right, darling.'

Daisy held onto her mother's hand throughout the service. Lots of grown-ups appeared, some she knew and some she didn't. She wondered why Nana, Aunt Ruth and Mr Bloum sat at the back of the church and didn't come and sit with her and Mummy at the front, because there was plenty of room. She wondered why Aunt Betty cried so loudly, and so did Alice. There were flowers, as nice as those in Mr Bloum's garden.

They put Daddy's coffin in the ground and only put a little bit of the dirt back in on top, then everyone went and had a cup of tea in Gran's parlour. After that she was sent to play with Graham, who was very serious and said, 'I'm sorry your dad's dead,' and let her hold one of his rabbits. Daisy went to bed that night still not knowing what the entire day had been about.

Alice understood the day only too well, though she

didn't understand why her sister felt obliged to outweep everyone else.

Alice went through the service automatically, as she seemed to have spent the days since Fred's death, in a mixture of shock, disbelief and incomprehension at simple tasks around her. She wanted Ruth by her side, as well, after all they had shared him in life, why shouldn't they in death? Alice was surprised at herself, she thought she would have coped better, demanded Ruth sit next to her, be more in control, but here she was beaten by it all, defeated, letting her mother lead while she followed. She was glad she had stuck to her principles about having her daughter there.

As they followed the coffin from the church to the prepared plot in the graveyard Alice looked across the fields. The Whittington graves were on a slight rise, which somehow managed to catch a chill wind even on a sunny day like this.

She looked back at the mourners. Ruth had tucked herself away at the back, discreetly. Alice knew there would be tears underneath the veiled hat. Then she saw her other daughter and her heart lifted.

Caroline had walked into place beside Gran. Her husband stood behind, solid and serious. She came, thought Alice, she never liked him, she never forgave me for marrying him, but she came. Alice had never expected or believed in a million years that she would, and she clung to this throughout the rest of the day.

Ruth did not go back to the house afterwards; she knew that she would be too much of a curiosity amongst the other mourners.

There was a momentary lull in the buzz of conversation around Alice as Ruth came forward to give her friend a kiss and bent down and patted Daisy's cheek. She turned

241

on her high heels and walked away without looking back.

As the funeral tea got under way Gran decided that Dorothy had seen enough of the funeral and sent her off to play with Graham. By that time in the proceedings the child was too bemused to put up any resistance, and neither was Alice. Besides, Alice had something very important to attend to. She found her older daughter and together they went and sat in Alice's bedroom.

They hugged each other tightly.

'Thank you for coming, darling, I mean it. I know that you and Fred . . .'

'Never really got on?' Caroline finished the words for her. 'We would have been here sooner, but there were roadworks at Stone. We crept in after the start and sat at the back, with a man and an old woman and someone, was that her?'

'Yes.'

'Oh.' Caroline was horrified yet fascinated by her Aunt Betty's tales that her mother could not only condone her husband having a mistress, but actually be friends with her as well.

'They've been very kind to me, all of them.'

Caroline nodded. 'So you're back with Gran?'

'Yes, until we can get back on our feet again. Fred lost the pub as you know, he'd been so ill for so long, the money just seemed to . . .' Alice found herself sobbing on her daughter's shoulder. They held each other close.

'Your gran has been very good to us.' Alice blew her nose loudly, went to the mirror and started to repair her make-up.

'I doubt it.'

Alice turned, surprised at her daughter's candour.

'Let's face it, Gran is not one of the world's most, well, sympathetic people for the want of a better word.'

242

Alice laughed. 'No, she isn't.' She sat down on the bed beside her daughter. 'She has me lined up for a job at Gill's Cables, and she marched Daisy down the road to the school. Or should I say Dorothy, because imaginary characters are not allowed in this house.'

'Is it hard going?'

'Very. Has she told you the rest?' Caroline said no. 'I will one day, but not now, it's too painful darling, suffice to say that if I don't toe the line, she has threatened to go to court and get Daisy taken away from me, and she would probably succeed. So here I am, getting ready to clock on.'

Caroline started to tug at her sleeves and Alice went on her guard; something was troubling the young woman.

'Mum, what I said at Graham's party. What you got upset about, about Dorothy coming to stay with me. I mean it. You could come too. There's lots of work round Manchester, you could get a job in a theatre even if it wasn't acting. It's nice where we live, not right in the city, on the edge. She'd like it, there are fields and we could get her a dog if she wanted. Trevor's always been keen on one. There's a good school in the village, supposed to be very good, what they call progressive, been written about in newspapers and everything. We've got a spare bedroom, until you found yourselves somewhere nice.'

Caroline wanted her mother back; she had never known her stepfather, never tried to. She was not at the funeral to say goodbye to him, rather to try and say hello to her mother.

Alice sat astounded. A month ago she would have said her older daughter hated her, now here she was inviting them to go and live with her. It was almost an escape route.

243

'Thank you darling. I'll think about it, I really will. That is so kind of you.' Alice kissed her and held her face cupped in her hands. 'Especially as I was a rotten mother to you, wasn't I?'

'I thought so at the time, but as you get older you can see things from someone else's point of view. Perhaps I've been a rotten daughter.'

'No darling, not you, never.'

Downstairs the funeral tea had got to the stage where elderly women were sitting in groups discussing their ailments and the men were all round the back door with glasses of beer, sneaking a cigarette and wondering how soon they could politely leave.

Gran, midway through her varicose veins with a neighbour, noticed Alice and Caroline and smiled. So some good had come of all this then, she thought.

Caroline collected her husband, who downed his beer in one gulp, shook hands and said the right words to the mother-in-law he didn't really know, before they set off to visit his parents. Alice watched and waved from the gate until their car turned onto the Huddlesford road.

Daisy was suddenly by her side. 'Graham let me hold his rabbit.' Alice noticed that her daughter sounded impressed, and had to wonder to herself if her mother was right, Daisy did need to get back to having a proper childhood.

'Alice.' She heard a grey voice behind her and turned to see the grey man it belonged to. He took off his hat.

'I thought I'd just stop by and pay my respects,' said Detective Sergeant MacCallum. As before, he completely ignored Daisy.

'Thank you,' Alice managed to keep her voice polite.

'We got those counterfeiters.' If it was his idea of a trap, to watch her reaction, to see if she would gasp and say 'Malcie!' he was disappointed. Poor MacCallum, Alice didn't know the script, she never watched *Dixon of Dock Green*. She stayed straight-faced.

'Yes, in Glasgow. Some of our chaps up there got them, with a bag of the cash and a haul of jewellery and silverware.'

'Oh?' *Chaps*, thought Alice, *haul*, he really should switch the set off occasionally, watching too much television is supposed to be bad for you.

'Of course, you went to Scotland, didn't you?'

'Yes, a friend of my late husband's gave my daughter and me a lift when he had to travel north on business; we stayed with my aunt in Paisley.'

It was the first time she had referred to Fred as her late husband. It hurt.

'This friend, it wouldn't be big Malcie MacFadyen would it?'

'Yes.' Alice held on tightly to Daisy's hand, terrified that the child might say something about his night-time visit to Nana's and how he had 'fallen over in the garden'. She needn't have bothered, Daisy was not the slightest bit interested in him, and with her other hand was picking dandelions out of the crack between the pavement and Gran's garden wall to give to Graham's rabbit. Perhaps Gran might let her keep one.

MacCallum continued, oblivious of the child, 'Only MacFadyen appears to have gone missing from his usual haunts. There are reports of a gangland fight. He could well be dead. City of Glasgow police are continuing their enquiries.'

Alice managed to look shocked. 'Well, he only gave us a lift to Scotland, we came back by train on Monday. He did say he had to meet some old business acquaintances.'

The policeman weighed her words. 'Thank you, you

245

have been most helpful.' He put his hat back on and left, after confirming where she was staying in case he needed a statement. Alice looked round: thankfully no one in Gran's had seen him.

Daisy asked if she could go and give Graham's rabbit the leaves. Alice agreed, and went back inside and poured herself a large glass of her mother's sherry. She winced when she realised it was British, not Bristol Cream, and raised her glass in a silent toast to Fred, and to Malcie, who according to police sources appeared to have joined him.

She sat down beside her mother and butted into the conversation. 'Veins? My friend Vi's mother's legs, poor soul, she's a martyr to them, bless her, a martyr.'

Chapter 22

Curtain up

Sums had never been Daisy's favourite. She sat in the classroom and tried to understand the mysteries of long division, but they eluded her. With one elbow on the desk she rested the side of her head in her palm, looked out of the window and started to dream she was with Mummy and Aunt Ruth. She wished she was anywhere but school.

Mummy and Aunt Ruth would have changed places with her.

They nearly lasted as far as lunchtime. The women they were working alongside took one look and said they didn't know why they'd been hired in the first place; the men took one look and knew very well.

They had been interviewed on the Monday and told to turn up in more suitable clothing when they started on the Wednesday. Before noon they were walking down the long drive from the imposing building that housed the cabling firm.

The first grumble from the foreman came when Ruth stopped to make herself a roll-up, then they were told off for laughing, then they were told off for talking. When Alice asked if they were going to get told off for bloody well breathing their careers came to an end.

They set off walking back to Nana's along the Lichfield to Tamworth road. The hedgerows were covered in dust from the road and a lorry went past sounding its horn, loose gravel spraying up in the summer heatwave. A car stopped and offered them a lift.

The clock on the kitchen mantelpiece just finished chiming midday as they walked in. There was only one thing they could do: change into some unsuitable clothes and go into Lichfield.

As the dinner-table monitor put a plate of grey mince and mashed potatoes in front of her, Daisy thought longingly of going into the Malt Shovel and being given a packet of crisps and a bottle of Vimto with a straw. She thought of the bars of chocolate that came out of the machine in the hospital at the end of visiting time. That made her think about her daddy; she wanted to see him so much it hurt, but she didn't know why. The first chink began to appear in the dam of Daisy's unhappiness.

Ruth bought some Gala nylons from Woolworth's, where Alice saw a sign saying they wanted an assistant for the sweet counter. She spoke to the manager, who said she wasn't suitable. He was looking for someone a big younger. What he didn't add was he always made a point of putting a pretty blonde teenager behind that particular counter, he thought it good for trade. If he's told her that, Alice would have slapped him. A mood of despair was beginning to descend.

They decided on the Malt Shovel, and walked down Market Street, stopping at Bert Reddington's old tobacco shop for a packet of Old Holborn for Ruth. The shop fittings hadn't changed since the time the narrow shop had been opened opposite Dr Johnson's house. Black mahogany and glass cases full of strange mixes of tobacco, rows of pipes, and a rack of walking sticks. It was the kind of shop where the all-male staff and customers stopped talking and stared when a woman walked in. Alice treated herself to a packet of Sobranie to cheer herself up.

They sat in a corner of the bar in the half-timbered pub on Conduit Street and considered the future.

'All hell is going to let loose when I get back home,' said Alice. The words echoed back across the years to when she was a teenager, sneaking home late to a bedroom window she had left slightly open for this purpose, reached by climbing onto the coal-shed roof from the rain butt.

Ruth bought them another couple of gins. 'But darling, what can she get on at you about? You tried. Daisy and you moved in with her, Daisy is in school. What more can she expect within a fortnight, dammit?'

The Malt Shovel was quiet so they decided on a visit to the King's Head on Bird Street. The barman said he was glad to see them, offered his condolences and poured them a drink.

Alice decided it was her last for the day; going back to her mother's jobless and smelling strongly of drink would have been the end, but she was glad of the false courage it supplied.

The landlord came over to them, with a scribbled-on Marston's beer mat. 'Had a bloke phone for you two last week, can't remember which day, now. It's on here, said he's work going if you was interested.' Prayers can be answered, even in the King's Head.

'It's Derek. Will he still be at this number, do you think? They've been moving about a bit,' said Ruth.

They asked the barman for change for the phone and shot up the street to the same box where Alice had called

249

the hospital and summoned a taxi, on the fateful night she left Mr Pickup's.

The stagehand who answered the phone said the *Hay Fever* production had left two days before. 'Where are they now? Darling, it's urgent,' Ruth asked. They stood in the box, the handset between their heads, and heard him call out, 'Anyone know where Derek's lot have gone on to?'

To Daisy's horror the teacher announced they were going to play rounders. Graham, who had received a talking-to from his gran, telling him to be nice to little Dorothy, picked her first for his team. Then he showed her how to hold the bat properly, and keep her eye on the ball. When it was her turn to bat Daisy hit the ball for the first time ever. She was so amazed that she just stood there and Graham and all his team had to yell 'run' at her until she got to first.

Alice and Ruth tracked Derek down in Oldham. They were moving on to Scarborough for a month, he said, was Alice interested in taking over as the maid?

'What about Ruth?' she called down the phone.

'Oh bring the old baggage along sweetheart, she can help somewhere. I could do with me own ASM, some of the ones we've had you wouldn't believe. But she'd better not expect top whack.' They accepted on the spot and all but fell out of the box, intoxicated now with their success.

Then it hit them. What About Daisy?

'We can't leave her with my mother,' said Alice. 'I couldn't. I just couldn't, and if we do a bunk she'll have the law on me like a ton of bricks. I know she will, she wasn't joking. Oh Ruth, what will we do?'

250

It had gone closing time so they grabbed a corner table in Melia's, chain-smoked, made each coffee last as long as possible and racked their brains. Someone had left behind a *Lichfield Mercury* and Alice began to flick through the pages. The new shopping precinct would be ready in three years, and foot-and-mouth restrictions were being lifted. The heatwave looked set to continue and there were fears about forest fires; soldiers were on standby at Whittington Barracks to go to Cannock Chase or Hopwas Woods.

They didn't know what to do. They wanted the work, it was the best offer they'd had in months, but leaving Daisy alone with Gran was unthinkable.

'Where is Oldham, anyway, Alice darlink? Scarborough I know, it's the seaside, bloody cold wind up there though, better take our woollies.'

'Somewhere north, you know, dark satanic mills, that sort of thing. Good television station up there, better than ATV, called Granada. Do you remember Lorraine?'

'Big beehive, bad eyeliner?'

'Yes, she picked up a really good contract on this show. Filmed at their studios in . . .' The penny dropped, Alice sat back, her smile almost splitting her face. 'They filmed it in Manchester!'

'So!'

'Manchester! Caroline! She almost pleaded with me to take Daisy. I'm not going to leave her with my mother. I'd choke first, and if I left her with Nana my mother would go crazy. But Caroline, why at Graham's birthday party all three of them, Mum, Betty, Caroline were all but forcing me to send her.'

They headed back to the call box. Caroline's bank-clerk husband was going places; they had their own telephone at home.

'Trent Valley, change at Stafford for the Manchester train, get off at Stockport. There should be enough time to telephone from Stafford to tell Trevor when to collect you at the station. The buffet car is usually near the back so don't get on right at the front or you'll have a long walk for a cup of tea.' Caroline was so excited that she didn't even say yes, just how to get there.

At afternoon playtime, Daisy sat on the steps and read a book her new teacher had given her. This one seemed pleased to hear about all the books she had read and had given her *Swallows and Amazons*. Daisy was lost in the Lake District. She dreamed through the rest of the school day, on board *Swallow* sailing to Wild Cat Island. On the way home Graham gave her the honour of an invitation to help him to clean out his rabbits.

'Then you can do it every afternoon if you like,' he said, overjoyed to find someone to take over the job.

Gran was waiting for them when they arrived home late in the afternoon: Alice smelling slightly of drink and Daisy very strongly of sawdust and rabbit.

Gran already knew about the lost job: news of a sacking as spectacular as that travelled fast in a village as small as Whittington. Betty was there, she wouldn't miss a chance like this; they stood like bookends either side of their disapproval.

How could she?

She definitely was crazy; there were probably grounds for having her committed, to throw over a good job like that.

'Then you will be glad to be rid of me.'

Alice told them she had a good job and Caroline would be taking Daisy.

'Dorothy,' snapped her mother sourly.

'My daughter is going to live where she can be called anything she bloody well likes.'

'You can't change her school again.'

'Why not? You almost had me handing her over to Caroline at gunpoint a couple of weeks ago.'

'I don't mind.' Daisy had been watching from the door. She didn't mind at all. She had enjoyed her day, but since her arrival at the village school she had been regarded as an oddity. 'Your dad's dead,' said one of the girls in reverential tones. Graham didn't help either; since Gran's order that he should be nice to his cousin, he had gone round introducing her, 'This is Dorothy, her dad is dead.'

Betty, who found it embarrassing enough to have to shop in the same city as her sister, had been mortified at the thought of sharing the same village. The loss of the job at Gill's Cables had confirmed her worst fears. How long would it be before Alice was going in the Dog or the Bell and chatting up men? Her nightmare had been the thought of Alice getting a job behind the bar, the only thing she had any experience of, apart from being sawn in half by that peculiar George.

'I think it's nice that Alice's family stays together,' she said sweetly. She had been surprised at how jealous she had felt when she looked out of the back kitchen window and seen Graham playing with Dorothy and the rabbits.

Betty would never have begun to admit it, but she had decided long ago that there was only room for one woman in her son's life: herself.

All that remained was to drag the old trunk back out again and decide what Alice would be taking to Scarborough. The rest of her clothes and all Daisy's belongings would go to Caroline's.

253

Gran spent the rest of the evening muttering, but, like Betty, she was relieved. The trouble with taking the high moral ground is that you can find yourself perched up there, unable to get down. She knew she had done the right thing insisting that Dorothy be taken care of properly. But when it came to sharing her house with a solemn-faced little girl who thought she was someone else, Gran discovered she was more set in her own ways and used to her own company than she realised.

Alice was excited as she kissed Daisy goodnight.

'Caroline says you can have a bedroom all to yourself and it looks out over fields, just like your old bedroom at the Jockey.' Alice thought about mentioning the proposed dog, but decided not to, no need to raise her hopes.

'Where will you sleep?'

'Oh, I told you darling, I'm going to Scarborough, you know, *Hay Fever* with Derek's lot.'

'But when you come home at night?'

'Darling, Scarborough is a long way away from Caroline's house. Mummy will have to stay in digs with Aunt Ruth.'

Daisy's face crumpled. 'But you said you were never going to leave me.'

'But you'll be with Caroline, your big sister, darling.'

'You promised, you know you did. You crossed your heart you hoped to die. That night Uncle George showed me the magic and Aunt Zita made me the party dress. You told me a big fib.'

'It's only until the show's over, darling.' Alice realised it wasn't. She'd been fibbing as much to herself as to her daughter. She told Daisy how much she loved her.

'But it's a big fib, you said you'd never leave me,' tears began to trickle down her face. 'You lied.'

It was the first time Alice had ever heard her daughter use that word.

Nana baked especially for the journey, enough to supply three travellers. From Manchester Ruth would carry on over the Pennines into Yorkshire, and await Alice.

'I know about Manchester,' Nana told Daisy proudly. 'I have a friend who lives there, she writes letters to me and I write letters back. Alvays she says to me, Nana come and visit. Perhaps now I vill. Perhaps I go to the shops to buy a hat with her at Kendal Milne or we could go to the Opera House. Maybe we could take you to see the Belle Vue Zoo, which goes for miles. Not a tiny thing like Hints Zoo up the road. It has a fairground there all the time and you could go every day like it was the Bower. See, didn't I tell you I knew about Manchester? You vill enjoy yourself darlink.' Daisy was lost to a hug.

'But who will read you *Kidnapped?*'

'Ruth will read it for me, but you can write me every week and tell me what book you read, so I will know.'

Mr Bloum took the big trunk out to the garden gate. Daisy sat on it and waited for the taxi to come; she hadn't wanted to stay in the house. The trunk and cases had been crammed into Betty's car and deposited, along with Alice and Daisy, at Nana's house. After a breakfast where no one spoke, Gran had bade them a cold farewell in Whittington, and Betty simply couldn't think of a word to say to the sister she did not, and never would, understand.

Throughout it all, Daisy had been silent. She could not believe Mummy had fibbed, that she was going to leave her behind.

Inside, Mummy and Ruth were fighting to shut Ruth's case again, and Nana was finding more food for them to

255

take. Caroline wasn't just getting Daisy: she was getting a fruit loaf, coconut cake and a quarry's worth of rock cakes.

Mr Bloum brought Aunt Ruth's overstuffed case out and put it beside the trunk.

'Mr Bloum?' He winced inwardly; he had hoped he was going to make a clean getaway, but Daisy had him.

'I called Mummy a liar.'

'That's very serious.'

'Because she promised she would never leave me and now I've got to stay with Caroline on my own. She crossed her heart and hoped to die.'

'If you cross your heart too tightly, I believe it can sometimes break. This I think is what is happening to your mother. Do you think she wants to leave you?'

'No.'

'Do you think she wanted to break her word on purpose to hurt you?'

'No.' If Daisy had known what the word obscene meant, she would have used it to describe the idea that her mummy would ever deliberately hurt her. 'Then it wasn't a lie, a big fib or even a little one?'

Mr Bloum sat down on top of the trunk and turned to her. 'No. Sometimes things happen over which we can have no control, no matter how hard we try.'

'What was it then if it wasn't?'

'Wasn't what?'

'A big fib, a little fib or a lie. You said no, when I asked if it wasn't a lie, a big fib or even a little one. It's not the truth, so what is it?'

She's got me again; the child could give Nietzsche a migraine, he thought, 'I would ask your mummy if I were you.'

Nana managed to get one last hug in. Ruth reckoned it

went on so long it added an extra one-and-six to the taxi's meter.

'I vill come and visit you in Manchester!' she cried out as the taxi set off, astounding Ruth that something had happened which might prise Nana from the rock of her kitchen.

They laughed in the taxi when the porter lifted the trunk out at Trent Valley station and said, 'Blimey, have you got a body in here?'

'Yes, he's called Malcie,' said Alice.

When they changed trains at Stafford a kindly guard gave them a length of string to wrap round Ruth's case when its hinges finally burst.

They shared their carriage and Nana's picnic with half a dozen junior soldiers on their way to band school. Daisy thawed; it was hard to be angry with Mummy and Aunt Ruth, because they laughed too much.

Ruth was still laughing when they waved goodbye as she stayed on the train and they got off at Stockport. Caroline threw her arms round Mummy and Daisy, and Trevor drove the car home at a snail's pace to stop the trunk falling off the roof.

Caroline had been true to her word: the bedroom really looked out over fields. She showed off her home to her mother, shyly, proudly.

Alice floated on a dream. Before they left Nana had told her, 'When someone you loves dies, you never get over it, but darlink, you come to terms with it.' Being reunited with Caroline had started the process.

Daisy and Trevor eyed one another warily.

Trevor only had brothers; he had gone to a boys' school and sometimes found being a bank clerk too exciting. Courting Caroline had been a big enough mystery for him to cope with; he'd never been around little girls

257

before. He didn't know that in Daisy he was in for a crash course.

As Alice, Daisy and Caroline fitted together like the last piece of sky in a jigsaw puzzle he bolted for the refuge of a Round Table meeting.

Alice had her doubts. Caroline had married a steady job and a nice young man. Suddenly Alice felt very guilty. I should have been there to rescue her, she thought. My daughter is me, when I was her age. Caroline has got back in touch, gone to all this trouble to get Daisy here, to get me here, so she can escape. Her whole bloody marriage is one of Daisy's big fibs.

When the time came for Alice to leave they all piled into Trevor's Ford Prefect and headed for the station. Daisy resigned herself to the fact that the days of riding in the leather seats of Uncle Malcie's Jaguar were over. It was push the plastic seat forward and climb in the back time.

Daisy decided as Alice finally let go and boarded the train that her mother had nearly perfected Nana's death grip. Alice cried, she waved, and so did her daughters. Trevor went and bought himself a copy of *Exchange and Mart* from the station bookstand.

The drive home was quiet. They missed Alice; she had been the catalyst between them.

Daisy could feel tears starting as they got out of the car. She was alone in a strange place with people she didn't really know. She was scared. As she walked in the house the handkerchief full of her savings fell out of her knicker-leg elastic.

Trevor heard the chink of coins. 'What's this?'

Daisy picked it up and held it tightly. 'It's my savings, I have got more than thirty bob,' she announced proudly.

'Good girl, you're never too young to start saving.

You and Caroline must come along to the bank and you can open a junior savings account.'

'No, it's my money,' Daisy didn't like the sound of that one bit.

'When you have a lot of money you should put it somewhere safe, in an account in a bank,' he explained kindly.

Trevor had admitted to the secretary of the Round Table, who had married a widow with two daughters, that he hadn't the first idea of what to do with children, especially girls. He had received what he considered to be sound advice: 'Take your time, be fair, but be firm with them. Let them know who's boss, right from the start. Start off on the wrong foot and they'll run rings round you for the rest of your life.'

Daisy stood sullenly and watched while Trevor decided to start as he meant to go on. 'You see, when we have money, we might drop it, or someone might steal it and then where would we be? So we put it in a bank. The bank uses our money to give to other people for loans and then pays us for doing this by giving us extra money back. It is called interest.' Am I going slowly enough? he thought.

'No. It's mine. I'm not letting anyone have it to give it to other people. I got it myself.' The idea of banking, of salting away surplus money, was alien to Daisy; she'd never been in a situation where there had been any spare cash.

'Don't be silly now.'

'No.' Daisy glared at him. Trevor could feel he was losing ground.

'What's the matter?' Caroline appeared.

'He wants to take my money.'

Caroline could see the idea upset Daisy. 'Oh let her

259

keep it if she wants, Trev. Tell you what, I'll give you a nice piggy bank and we can put some of your pocket money in it each week.'

Trevor remembered his friend's advice. 'No, dear. I've said she's to open a savings account and she will. I'm not going to be contradicted in my own home. You'd better remember that, young lady.'

'Trevor's right you know, what if we had a big nasty burglar who took your money? It would be nice and safe in the bank.' Caroline tried the role of peacemaker.

'No.'

Trevor had no way out but forward; he held out his hand. 'Give me the money. We'll have an end to this nonsense. I'll open the account for you myself.'

'No.' Daisy's voice went higher. She had never faced an ultimatum before in her life, and, unbeknown to her, Trevor had never issued one either. All she knew was it was hers and she was keeping it.

'Now!'

'No.'

'Trevor, could she just —'

'Leave it to me Caroline. Come on, hand it over.'

'No.'

He reached over and prised the handkerchief out of her fingers, she tried to pull it back and coins flew everywhere.

Both Trevor and Daisy were out of their depth. Daisy decided to scream and sob, drowning in her terror of being alone, a sudden fear of Caroline and Trevor and the fact she wanted her mummy. Trevor was appalled that the child had been alone with them for less than an hour and he'd managed to reduce her to a tear-sodden, red-faced howling wreck. He tried to wade ashore and salvage his authority and dignity by giving her a slap across the legs and ordering her to her room, just as his father had always done to him.

No one had ever slapped Daisy before; the pain and indignity merely compounded her misery and she sobbed herself into exhaustion.

They left her to it, partly because neither of them had any idea what to do next with a sobbing eight-year-old but mainly because they were busy having the biggest row of their entire married life.

When Daisy woke she was hoarse, with sore ribs and a headache. She felt hungry, thirsty and very alone. She sat on the edge of her bed and looked at herself in the mirror.'

'My God your face looks hellish, darling,' she told herself. It was what Mummy would have said if she had been there, and it comforted her.

She went and sat on the dressing-table stool in front of the mirror, remembered, and fumbled in her cardigan pocket.

Yes, there it was. Mummy had given it to her just before she left. Her best lipstick, the one they bought that afternoon after she peed herself in Sutton Coldfield, Clover Blush from the House of Dorothy Gray. Daisy put her elbows on the dressing table and leaned forward to the mirror. She twisted up the tube and applied it carefully, pressed her lips together, turned her head this way, then that, and finally used her ring finger to wipe each corner of her mouth.

She was sitting back admiring her handiwork when Caroline came in and sat on the bed; Daisy didn't know her sister had been standing outside the door, anxiously waiting for the first sound of movement before daring to enter.

261

'That looks nice.' Caroline's eyes were as red as Daisy's.

'You can try it if you want.'

Daisy moved up and Caroline sat on the stool beside her. Her big sister applied the lipstick carefully, pressed her lips together, turned her head this way, then that, and finally used her ring finger to wipe each corner of her mouth before sitting back admiringly.

Side by side they looked at each other in the mirror.

'What we need is an adventure, darling.'

The other one nodded, because if there was one thing Alice had taught her daughters, apart from how to put on lipstick, it was that life should always have adventures.

Three Women
Marge Piercy

"Every new novel by Marge Piercy is cause for celebration"
Alice Hoffman

Suzanne Blume has survived two marriages, financially
supported two children through college and her teaching
duties at a Boston university allow her just enough time to
take on important legal cases and spend time with her clos-
est friend. Life in her forties has also yielded some unex-
pected pleasures – she is enjoying her first sexual relationship in over ten years.

But her neat, buttoned-up life starts to unravel when
her daughter Elena returns home, angry and unemployed.
Can mother and daughter rebuild their fragmented
relationship? And what of Suzanne's own mother?
Having devoted her life to men and politics with equal
passion, fiercely independent Beverl
y is now coping with the effects of a stroke, and is also
forced to share Suzanne's home and rely on the conven-
tional daughter she has never had much time for...

Praise for Marge Piercy and *Three Women*:

"Vividly imagined and deeply satisfying" Marilyn French

"Marge Piercy is one of the most important writers of
our time"   Erica Jong

The very best of Piatkus fiction is now available in paperback as well as hardcover. Piatkus paperbacks, where *every* book is special.